MOTHER DOLL

MOTHER DOLL

KATYA APEKINA

A NOVEL

THE OVERLOOK PRESS, NEW YORK

This edition first published in hardcover in 2024 by
The Overlook Press, an imprint of ABRAMS

Abrams books are available at special discounts when purchased in quantity
for premiums and promotions as well as fundraising or educational use.
Special editions can also be created to specification. For details,
contact specialsales@abramsbooks.com or the address below.

Library of Congress Control Number: 2023946469

Printed and bound in the United States

1 3 5 7 9 10 8 6 4 2
ISBN: 978-1-4197-7095-1
eISBN: 979-8-88707-153-4

ABRAMS The Art of Books
195 Broadway, New York, NY 10007
abramsbooks.com

For my parents, my grandparents, and for Fais

Take your hands out of your pockets—
Grab a rock, a knife, a bomb!
And for those who don't have hands,
just use your forehead!

. . .

Come on!
Let's paint Monday and Tuesday
with enough blood that they
become holidays!
       —Vladimir Mayakovsky, "A Cloud in Pants"

PART 1

CHAPTER 1

It was ironic that Zhenia and Ben would come home from spending time with people who had kids and be so giddy with relief and self-righteousness over their decision not to have any that it would make them want to fuck.

They had just gotten back from seeing a high school friend of Ben's who was in town to fundraise for the Obama campaign and had brought along his whole family. It was watching this friend try to hold a conversation while also wrangling his toddler and switching off with his tense wife on something ominously called "The Baby's Bedtime Routine" that made Zhenia and Ben, now in their empty, quiet apartment, feel engorged with smugness.

"You can't really go anywhere," Zhenia said, leaning out of the bathroom midfloss to continue the shit-talking they'd started in the car. "You can't even have a conversation. Having kids makes people so rude. Can you imagine just letting your kid stand in front of your face, yelling and interrupting like that?"

Ben was naked in bed already, absentmindedly stroking his nipples. "It's true. What did we even talk about? He'd ask me about work, and then as soon as I'd start to answer, he would shift his attention to his screaming child, and I didn't know what I was supposed to do in that situation. Like, am I supposed to wait? Am I supposed to answer *over* the screaming child?"

Zhenia spat in the sink and dried her mouth with a towel, laughing. "I would have loved to see you yell over that kid like you were in a loud bar or something."

When she stepped out of the bathroom, Ben was using the sheet to fan at his erection.

"What are you going to do with that mouth?" he said in a funny voice.

"I cleaned it just for you." She bared her teeth.

Then they had sex freely, with all their fluids sterilized.

A strange image appeared to Zhenia right after she came, of her grand-mother boiling the drinking water—vivid and metaphorical. She thought her grandmother could visit her like this only if she were dead, so even though it was late, and even later on the East Coast, she called to make sure that her grandmother was still alive.

Zhenia thought about that visitation again a few weeks later when she noticed that her period was late. Ben had gotten a vasectomy as soon as the union gave him health insurance, and she'd been on the pill for years, so she wasn't really worried. She took a pregnancy test just to confirm what she knew—that pregnancy was impossible—but the test was positive. She'd gotten the first pregnancy test from the dollar store, so she got three more from CVS, in case the first one was defective.

Why was it so cheap? It must have been wrong, she assured herself, as she peed on the more expensive ones in the pharmacy bathroom. It wasn't wrong. She was pregnant. The nausea started almost immediately.

That day during her shift at the hospital where she was working as a translator she had frozen several times, midsentence, hand up, eyes closed, waiting for the wave of nausea to pass over her.

She knew that she would need to have an abortion. What other option was there? She'd had one before, and unlike in the dramatic way it was portrayed in movies and on TV, it wasn't a difficult choice, she wasn't traumatized afterward, and no part of her regretted that decision. Yet now, somehow, it did not feel like a possibility at all. Why was that? Ben had always been clear about not wanting children. Forcing a child on someone who didn't want one was barbaric. But hadn't she also been sure that she didn't want one until, suddenly, she did?

She called her grandmother to tell her the news. Her grandmother had stopped being able to outwardly understand things, but it was still possible,

Zhenia thought, that she was at least partially in there. Anyway, she was the only person whom Zhenia wanted to tell.

She called the house and her mother answered.

Zhenia had been hoping that it would be Nathaniel, her stepdad, because he lacked curiosity and never asked questions. He'd married her mom when Zhenia was six years old and was the only father figure Zhenia had ever known, and yet she never thought of him as "dad." But, he was a reliable presence. He could be counted on to shuffle up the stairs with the cordless phone and hold it to her grandmother's ear and not think anything of it afterward.

Her mother, though, was a different story.

"Zhenichka." Her mother, Marina, was already sighing. "What gibberish. Don't use your grandmother's dying body as your confessor. You want to help your grandmother, come back here once in a while and help me take care of her. Change her sheets. Brush her hair. Massage her legs with lotion so she doesn't get sores. Do something practical for once. Don't whisper bullshit into the phone while I hold it to her unhearing, unseeing, unthinking, but still somehow living, head. It's grotesque." Then she hung up.

But what did her mother know about what Baba Vera could or couldn't hear? And if her grandmother had been able to speak, she would have surely disdained the "practical." She would've wanted exactly what Zhenia was offering, the contents of her heart.

A FEW DAYS later, Zhenia and Ben went out to dinner at the Thai place in the strip mall across the street. She thought she would tell Ben then, but she didn't. She felt instinctually protective of what was growing in her. Telling him, she sensed, would let the air out. Or, in. Wasn't that how Hemingway described an abortion in "Hills Like White Elephants"? "It's an awfully simple operation. Just let the air in!" The characters never talked about it directly. She'd read that story in a high school English class after having her first abortion and laughed at the melodrama of it, laughed hysterically enough to be sent out into the hallway. Part of why she couldn't stop laughing was because the boy in her class who'd impregnated her had thought the story was about a lobotomy.

And now, what? She could at least feel the pain of the woman who was being strong-armed into something she didn't want.

Ben was telling her about the reality show he edited—how one of the women was on a weird citrus diet and was eating oranges with the skin on. He'd edited a reel of her spitting seeds constantly into her hand. That woman's husband was rumored to be a psycho, maybe even a murderer or serial predator. What if there was footage of him in the background of a scene they'd shot at their house, holding a murder weapon?

"It's funny," Zhenia found herself saying, as though it related to what he'd just been talking about, "that something can be nothing or everything depending on what value you assign it." She was thinking about how the last time she'd been pregnant, she had definitely thought of what was growing inside of her as cells, and this time, already she'd begun thinking of it as a baby.

Ben stared at her, waiting for her to follow up that vague statement with an example or an explanation, but she didn't. Instead she lurched across the small restaurant to the bathroom and vomited up shrimp.

Zhenia had met Ben at NYU, six years ago, when she was a sophomore and he was a grad student—they'd met in her dormitory cafeteria a year after the Twin Towers had collapsed. Their first date was to Kim's Video and then to his grad housing, where he kissed her, finally, on the couch in the common room in the blue glow of the DVD menu. A few months later, halfway into the spring semester, they dropped out of school and moved to L.A. for pilot season together with their friend Naomi, imagining a life in which they would all become successful actors.

Zhenia's mother had not taken the news well. "You're not even in the acting program!"

Marina was a biologist who studied how bacteria communicated. As for how *humans* communicated or searched for what was in their hearts—this did not interest her. Any academic discipline without a clear and direct path after graduation was questionable. That Zhenia was an English major had already seemed stupid but not nearly as illogical and arbitrary as this decision to pursue acting in Los Angeles.

"I don't need the school's permission to be an actress," Zhenia had said, though whether she believed this or not, she wasn't sure.

"Marina, let her go." Zhenia's grandmother had picked up the phone in the other room and interceded on Zhenia's behalf. She'd blow into Zhenia's sails herself if she had to. "Let her become an actress, that's a great idea," she'd said.

The fact that Zhenia had never acted or expressed a real interest in acting, that she hadn't even made it past the first rounds of auditions for her high school plays—were these not valid points to make?

"Mama, you know that's just because I have a quiet voice."

"In Hollywood they'll have microphones," her grandmother agreed, "and in movies the acting is different, it's not even acting. That is the point, I think. You can talk quietly, but with intensity."

Who knows what her grandmother had actually believed. Anything would have been a great idea, to just get her away, to protect her from Marina and from herself. She knew that her health was failing, that her mind was failing, and she did not want her little Zhenichka to bear witness to any of that. Whether Zhenia wanted to bear witness to that was beside the point. "Let her get to L.A. and if not acting, she'll find something else."

"Idiocy," Zhenia's mother exclaimed, finally angry enough to switch over to Russian. "Total idiocy! What have I been paying for the last two years? You and Babushka plotting and scheming . . . Take her with you. You two headless dodos. Nothing she has done in my entire life has made any sense, and all of it has been with the end goal of irritating and hurting me because she knows that as much as I would like, I can never be rid of her!"

AFTER SHE MOVED to Los Angeles, Zhenia would call every week—she'd save up funny stories about Hollywood ladies with dogs in baby strollers and men with misspelled tattoos—but as the months went on, her grandmother grew vaguer and quieter, hiding her confusion as much as she could, missing and postponing their calls more and more frequently until eventually she became indisposed. Zhenia tried to get information from Greg, her little brother, really half brother, if she could catch him between his cello lessons and soccer games. Her mother did not like them to have an unmediated relationship because she worried Zhenia would contaminate him with her impractical and poorly thought-out worldview.

"Wouldn't it be cool if you went to the Chestnut Hill Cinema and there I'd be on the screen, my face the size of a house?" Zhenia would ask.

"That *would* be cool," Greg would say uncertainly. "Did you get a part in a movie?"

"Not yet. How's Babushka?"

"I'm not allowed in her room. She doesn't like me in there."

"Is she in her room right now? Mom said she went out."

"She's in the hospital."

Which is how Zhenia found out that it was serious. The hospital didn't keep her long. There was not much they could do for her. Instead, she deteriorated slowly at home, and Zhenia stayed away, diligently going to auditions, using her mom's credit card to take improv classes and get headshots. Zhenia got a job, first at a coffee shop and then, putting her Russian skills to use, as a medical translator. Zhenia's Russian had been a huge point of pride for her grandmother—it was their private language. Vera would brag to anyone who would listen about how unusual it was for someone who immigrated at the age of five to hold on to their mother tongue so well, especially since Zhenia's mother spoke English exclusively at home to Nathaniel and Greg.

IN HER FIRST and second years in L.A., Zhenia had flown home to visit a few times, but she could see that it put too much of a strain on her grandmother to make things look normal, to try to hide from her beloved granddaughter the truth of her condition. And when Zhenia had said something about moving back, her grandmother had howled—"I don't want you taking care of me. No! What gibberish. This is the last thing I want!" Zhenia understood then that she was being banished, and when she didn't come back for Christmas she could tell that everyone was relieved, maybe herself included.

Everything felt temporary, and since there were no seasons in Los Angeles to track time, you could avoid accounting for its passage. Five years went by in this way. Naomi got a part on a TV show that went to series pretty soon after they'd moved, and Zhenia and Ben auditioned for things endlessly until Zhenia eventually gave up and then they married each other.

THE NEXT NIGHT, Zhenia was lucky because her mother wasn't home, and Nathaniel was bland but helpful. She lay in bed next to Ben, talking to her grandmother in Russian, about the thing she wanted to talk about with Ben but was too scared.

"You're disappearing and this baby is appearing," she said to her grandmother, "and the two feel connected to me. I can't afford any of this, that is definitely true, but poorer people have had babies. Mom had me under much worse circumstances. But, she had you to help take care of me. To love me. There's also the fact that my husband doesn't want a baby. He has always been completely certain about this."

Her grandmother's breathing was an even whistle. Zhenia heard Nathaniel clear his throat. The phone must have been on speaker, and though Nathaniel's Russian wasn't great, he'd taken enough evening classes early on in his relationship with Marina that he must have been able to understand the gist of what Zhenia was saying.

He cleared his throat again, this time in order to speak. "We could help you," Nathaniel said, "if you moved back here. I'm sure your mother would be happy to—"

Zhenia hung up. The broken fourth wall. She could see how in his eavesdropping, it must have felt to him like she was making a confession.

Laying herself before him for the saving. And her grandmother was just a pretext. A bearskin rug to lie on top of.

Ben turned the page of the script and looked up at her. He pulled the cap to the highlighter out of his mouth. "What's up?" he said.

Take a picture in your head, she thought, this is the face of the person you are about to betray. The thin strand of saliva connecting his lip to the neon pink cap.

"Do you believe in reincarnation?"

"What?"

He obviously didn't, so she didn't know why she was framing it like this. She was wondering whether the baby growing inside of her could be the reincarnation of her grandmother. This felt both irrefutably true and completely irrational.

"Like, say you did," she went on. "How would it work, do you think? Does one person need to die and the other need to be born at the same exact moment? What if someone was half-dead, their body still on earth? And what about the whole question of new souls, and the population growing? Do souls split, and in the process do they deteriorate? Or do they split and grow the way cells do, multiplying continuously?"

Ben wiped his chin and put the cap back on the pen. "And by soul you mean . . . ?"

She felt absurd, because she didn't really believe in souls, or maybe she did, but she still realized that it was absurd.

"You're so Russian." Ben laughed, looking down at his script. He flipped a few pages back, then smacked his chest with his fist. "My Russian soul!" he said emphatically, with a thick accent.

She stared at him, until he stopped snickering. He had an audition the next day for a prestige series about Nikola Tesla. He still went on auditions occasionally, even though his career as an editor for reality television was thriving. She picked his hand up, lifted it high, and let it drop limply onto his lap, knocking the script off the bed. He looked at her, still smiling but with a building sense of dread. The dread was catching up.

Maybe she could wait until she began showing to tell him. She should at least wait until after his audition because it could be a big break for him. He didn't get auditions like this very often, and the role—hairy, large nosed, wiry—it was basically written for him. This news could sabotage him. It might distract him and get his head out of the game.

"We're pregnant," she said, which sounded weird as soon as she said it. The "we" a little try-hard.

He nodded like he understood the joke. She was getting back at him for the Russian-soul stuff. They nodded at each other like two bobbleheads until she got up and brought him the four pregnancy tests. They were a week old now and yellowed, but the blue plus signs in the second windows were still visible against the discolored backgrounds. She kneeled before him with the plastic sticks and put her head sideways on the bed, so she wouldn't have to look at him.

CHAPTER 2

We are an undifferentiated cloud. We are all dead and none of us have been able to move on. We talk at once. We are aggrieved. Our chatter is endless.

—*Pardon, excuse me, pardon me.*
—*During the war the things that would pass for caviar, grainy, thick-skinned rubbery balls, some kind of industrial by-product!* . . .
—*My life was a series of misunderstandings, and my death too. Clumsy misunderstandings, this was my organizing principle.*

Sometimes, piles of zygotes and embryos, big and small, pulled out by the root, show up and then we dig holes with our collective claws, and plant them back into the ground. Can we bury ourselves back into the earth? Can you bury a cloud with dirt? And who would want this? We do not want this.

—*Obviously, it was the work of many men like me, but together we short-circuited entire Soviet apartment buildings. The key was to organize.*
—*Why are there so many Russians here? Do we get grouped together by language? By character flaws?*
—*Speak for yourself, character flaws!*
—*Do we share a defect of national character? Are there other outposts of French and Germans?*
—*I am French. I was born in Russe, but I was really Français. In my soul.*
—*Sounds unlikely.*
—*Where is the tsarina? She was in here earlier.*

—*So young, such a tragedy.*

—*She must have evolved past all this. It's only natural that she wouldn't be here very long.*

—*And the oysters during the war, they were no good at all. What were they contaminated with? They were orange and green. Fry them up and serve them, but they tasted terrible. They tasted like heavy metals. Maybe they were barnacles stuck to the bottoms of submarines.*

—*Gorge on pineapple, chomp on grouse, your days are numbered, bourgeois louse!*

—*The pineapple! Now, the pineapple was always very good if you could get it.*

—*There was really a tsarina here?*

—*She added a certain something to the group, certainly.*

—*You would think so.*

—*Why even in death do I feel like I am on an overcrowded subway train? Some air. I need some air. Where am I?*

—*The tsarina was never here. Give me a break. None of the tsarinas were ever really tsarinas. You think because we're dead we stop lying? Maybe if any of you told the truth for once in your goddamn lives, you wouldn't be in here.*

—*Speak for yourself. Lying was never my problem.*

—*Pardon, pardon, where am I?*

—*If we all move together . . . This way . . . No, this way . . . You're pulling us. Keep moving and we'll get somewhere. There are apartment buildings we could be short-circuiting right now.*

—*Stop tugging on me. Who is tugging on me? I need some space. I can't catch a breath in here.*

—*You don't need a breath. You're dead. All that's left of you is your hysteria, free-floating.*

Sometimes, a flame emerges, and inside of it, an object. An offering by a living person sent to us, usually in error. Some of the objects are mysterious, others familiar but completely useless:

A phone with all of its buttons melted together.

Piles of foreign currency that we can't buy anything with. It mildews quickly and disintegrates.

A convertible with no gasoline, but pushed by the force of our wills, in circles, rusting in our atmosphere of gaseous tears.

And sometimes, but this is not often, a person will come from the other side, usually on a hired errand.

"Hello? Hello? Coco? Coco? Can you hear me?" *A distant voice, not our own. It is apart, and yet inside of our cloud. It causes us all to ripple. It exists on another plane and dimension and yet is somehow audible to us.*

From our cloud emerge five Pomeranians, translucent like jellyfish, all responding to the name of Coco. Where have they come from? They pant and nip at the ankles of the man. A silhouette in our midst. A solid tree of meat.

—Excuse me. Excuse me. Sir? Madam? Sir. Excuse me. You!
—He can't hear us. They pay him to find their dogs.
—Who does?
—The people whose dogs died.

"Coco! Coco! Which one of you is Coco?" the man asks the dogs. He crouches and pets them all, looks at their translucent bodies for the indicated markings—a patch on a paw, a sly look, a slightly crooked tail that points right. These clues are sometimes helpful, sometimes not. Another Pomeranian emerges, but this one is the size of a couch.

—Sir!
—He can't hear you, I told you. You broads never listen.
—Sir! Sir!
—Quit tugging on us.

—*Ironic this Communist revolutionary can't cooperate with the rest of us. Her needs, her needs. They were all like that. Liars.*

—*Listen, if you were so perfect you wouldn't be here, okay.*

—*Where would I be then?*

—*Wherever the others are sent.*

—*Nobody is sent anywhere.*

—*We are all just the remaining garbage. The best we can hope for is to get dissolved.*

—*What is in that for me, might I ask you? Why would I want such an outcome?*

—*You wouldn't. Clearly. That's why you're here.*

—*You're here too, might I remind you.*

—*Sir! Sir!!!!*

The man looks up. What was that? A sense of movement in the fog? It has taken him a while to get here. Perhaps he is not even in the right place. All these Pomeranians seem to be named Coco.

—*Sir!!!! Excuse me!!*

"Hello?" he says uncertainly.

It is very cold here. The dogs are nipping at his pants legs, chewing on the shoelaces of his sneakers. Ghostly little fox jaws snapping inside puffs of fur. The large one circles him twice, then begins to lick his neck, leaving something viscous on his skin that freezes in crusts almost immediately. Ghosts look like the dead's own self-conception, so why is this Coco so large? Is it the most loved? Or does it just have the most inflated self-regard?

He hears the sound again. Faintly, but this time unmistakably, "Sir!"

He stops petting the dogs, stands up, shivering.

A girl tumbles toward him out of the mist. She looks about sixteen.

"Do you see me?" the girl says. "Can you hear me?" There is a slight accent warbling underneath her mid-Atlantic English.

"Yes," the man says. The girl is wearing a pleated gray wool dress with a white pinafore and lace collar. A school uniform. There has been a clear struggle for her to get out of wherever she'd been hiding. Her braid is undone on one side, and she's missing a boot. The sleeve on her dress is torn, shredded, as if by claws.

She takes his wrist. "Help me. Please."

The man was warned many years ago by his teacher at the Institute that you should remain open to the gifts of the dead but also that you must not overstay your time there. Time is an elastic concept in the afterlife, and really on earth too if you know how to work with it, but bodies conform to rules of gravity and you must always prioritize and care for them because crossing into other realms taps the body's resources.

The part of his wrist that the girl is holding has gone numb, as though a nerve were pinched in his back.

"How do I leave here?" she asks.

"Do you know that you're dead?" Some of the spirits he has talked to do not. Or rather, they know but they don't. This type of self-deception exists even in death.

She nods vaguely. "Of course."

"Can I help you find peace?" he asks her, loosening her grip on his wrist and beckoning to the largest Pomeranian. The dog ambles over to them, then stands there like a table. The girl runs her hand through its fur, in both directions, lost in thought.

The man wraps his arms around the dog and lifts it by the armpits. The dog does not seem to mind this at all. It blinks and pants as the man whispers something in its ear. A message relayed from the owner. The dog begins to fade, its twitching tail disappearing last.

"I think all ghosts are looking for peace," the man tells the girl, wiping his hands on his knees when he's done.

The other dogs do not know what to make of what happened to Big Coco. One begins howling; the others bark apoplectically.

The girl does not seem to notice any of this. She brings her hand up to her jaw and nods vaguely. "I don't think it is possible. Peace. After what I've done."

The man nods. "What did you do?"

"Oh, it's horrible." They stare at each other. He's been doing this for a while and this is the farthest he has wandered. It's very cold here. He clenches his jaw to stop his teeth from chattering.

The girl takes the man's hands and wraps them around her translucent waist. "Will you help me disappear like that?" she asks, staring into his eyes. "If I tell you everything, will you help me?"

A dog faithfully awaiting instructions from its master—this is one thing. They can be released fairly easily. People are trickier.

"I'll try. Sure," he says. "Is there someone who needs to see you and hear you? Someone from whom you need forgiveness?"

She gives a small nod. "But she's no longer there. She's not dead exactly, but she's gone."

Yes. There's standard protocol for this. "Does she have descendants? Usually these things get carried from one generation to the next. And of course, whoever it is has to be open to this sort of thing. Some people are and some people aren't."

Another nod. Her eyes are clear and gray and when they lock onto his, they immediately give him a feeling of connecting to the infinite. Something in him dilates. It's a slightly uncomfortable sensation that can still be reframed as pleasurable.

"You died young?" he asks.

She squints, trying to remember. "In a sense, yes. But, no," she says carefully. "I died at ninety-six on Long Island. But by then it wasn't me who died. That woman has made all her necessary amends. That woman I don't think is here. She's dissolved, reincarnated, whatever else happens. But I am the part of her that she never successfully buried. She cordoned me off from the rest of herself, from her new family. I'm her true self. Though, she would have probably said she was just as true as me. And she wouldn't have been wrong."

As she looks at him, he can feel something of hers moving through him and this makes him shake. Is it with excitement, fear, or simply exertion? It's taking a lot of effort to keep himself here.

"Will you come back for me?" she asks.

Her sad gray eyes, just the thought of them, will make him start shaking violently again for days to come.

"Yes," he says, but he is already going, gone. Filled with the sensation of falling backward out of the portal he'd managed to find and pry open for the length of his visit.

CHAPTER 3

Ben got the part in the show. The bad news about Zhenia's pregnancy gave him an aloofness that the casting directors found intriguing. Or, at least, Zhenia kept trying to spin it that way as she helped him pack for the shoot in Atlanta.

"See, the baby is helping you already. You're leveling up." She folded a sweater, which he then refolded more carefully and zipped into a specific compartment in the open suitcase.

He was the neat one in their relationship, or not even that, just more particular. Fussy, Zhenia might say if she wasn't feeling charitable, which she wasn't. How can a person feel charitable and nauseous at the same time? The nausea was unceasing, a wobbliness behind her eyes. The feeling that everything was made of dirty jelly. It could only be cured with eating, which she did not want to do, but did constantly. A trail of saltine crumbs following her everywhere she went. She could always find her way back with crumbs like that. Find her way back to where though? There was nowhere to come back to. The home she had made with Ben was gone. She had destroyed it with her decision. And though he didn't say it, she knew that he didn't think the baby was his.

She began to cry again and Ben held her, even though he was hurt and annoyed and excited to be leaving, to finally have a part in a real TV show, not an Applebee's commercial, not a network pilot that never made it to series, but an HBO drama with actors whom most people would recognize if they saw them, even if they didn't know their names.

Ben comforted Zhenia. Kissed her hair. Rubbed the tears into her cheeks with his thumbs. This led to them having sex, even though neither of them particularly wanted to. Ben insisted on using a condom, which he admitted was pointless since she was already pregnant, but he wouldn't budge about it. Every time from now on, out of principle, there would be this layer of rubber between them.

As he was about to come, the condom squeaking back and forth inside her, Zhenia bit his shoulder. He yelped but kept thrusting. She masked it as passion but she'd wanted to hurt him.

She drove him to the airport and secretly hoped that a semitruck would turn over in front of them, and he would miss his flight and somehow decide not to go, not to leave her. But traffic was light and they got there without incident.

ZHENIA WAS TRANSLATING that day for an elderly Russian woman. This job often felt like a form of penitence, or maybe transference. As Zhenia's favorite person in the world was dying in Boston, she was helping these other babushkas in Los Angeles. She bore witness as these stand-ins decayed, and transferred whatever kindness she had onto them.

This was her third or fourth time taking this woman, Elizaveta Ivanovna, to a specialist. Elizaveta Ivanovna was from a small town near Siberia. She had moved out here because of her son, but he worked three jobs and could never come to these appointments with her. Aside from being from Russia, she seemed nothing like Zhenia's grandmother. Baba Vera had a slyness and enjoyed working the system—she'd charm clerks and bureaucrats in broken English, much to Marina's annoyance. "Stop with your stupid idioms, stop reciting poetry," Marina would growl, but to Zhenia's delight, Vera's antics did the trick more often than Marina would like to admit, getting them a steep discount at a yard sale or a shortcut to the front of a line. Elizaveta Ivanovna did not have this sort of flair. She wore a kerchief on her head and crossed herself a lot and seemed to be in a constant state of deference. If a doctor mentioned the name of a disease or if anyone talked about something that would happen in the future, Elizaveta Ivanovna would cross herself and say, "God have mercy, God have mercy."

Zhenia looked over at the clock in the waiting room.

The Tin Man was keeping them waiting. The Tin Man was Zhenia's nickname for the cardiologist, Anton Kirov, whom she had hooked up with several times in a supply closet a little over six months ago, shortly before signing her marriage license with Ben. The Tin Man spoke Russian fluently, probably better than Zhenia did. His English even had a slight . . . not accent exactly, but foreign lilt. There was absolutely no need for Zhenia to be there, but she assumed that the agency had sent her by accident, or at the old woman's request. She and Elizaveta Ivanovna had formed a bit of a rapport across these visits. It was hard not to feel affectionate toward a woman who was her grandmother's substitute.

Zhenia stood up and paced by the receptionist, who was studiously avoiding eye contact. The reason Zhenia called Anton the Tin Man was because she got the feeling that he didn't have a heart, a deficiency that probably also fueled his interest in cardiology—don't we all want to study and understand what we lack? He was married and had left his wife in St. Louis or somewhere to take over the cardiology department at Huntington. And even though he'd been the one to initiate the hookups with Zhenia, he'd had a brusqueness and ambivalence that Zhenia found offensive.

Zhenia glanced at the receptionist again and sat down. She didn't know whether their hookups in the hospital closet had been common knowledge. Part of why Zhenia married Ben had to do with a feeling that if they *were* married, she'd finally feel confident enough in their relationship to stop trying to sabotage it. Maybe it had worked? Since high school she'd had the habit of acquiescing to anyone's desire, as long as it was strong enough for the both of them. She'd been unfaithful numerous times before, but since *marrying* Ben six months ago, she hadn't slept with anyone else. Though, really, the times before, when she'd been unfaithful, were also the times she'd appreciated Ben the most. A steady and reliable person to come back to.

Elizaveta Ivanovna yawned and immediately made the motion of a little cross over her mouth.

"Why do you do that?" Zhenia asked her gently.

"So the soul doesn't escape," Elizaveta Ivanovna explained.

Zhenia wondered if Ben would say that the reason Russians were so obsessed with their souls was because their souls were always on the verge of vacating their bodies.

Ben was probably midair by then, glancing out the window at the clouds, leafing through a magazine. When he traveled she used to hide surprises in his suitcase—once she filled a sock with jelly beans; another time she put origami animals in his toiletry bag. It had been over-the-top twee. A joke, but still sweet. This time she hadn't done anything like that.

The receptionist finally called them in. Zhenia helped Elizaveta Ivanovna up and walked her slowly down the aisle of the waiting room. The Tin Man had just finished eating at his desk. He balled up his empty deli wrapper and threw it in the trash, then got up to greet them. He was tall and his face was long, horsey and appealing. Zhenia enjoyed when work brought her back to him. She liked the opportunity to touch whatever splinter it was he'd left inside her.

He shook Elizaveta Ivanovna's hand, then smiled professionally at Zhenia. He tried to shake Zhenia's hand too, but she instead pumped a glob of hand sanitizer onto her palm and began to spread it methodically.

"Do you want to just speak to her in Russian?" she asked him.

"I don't speak any Russian," he lied, then blushed. "That is why I asked for her to bring you."

Zhenia stared at him, blinking, not quite understanding this game. She'd been the one to end their tryst, yet she hadn't felt like she'd ever had the upper hand. He'd say things to her that made her feel like she'd bitten into gristle. Like when they were leaving the supply closet for the last time, he'd casually said how when he'd seen her in the hallways, she'd seemed so gentle and nurturing with the old people and that he had hoped she'd be that way with him too. Whether this was a neutral observation or a rebuke, Zhenia wasn't sure, but for days she kept thinking about it.

Standing now in his office, Zhenia felt flustered. She summarized and skipped over some of the pleasantries, which sped things along awkwardly, especially since the Tin Man, at least, knew what she should be saying and must have been thinking that she was not competent at her job. They sat down and he pulled up Elizaveta Ivanovna's file on the computer. He glanced over it and nodded, belched quietly into his hand.

"Tell her," he said to Zhenia, "that the results of the cardiogram are not good."

The old woman put her hand on Zhenia's wrist and clasped it as Zhenia turned to her and repeated what he'd said.

"Tell her," the Tin Man continued, "that I recommend a very simple procedure. An electrode in her heart."

Zhenia translated. She waited for Elizaveta Ivanovna to cross herself, but she didn't because she was too shocked. "He wants to put a metal spike through my heart?!"

"I don't think it's metal," Zhenia said. "Is it a metal spike?" she asked the Tin Man. He seemed irritated, as though the question were hers and not the patient's.

He repeated that the prognosis was dire. Zhenia could tell he wanted very much to repeat himself in Russian but held back. "Does she understand?" he asked Zhenia.

Zhenia dutifully repeated what he said. Elizaveta Ivanovna wouldn't look up; she was holding Zhenia's wrist, stroking it with her thumb.

"Okay," Elizaveta Ivanovna finally said in heavily accented English. "I will try." She stood up.

Zhenia stood up with her, as did the Tin Man. He was smiling in a way that made it seem like he had accomplished what he had set out to do with the patient. Had there been other options, then? Could they have said no? Zhenia wondered. Should they have?

He looked like he wanted to say something else to her, but there was really no way for him to do this and Zhenia did not help. She followed Elizaveta Ivanovna out and blinked away the feeling of the Tin Man pressed up against her in the dark closet, panting in her ear.

The old woman was breathing loudly as she walked to the elevator. She held on to Zhenia, and several times put her hand out to the wall for support. As they waited for the elevator, Zhenia couldn't help it—she leaned over and made the gesture of the cross over Elizaveta Ivanovna, but the old woman batted her hand away. She wasn't in the mood. "You're doing it backward," she said. "And you're a kike."

Zhenia put her hand down at her side, shocked.

Zhenia told the story later to her mother, who snorted so loudly it made Zhenia's phone vibrate in her hand. Marina acted as if she'd seen the story's conclusion from a mile away, that this was the natural conclusion to any story. Marina wasn't born yesterday! Their life in the Soviet Union had been haunted by hags like this who sat on the benches in the courtyard and called them names. Of course this nice old Russian lady was an anti-Semite! What would be truly shocking was if she weren't.

And though Zhenia didn't tell her mother about the married cardiologist, the same went for him being a rat. There was no need for Zhenia to pinpoint the exact ways in which he was. No need for her to investigate and poke around or feel too flattered by his attention.

CHAPTER 4

The first time Paul called, Zhenia was lying in bed, looking at the succulents on the windowsill. They were furry with dust. How long had it been since anybody watered them?

Ben was asleep next to her. He seemed different since coming back from the first round of filming in Atlanta. They'd given him an old-timey haircut and the pomade he'd started using left halos of grease on the pillowcase.

Why hadn't it occurred to her to water and wipe these plants while he was gone?

Zhenia let the phone vibrate on the bed between them. She didn't recognize the number so she let it go to voicemail. Ben groaned, turned toward the wall, and rearranged the pillow between his knees. She wondered when she would start feeling the baby inside of her and what that would feel like. When she'd googled "quickening," somebody on a message board described it as a flutter, but she couldn't really picture that feeling. A phone, vibrating inside of her womb, this she could imagine. The call was coming from inside the house!

She got up and boiled water for tea, then played the voice mail in case it was something work related. There was a silence at first, and though she couldn't hear breathing exactly, there was clearly a person on the other end. Then, finally, a man's voice: "Hi, Zhenia."

Her name in his mouth sounded like a tangle.

"We haven't met. I'm calling about something . . . Well, I'd rather explain it to you, not to a machine. It's about a relative of yours."

Zhenia set the teakettle down. She turned to Ben on reflex but didn't wake him. Which relative of hers could this message be about? Her brother, probably. He was just starting his freshman year now at Northwestern, a DJ on the side. Maybe he owed somebody money? After being under their mother's thumb for so long, it would make sense that he would now find an area in which to be immoderate. Her curiosity was piqued.

She poured herself tea and called the number back. A man answered.

"Zhenia!" he said before she had a chance to introduce herself. "I'm so glad you called. My name is Paul Zelmont." He had a wet way of speaking. She pictured him having thick, damp lips. "I'm a medium. Perhaps you've heard of me?"

She hadn't.

"I'm well-known in some circles. I have a website."

She went over to her laptop and googled him as he talked. The man who came up in the images looked eerily like what she'd been picturing, or perhaps what she'd pictured was vague enough that it transformed into this man. Head shaved bald, white stubble on his cheeks, prying eyes, and yes, thick, wet lips, she was right about that. On the website it said he charged $350 for a fifteen-minute consult.

"I've been talking to your great-grandmother," he continued, "and I need your help."

"Okay." Zhenia tensed and stepped out onto the balcony. For a scam, this seemed weirdly involved. "Did she leave me an inheritance and you just need to know my bank account number so you can transfer me the money?"

The man laughed. "Nothing like that. I know it's strange for you to be getting this call out of nowhere. Her name was Irina Petrovna. She's on your matrilineal line."

Zhenia's grandmother had been raised in a Soviet orphanage for children of spies. This Irina had left her there and sailed to America. Baba Vera had been four, old enough to understand abandonment both viscerally and cerebrally and be haunted by it for the rest of her life. What would Irina's ghost want with Zhenia? Not that Zhenia even believed in this stuff. But if she did, it wouldn't make any sense. The whole thing was preposterous.

"She needs to tell you her story, her full story, and then once you have a complete picture you can, if this feels right to you and I very much hope it will, you can offer her forgiveness. We've discussed it and the best way to go about all of this is to have her dictate us a memoir. She speaks English, Russian, Yiddish, German, and Hebrew, but she says she needs to dictate this in Russian to get anything honest. Her English-speaking self was founded on deception. So she can dictate her story to me and you can translate. Then, I'd like these memoirs to be published and for us to split the profits. This would be her legacy, as well as your inheritance and my remuneration. I don't work pro bono for ethical reasons. It's a way of keeping healthy boundaries around my work."

Zhenia turned and looked through the glass at Ben, who was sitting up in bed awake now, looking at his phone. She raised her eyebrows to try to get his attention, but he was looking down, typing something into his phone and smiling.

"We can split sixty/forty, which is unusually high as far as translation fees, but you'd be doing more than just translating. Her story is for you. You'd be the one receiving it, so this seems fair to me. How does this sound to you?"

Zhenia paused. It sounded insane.

"As I mentioned, I don't speak Russian," he continued. "So you will have to transcribe and translate, then send me what you have. She really is a fascinating woman. I've never done anything quite like this. It's taken a lot of legwork on my part to track you down."

"You couldn't just close your eyes and see my phone number?"

"No, that's not how it works at all," he said wearily. "I could see it had a seven in it, but that was all I had to work with. Anyway, would now be a good time to start?"

Zhenia picked up a plastic water bottle next to the lawn chair she was sitting on. It was filled with cigarette butts. She shook it like a dirty snow globe. There was a strong impulse to stall.

"She had other children, other grandchildren and great-grandchildren who she was probably much closer to. Why wouldn't she go to them?"

"No. They have nothing to do with this. She wanted it to be you. Your grandmother is indisposed. Your mother is not open to these sorts of messages—"

"Because she's a scientist?"

"No, I don't think that has very much to do with it. She's just closed off. Anyway, that leaves you, and I guess also the life you're carrying inside of you."

Zhenia froze. Her pregnancy wasn't a guarded secret, but who knew besides Ben, her grandmother, Nathaniel? Was this Ben's idea of a joke?

"Did Ben hire you to scare me?" She set the ashtray water bottle down carefully and turned to look back through the sliding glass door, but it was her own reflection she was seeing, not Ben.

"I assure you nobody has hired me. And my intention is certainly not to scare you. Your great-grandmother has enlisted me in a project that I think could benefit all of us. And she's eager, she's eager to start."

"How did you know I was pregnant?"

"Knowledge exists all around us and as a psychic I know how to interpret it."

Zhenia blinked, not knowing what to believe. "Is she here with me now?"

"In a sense. Spirits are in their own world, but there are places where you can overlap."

"Can she see what I'm wearing?" Zhenia looked down at her peach terry-cloth bathrobe. "Can she see inside of me?"

"I don't know. I don't think she can see your physical body. She's not near you in that sense."

"Then in what sense is she near me?"

"Through me. I'm the channeler. Listen, do you have a pen and paper? I would like to begin?"

There was a level of genuine alarm in his voice. The way she sounded when she asked people in stores with "No Public Restroom" signs if she could use their restroom.

"Fine," Zhenia said, not certain she believed in any of this but also curious about where this was going. She went back inside, got a pen and a notebook.

"If this is even real, then why does she feel like she needs my forgiveness?" Zhenia muttered, adjusting her chair at the kitchen counter. "She's dead. She got away with it, whatever 'it' was."

"I'm starting," Paul Zelmont squeaked, not seeming to hear her.

The words began to pour out—it was his voice still, not a falsetto or anything like that. But he was not a Russian speaker and he clearly was struggling to make the necessary sounds with his face and tongue muscles.

Zhenia translated in her head and transcribed the results as she went. Her hand moved quickly over the page, the Russian words coming out smoothly in English; she felt almost like she'd entered a trance.

"What?" Ben asked, peeking out of the bathroom, the only other room in their studio apartment. "Oh, I thought you were talking to me," he said, and closed the door behind himself.

CHAPTER 5

Every time someone leaves the cloud they have to reconstitute themselves from our shared pain. The suffering is communal and the girl gives it shape temporarily and then returns it to us.

—*He won't come back. Even if he wanted to, he wouldn't be able to find you.*
—*And what to say about the grouse! It was no good. Full of metal pellets. You would spit them out and let them clank against the plate. Lead pellets, probably.*
—*It was lead in the water that made the Romans go mad.*
—*But even that terrible grouse, what I wouldn't give for it. I'm so hungry.*
—*Hunger doesn't exist here.*
—*Time doesn't exist here.*

Time does not exist, this is true, but it's also interminable. It might not correspond in any way to the passage of time on earth.

—*Has anyone seen that man who comes here sometimes?*
—*He's probably dead already.*

It is also possible that it has just been a moment. The girl thinks about how when she was alive, time had not made any sense to her either.

Her first husband, the man she'd betrayed, who had fathered her daughter, Vera, he'd had an impeccable sense of time. His brain was a device that tracked himself in relation to the world around him— he'd had an internal clock and an internal compass. He'd been thoroughly decent too, clear, uncompromising. It was automatic for him and it overrode his sense of self-preservation. Even at the end he didn't turn on anybody. Did this ironclad decency make him more like a machine, or less? She'd never met anyone with this kind of decency in America.

Her second husband, her real husband, the one with whom she'd spent half a century, would have been offended by this—he had considered himself decent. But his definition of decency was very narrow. He helped other Jews, for example. But it was only Jews who interested him. And he helped them only in the ways that he considered helpful. And anyway, it was easy to pass as a decent person if very little of your own was ultimately at stake.

For her first husband it was his decency that got him killed, so what use was it?

The rest of us in the cloud, we have little interest in her musings.

We respond to her not in one voice like a Greek chorus but like bored people on a train who have all been crammed together for too long. Nobody wants to listen to these abstractions about goodness. Who cares? The man visitor. Now this is *what we want to know about!*

—Two husbands aren't enough for you? You want a third? I bet he's dead by now.

—Most certainly.

—You're not the first one to have made contact, you know.

"Hello? HELLO? Am I in the right place? Hello?"

It's his voice. She has summoned him!

"Yes," *she says, but so do the rest of us. Everyone is excited again for a visitor.*

We want to take him from her. We were not interested in him earlier, but her desire for him is so intense it has infected the whole cloud.

Through the fog she sees a hand, large and strong like a futurist statue's. Defined knuckles. She holds on and the man drags her out, even as several of us hold on to her waist and legs.

"One at a time, one at a time," *the man says.*

"We have stories too," we whine.

A lady's voice is delivering her tale of woe about the blockade and having to boil books for soup.

"You'll get a turn," *he says, placating us, pulling us off one by one like leeches and letting us get reabsorbed into the teary cloud of regrets.*

"Listen," he says, "it's you, isn't it, Irina Petrovna?" She looks different to him today. The same school uniform but her texture is wispier.

Our shared sadness is stuffed into her slightly differently, that's all.

"It's me." She nods.

"I found your great-granddaughter like you asked."

They've managed to float off a distance from the rest of us.

They're in a barren landscape. The rolling hills gleam strangely in Paul's light. Their scale is unclear—they could be on another planet, or inside of a body.

It reminds Irina of the colonoscopy photographs her grandson from her second life brought home from work.

"Lean in and talk," Paul says to her. "I'm ready." He opens his mouth very wide. She leans forward, clears her throat, and speaks.

"Vera's granddaughter?" she says, peering into his blinding gullet. "Zhenia? Can you hear me, then?"

Paul nods, gurgles.

Oh. This might work! I worried that you'd be like your mother, difficult to contact, and that my words would just sink like rocks inside of you, and what good would that do either of us? But I can tell you're different. You have an openness. Some might call it a gullibility!

Zhenia cleared her throat. "Is she insulting me?" she asked Paul, setting down her pen.

"Well, I don't know what she's saying, but I don't think so. That's not the sense I'm getting standing next to her. Maybe she's just not expressing herself well?"

"I'm not insulting you," Irina says in English. "I am saying that this quality in you . . . this pliability . . . maybe it's what I need. You are *listening*, after all. And what I'm about to tell you, I haven't told anybody. I lived many, many years with secrets that I repressed and repressed until I was formed from them. I am the shame that nobody in my second life knew about."

"We think that if you witness her, she might be released. Surely her actions have rippled into you. If you offer her forgiveness you may also find this useful?" Paul was trying to sound casual and wise, as though he had no horse in this race.

Zhenia blinked a few times. *Forgiveness* . . . that seemed a bit much. Probably not something she would realistically be able to offer.

"My daughter, as you know, is in an in-between state, unable to receive messages, but you're the closest thing to her. Receive this story for Vera's sake if nothing else."

Zhenia could hear Ben turning on the shower in the bathroom.

"May I begin?"

Once Baba Vera was invoked Zhenia couldn't say no, and a begrudging curiosity began to claw at her insides. "Yes, okay," Zhenia said.

She creased down the notebook page with the side of her thumb.

I was born to a mother who was wealthy and Jewish. Her family had survived atrocities. She was beautiful and pathologically stupid. My father was charming and a goy. This meant that by Jewish law, I was considered Jewish, but by Russian law I was technically not, and this made my life considerably easier.

I loved my father very much—it seems everybody did—though when I met people charming in that way as an adult, I knew not to trust them. He gambled away my mother's inheritance and then died before he had a chance to win any of it back. A heart attack at the dinner table the week I was supposed to go back to school.

Word of my father's death spread quickly and later that day people came by and took the table and most of the furniture to begin collecting on his debts. My mother was running from room to room, fighting them. My father's body was laid out on an unhinged door. I stood over him, not comprehending how one moment he could have been teasing me, laughing and blowing on his soup, and then suddenly his heart could stop and he could leave me so completely alone in the world.

I was the only child there to mourn. One of my brothers was dead; the other was in the army. My mother and I sat shiva for a week in our empty estate. Then she lost her mind and moved into a convent, and I went back to school.

The estate in Volohonsk fell into disrepair quickly. There was some legal confusion in its conversion into gambling debt and as it sat empty, and unrest in the country grew, peasants who had once worked for my father raided it and tried, drunkenly, to set it on fire. The house was so damp, I don't think it ever caught. I believe it's still standing, subdivided into communal apartments—though I've never been back to look. It's not a place I've given much thought.

It's where I came from, but it didn't form me. Not like Petrograd.

"Petrograd—is that St. Petersburg?" Zhenia picked at her cuticle. She had only a vague memory of the city she was born in, having left when she was five—a muddy park, a polyester curtain over a tall window, a row of tulips, a stuffed bear. Memories that could have been gleaned from photographs and might not have been her own.

"St. Petersburg, Leningrad, Petrograd, yes. They kept renaming it. We as a people have always stupidly believed in fresh starts. When I was there, St. Petersburg sounded too German so they changed it to Petrograd and that is how I knew it. When I moved back there again with Osip it was Leningrad. I never got used to that."

For me, it was also a place of fresh starts. When my father was alive, he'd used a winning streak to get me a spot at a finishing school of some renown. It was a relief to be out of the provinces, where all there was to do was ride my small horse in circles in the orchard and watch my governess blow her nose. I was not raised with ideas. That is why when the German teacher, Fräulein Agata Brunweiller, took me under her wing it was the most exciting thing that had ever happened to me. All of her ideas, no matter how borrowed or half-baked, seemed to me absolutely brilliant.

After my father died and his unpaid debts to the school put me in precarious standing, Fräulein Agata's interest in me only grew. Perhaps this was kindness, perhaps something else. I was eager and pliable too—this trait I was admiring in you earlier and which caused you to bristle. And I don't blame you for that because who would admire pliability other than a person who wants to bend you to their will?

The school allowed me to finish out the year, but I was unceremoniously forced from the dormitory and into my aunt Gittel's house, where she put me in a small room with a sloped ceiling next to the servant's quarters.

My aunt was as shrewd as my mother was dumb. She had a chapped, red dog-face and was always dressed, incongruously, in the latest fashions. They were wealthy and aspiring to be in Petrograd society, but unable to, on account of being Jewish. She took me in because she hoped that I could be her daughter Hanna's entrée into this gilded world that my gentile father had been able to sneak me into. Of course, she came to regret this.

At school, Fräulein Agata had formed a group of us as her entourage: me; a girl named Olga, who was so staunch and uptight it amused Fräulein Agata to poke at her—Olga ended up with a lot of blood on her hands; and Elsie-something, a very good piano player. Fräulein Agata would have her play for anyone she was trying to charm. Elsie was sickly and spent much of that year before the war in bed or visiting sanatoriums. She would have been the one we expected to die first and yet, it was her sickliness that probably saved her, because she was out of the city when the fighting started in earnest. My cousin Hanna wasn't a student, but she was also in the group because I wasn't allowed to go anywhere without her.

Hanna, sweet Hanna. She'd seemed to me then as bland as a big, mealy peach. Beautiful, healthy, spoon-fed almost into adolescence, no absence of parental love to make her devious or clever. She was one of the few people in the world who loved me, who showed me physical affection.

Though Fräulein Agata was the teacher, she was really only half a step ahead of us in life. She was quite "boy crazy." She didn't have many friends of her own, since the other teachers were old and stodgy and suspicious of her on account of how she'd been hired.

She'd come to Russia as a governess for a prominent family and had been caught having an affair with the father, a general who we all thought was much, *much* beneath her. His wife had found out, or at least became suspicious, and so the general had arranged this teaching job.

The general would come around once in a while and take her out of class and she would leave me or Olga in charge. I don't know what they did exactly, but her stories always seemed to end with him declaring his love and weeping into her bosom as the medals on his chest jangled. Then afterward, as our classmates followed the work that Fräulein Agata had copied onto the chalkboard from a stack of inherited lesson plans, Olga, Elsie, and I crowded together around Fräulein Agata's desk, and she talked to us about life.

She had very romantic ideas. She was interested in educating us fully. Our favorite topics were love, lovers, and revolution. Sometimes one of the regular girls would wander over as Fräulein Agata was talking in hushed, rapturous tones about the French Revolution, the city on fire, the guillotine sharpened and zinging, the oaths made on tennis courts by men of substance, *brave* men who were willing to risk everything, upend their comfortable lives. And right as Fräulein Agata was winding up her oratorical whisper, one of our simpering classmates would ask her something about conjugations or declensions, and it would give me such pleasure to watch Fräulein Agata go apoplectic.

She felt confident in the general and his ability to safeguard her even as the general's wife started a campaign for the school to only offer French. A few months earlier, an angry mob had stormed the German embassy and pushed the horse statues off the roof. The climate was not friendly to Germans on account of the Great War. So unfriendly that we made a point of walking Fräulein Agata to her dormitory in the evenings as a group, because either some anti-German protestors or perhaps the general's wife had left a flaming pile of shit on her balcony once, and another time had thrown a brick through her front window.

She showed us the note that had been tied to the brick with a piece of twine. We were all in agreement that the handwriting was a woman's made to look like a man's.

The general's daughters were in the younger grades, and sometimes our teacher would have me or Elsie (Olga refused) visit the elementary school to spy on them and report back. Fräulein Agata said that she missed them terribly and wanted to know how they were, but I did not believe this for a second. There was something thrillingly unmaternal about her. Those girls had been paths to the general, and the general had been a path to a wider world. It was through him that we'd gotten the invitation to the luncheon.

And that luncheon was when my life began in earnest, with all of its accompanying troubles.

Paul leans away from the girl and coughs for a little bit, rubs his aching jaw.

The girl is so lost in her monologue that her lips are still moving, though no sound is coming out.

Distantly, he can hear the other one on the line of the phone.

"What?" Zhenia said. Her hand was tired from writing. Rather than turn the page, she'd written very small up the margin and then between the lines. She massaged her hand and stared down at her scrawls.

The sounds Paul was making on the phone were no longer words.

He cleared his throat. "I lost her, I think."

Paul and Zhenia breathed into the phone, not saying anything for a while.

"That was something," Paul panted, finally breaking the silence. "I've never had anyone speak through me like that. In a different language and everything. Did you write it all down? Did it make sense? What did she say? Does it seem like there's a book in there? My agent's going to flip."

"She just talked about her childhood. A teacher that influenced her. A luncheon that changed her life. Did you know that she was a revolutionary?"

"She was? In the Russian Revolution? That's fascinating. Yes! My agent will definitely flip!"

"She probably killed people," Zhenia said piously. "My grandmother thought she must have. Where did you find her? In Hell?"

"Hell?" Paul repeated as if this were a place he'd never heard of. Zhenia ignored this.

"My grandmother didn't like to talk about her very much—or maybe she didn't have much to say. She barely knew her. But, I don't know. Do you think this could give her peace?"

"I think that's why she's telling us!"

"No, I meant, my grandmother. Do you think knowing her mother, the details, could that give her peace before she dies? Is this what she's been holding on for?" She thought about the way her grandmother would cry quietly next to her in bed sometimes and wipe her eyes with Zhenia's hair.

"How would I know? I've never met your grandmother." Paul dismissed this like she had just asked him something stupid.

How was Zhenia supposed to know the limits of other people's knowledge? Especially when they had psychic abilities and spoke to the dead? She felt suddenly irritated, like her feet were tangled in a blanket, or she had just walked face-first into a spiderweb.

"All right, bye then," she said abruptly.

"Don't forget to send me a photo of your notes!" she heard him say before she hung up.

CHAPTER 6

Zhenia's irritation lingered. She went driving to get rid of it. Why had she agreed to do this project with that strange man? Why was she always doing things that other people could see from a mile away would not serve her interests? The pull of curiosity, she supposed. She found herself at her friend Naomi's house in Malibu. Zhenia had only been here a handful of times—the house was purchased after Naomi's television show had gone into syndication, and soon after that Zhenia had stopped returning Naomi's calls and their friendship was short-circuited by Zhenia's jealousy. Zhenia sat on her friend's front steps and waited, listening to the ocean and the birds.

When Naomi pulled up, she acted as though she didn't see Zhenia, or Zhenia's car. She unloaded her surfboard and leaned it against the wall of the house, then turned on the outdoor shower.

Zhenia assured herself that she was really there by unwrapping a saltine and nibbling it as her old friend rinsed off. Naomi's success, Zhenia assumed, should have been enough salve to heal any wound.

"I haven't heard from you in a long time," Naomi finally said, coming out of the shower stall, toweling off.

Online, Zhenia had heard of people referring to her friend as a homunculus because of her largish facial features. Zhenia knew it was wrong, but she had felt some pleasure when she came across this. She'd read it to Ben with false incredulousness, and he'd shaken his head about the cruelty of people, but really both of them had been a little relieved that there were people out there, not them, but other people, who would take Naomi down a peg.

"Do you want to come in?" Naomi said. She was obviously hurt, but at the same time there was a small opening there that Zhenia could sense might be pried open further.

Zhenia lay back on her friend's scratchy welcome mat, saltine crumbs on her chest.

"I'm sorry I haven't called," she said. She caught her friend's bare foot as Naomi unlocked the front door and tried to step over her. "I'm sorry," Zhenia said again.

Naomi held on to the doorframe for balance. She looked down into Zhenia's familiar face, her long, cracker-filled mouth. Why was it that when you got something good, people assumed you were from then on somehow impervious to pain? Naomi's mother had died a short, horrible death, and none of her friends were there for her anymore. She hadn't reached out to Zhenia because Zhenia had betrayed her, she felt, by giving up on their dream and marrying Ben, of all people. Ben was Zhenia's first real boyfriend and he was perfectly nice and this was apparently all it took. Zhenia had the infuriating quality of being like a suitcase, just set her down and that's where she'll stay: blink, blink, blink. Not taking any responsibility for anything. Now she was lying on the doormat, and Naomi wanted very much to kick her, but also to help her up, and the latter is what she did.

She gripped Zhenia's forearm and led her inside into the living room. She dropped her friend onto the couch next to the long window overlooking the beach.

"Do you want tea?" she asked. Zhenia nodded, staring out at the ocean and the overcast sky. Some fins or tails popped out of the water at a distance. Dolphins.

"Remember that bald guy with a convertible?" Zhenia asked.

When they'd first arrived in L.A., Zhenia and Naomi had gotten picked up at a coffee shop by a bald guy with dimples and spent a bizarre afternoon riding around town with him. He was not much older than they were but Zhenia thought he looked like a large baby. Naomi found his confidence attractive. She sat in the front and Zhenia sat in the back, as he drove really fast down the winding canyon roads. It was an afternoon that did not have much of an impact on Zhenia's life, and yet that feeling of the whooshing road, the city lights below twinkling in the smoggy sky, the dusty smell from the drought—it had folded itself into a cranny of her brain and every once in a while it would shoot off, and she would think of it for no good reason.

Naomi brought the two mugs and set them down. "Keith. What about him?"

"Oh, you know him now?"

"He's at CAA. He works with my agent."

Zhenia realized that any initial impressions would have been overwritten for Naomi long ago because it was not a memory that stood on its own but part of an ongoing relationship.

"I was just thinking about how it felt to be new here, and riding around in the canyons," Zhenia said.

"It was fun," Naomi said neutrally.

"It shows up in my dreams," Zhenia said. "Me in the back seat, a car speeding along at night without a driver."

Naomi nodded. "You feel out of control, I guess." That didn't really take a trained dream therapist to parse.

Zhenia traced the outline of the banyan leaf right outside the window, then put her hand down when she saw she was leaving smudges. She tried to take a sip of tea, but it was too hot. Naomi's silence was ostentatious.

"I'm pregnant," Zhenia said, lying back on her friend's couch as if the two of them were friends still.

Naomi said congrats, but she was madder at Zhenia than she'd realized. "That's great," Naomi said, and got up with the tea she'd made them, went back to the kitchen, and dumped both mugs down the drain. Then she ran the disposal for no reason at all.

Zhenia wondered whether Naomi was jealous. She'd always thought of the jealousy between them as entirely her own, thick and clumpy with veins, a secret counterweight that held her and Ben's relationship in balance, even after Naomi was no longer in their life. But maybe Zhenia entering this new life stage first was bringing something up for Naomi? Maybe it was one area where Zhenia had won?

"And Ben is leaving me."

This wasn't true, but it felt true in the moment so Zhenia said it. Maybe she thought it would make Naomi more sympathetic, or maybe Zhenia just wanted to hear it out loud and feel a little jolt of fear. "Because he doesn't want the baby."

Naomi just shrugged and stayed behind the counter with her back to Zhenia.

Zhenia watched the tip of her friend's wet ponytail spread a dark circle across the back of her T-shirt. For so long Naomi had been an abstraction to her, an idea of a person who had gotten all the things Zhenia had not—a normal American upbringing, and then fame and fortune. Zhenia wanted to talk about the call with the medium, but it seemed obvious, now that she was here, that reappearing this way with her news and her emotional needs was not going over very well.

"That drive," Zhenia said instead, bringing them back to the conversation they were having before Naomi got up, "do you think that was like . . . the moment for you when everything changed?" She was thinking of what Irina had said about a luncheon and an invisible line after which "life began in earnest." Zhenia felt greedy for a moment like that.

Naomi turned and looked at Zhenia, a person who used to sleep beside her in her narrow dorm room bed, head to foot—there was a word for this in Russian, Zhenia had taught her, *valetom*, like Jacks on playing cards. Both of them in oversized T-shirts and socks, talking into the night, even though they talked all day and Zhenia had her own bed two floors down. Zhenia didn't do many sleepovers in high school so this was novel to her. Growing up, she told Naomi, her grandmother had been her closest friend. Naomi gathered that Zhenia had been a strange and anxious child, and as a teenager Zhenia had slept with too many people's boyfriends.

Zhenia often talked about her grandma—something about an orphan-age, a textile factory, a great love sent away to a labor camp. The grand-mother seemed like an interesting person, but a child whose closest friend was an adult . . . it was strange and explained something stunted about Zhenia. The way she managed to be both feral and spit-shined.

"Was that drive like a tripwire you crossed, that set everything else in motion?" Zhenia continued.

That drive had been that moment for Naomi, Zhenia was sure of it. But she'd been there too! She'd been present for a life-changing event and it hadn't chosen her to change. She hadn't even known it held that power. Though maybe she *had* known: Why else would she find herself returning to it so often?

Naomi shrugged. "I don't know." She found Zhenia's thinking weirdly passive and fatalistic. Like a moment is what matters, and not all the moments that surround it. Like Naomi had just pulled on the right rope and been drenched by success.

"I haven't had that life-changing moment yet," Zhenia was saying. "All the events in my life feel horizontal."

She looked at Naomi then and the sudden naked desperation of her gaze made both women look away from each other.

"I don't really believe things can be pinpointed to a moment like that," Naomi said after a while. She had allowed Zhenia to treat her poorly in their friendship because she'd felt guilty for being luckier and more talented, and, maybe most importantly, for having an instinct not to always do the opposite of what she really wanted. "What's that story about a thirsty person waiting for rain with their mouth open?"

"I don't know, what is that story?" Zhenia said, rubbing her arms as if she were suddenly cold. She wasn't interested in her old friend's condescending wisdom. "Maybe having this baby will be that event for me."

Naomi pursed her lips. She wondered whether Zhenia really could think this way, or if she was just trying to get a rise out of her. "It will probably change your life." Naomi straightened.

Zhenia shrugged. "Maybe it's too much to put on a baby. The wrong attitude to have going in." She said it without meaning it.

But Naomi was no longer engaging. She walked up the floating staircase and disappeared. Zhenia was surprised by Naomi's anger. It had honestly not occurred to her that Naomi, in her new and exciting life, would care one way or the other what Zhenia did. Naomi had always had this sort of benevolent superiority that Zhenia resentfully took advantage of.

She could hear things thumping around upstairs. A white cat Zhenia had never seen before walked halfway down the staircase, then noticed Zhenia and paused.

"You can let yourself out," Naomi called from upstairs.

Zhenia sat up from where she had splayed herself on the couch. She gave a small nod. Even as she gave it, it felt ridiculous. Theatrical. A high school production of Chekhov. *I have nobody, but I am so brave*, it projected out stupidly into Naomi's empty living room.

The cat was so absorbed with licking its paw that it didn't stop to watch as Zhenia got up and opened the front door.

CHAPTER 7

Creating stresses in the social fabric was one of Fräulein Agata's great joys, so when the general's friend, a society lady, asked her to bring the school's top students, my German teacher brought us instead. None of us marriageable by real standards—me, basically a penniless orphan, Hanna, not a student and Jewish enough not to mix her milk and her meat, and Olga, with a pince-nez and stern expression that Freud would have described as castrating. It's possible Elsie was with us too. I keep forgetting about her.

We arrived sweating from the bike ride. The house was quite grand and beautiful. Girls from my school lived in houses like this, but I had never been invited inside of one. The servants wheeled away our bikes and took our coats, leaving me self-consciously crossing my arms. I was in one of Hanna's old dresses and the silk pattern hung loosely where it had been filled out by my cousin's ampler breasts. We had arrived fashionably late, and were led through the halls past paintings of the hostess depicting her as she had been in the previous century. I remember thinking that the house must have been designed by the architect to build anticipation, the echoes of the party bouncing toward us as we approached. It took everything in me not to be overcome with excitement, break into a trot, and rush the dining room at full tilt.

Fräulein Agata could feel the excitement too. She was blushing, readying herself for trouble. We passed a room full of wicker birdcages; the tiny colorful canaries inside flitted about and sang nervously. Our teacher made us stand and look at the birds for a moment, let us smooth down each other's hair and regain our composure, as the servants waited, holding open the doors to the dining room. The guests were seated at a long table with a dark green tablecloth. It was a beautiful room, with silk walls, exquisite wood, a chandelier fitted with little electric bulbs, an enormous fireplace in full flame. Outside, it was already starting to get dark because the days were getting shorter and the clouds were hanging low over the river.

The general wasn't there, but there were other inbred aristocrats. Lots of golden epaulets and wives with heavily powdered faces. Scattered among them were guests like us, meant to evoke "exotic color"—a political prisoner recently returned from Siberia, a French perfumer with a bell-shaped nose. Seated next to the hostess was her brother, who wasn't all there. He had a napkin tucked into his collar. He gave the impression of being slovenly, though there was nothing specific that I could point to as being out of place. He was focused monomaniacally on the arrival of the food, a fork and a knife in his hands, like he was in an illustration in a children's book.

"He's a very talented mathematician," Fräulein Agata whispered to Olga, and maneuvered her to the empty chair beside him.

The perfumer was already holding Hanna's hand and kissing it up to the elbow in the French fashion, so she was stuck sitting by him.

The hostess introduced me without getting up from her seat to the man who had just returned from Siberia. He was dressed strangely, with a yellow silk scarf tied in a bow around his neck, a splotch of blood on the lapel of his jacket, an aloof look that Fräulein Agata and I both found quite intriguing. Fräulein Agata seated me beside him so I could be her little puppet.

She arranged my arms and tilted my head at a becoming angle. It was a game we called: "Doll."

"Isn't she a beauty," she said to the man. She used me often in this way. The attention was ostensibly on me, but the interesting stuff was happening between them.

"Beauty," I said to the man, "is, in my opinion, entirely overrated. My mother was beautiful, and it got her absolutely nowhere."

Fräulein Agata nodded. She'd heard me talk about my mother like this many times. She rearranged my hands and squinted at the results.

A man across the table tried to join our conversation. "Isn't beauty enough for its own sake?"

Fräulein Agata ignored this idiotic sentiment.

"She wasn't using her beauty for good," Fräulein Agata said. "We all are given talents, and it is a crime"—she tilted my head—"a sin, to waste them."

This got the man next to us to crack a smile. "A sin," he whispered dramatically, and crossed himself.

"You laugh, but you don't agree?" Fräulein Agata said, turning the force of her charm on him like a hose. He got wet.

She took my hand under the table and squeezed it. I could imagine that in her sleep she might appear quite ugly. But awake, her face was full of such cleverness and animation, I didn't know how it was possible for any man to resist her.

On the other side of her was the empty chair at the head of the table reserved for the guest of honor.

"Who is the guest of honor, I wonder."

"Probably Elijah," Fräulein Agata said to me, but for the benefit of the man, perhaps to show him I was Jewish, or merely to show off her knowledge of these things.

The hostess was seated far down the table on the opposite end, looking at each of us through her lorgnette with disappointment. Marriageable or not, Fräulein Agata reminded us on our way there, we had the commodity of youth. And it was true! The powdered women tensed and exchanged looks when their husbands tried to engage us in conversation.

One man with whiskers who was in charge of something in the customs office told us a story that was meant to be amusing, about someone who had tried to smuggle fabric without paying the necessary tariffs on it.

"How did he smuggle it?" my teacher asked, trying to rush him along to what must have been the good part.

"He had hidden it under another bolt of fabric!" the man said.

Nothing about his story was proving to be interesting. "I thought you were going to say he tried to smuggle it in a horse," my teacher said.

"Like a true Trojan." I giggled.

"How would that work?" Olga said, squinting at us across the table.

"In a carved-out compartment!" We were laughing, though it was very stupid.

"Gibberish," Olga scolded us, though she was laughing a little too.

Hanna tried to join in our fun, but the French perfumer was using her fingers to stroke his own nose.

The shape of it, I heard him tell her, amplified smell. Then he began to list the flowers that did and did not keep well in suspensions.

"Unsurprisingly," he said, "night blossoms work best."

Fräulein Agata leaned over me to talk to the man with the yellow scarf. There's no reason to be coy here. I might as well tell you who he was. Osip Valeiravich. Perhaps you've heard of him? He was a figure of some significance. To me, certainly, because I married him, but to the larger movement as well.

Zhenia was sitting in the car, parked in front of her apartment building. The air conditioner was blasting cold air in her face. She cleared her throat because it had been so long since she'd spoken.

"No," she said. "I've never heard of him. Babushka only ever talked about you."

Irina seemed not to hear this. "There was a time when most cultured people would have recognized the name. Well, a small window since history books erased almost everyone. All of us who made the Revolution possible disappeared after the Bolsheviks took over."

"Babushka only ever talked about you," Zhenia repeated.

"Yes, I heard you the first time."

Osip was back after being sent away for two years to Eastern Siberia for organizing against the imperial government. He was at the party to gather money for striking factory workers. It was fashionable to give money to liberal causes. Everybody in these aristocratic circles liked to act as though they were sympathetic to the workers and the peasants. Up to a point, of course!

"What was it like in Siberia?" Fräulein Agata asked Osip in a voice that to me did not sound entirely natural.

"Cold," he answered, and looked at me as though I were the one who'd asked.

"How cold?" she asked breathily.

He got up and scraped his nails along the frost on the window, then stood behind my chair and pressed his icy fingertips against my neck.

I gasped.

"I see," Fräulein Agata said. "Very cold." She took his hand off my neck and rubbed it to warm it up.

The hostess called down the table and asked if she was giving palm readings, and if so, to do her.

But then, suddenly, it was me who was up and kneeling before the hostess. It felt like Fräulein Agata had an ability to bend things around to her will, so no matter what you did you always ended up where she wanted.

I took the hostess's skeleton hand, loose glove of skin held in place with many large and heavy rings. All eyes were upon us. Hanna looked on hopefully. Olga pulled her pince-nez out of her sleeve and scowled.

I looked at the faint lines crossing the hostess's palm.

"I hear . . ." I began, "the galloping of hooves."

The hostess furrowed her brow and nodded.

"It's getting louder. Louder!"

And then, in truth, I did see a vision: Blood! Buckets of blood pouring through the street! The hostess's severed head, rolling like a cabbage down a stairwell!

I stopped at "Blood! Buckets of blood . . ." and trailed off. Even that was too much. The hostess withdrew her hand sharply, her rings banging against the table.

I heard Olga snort as she suppressed a laugh, and a man with golden epaulets shook his head and looked down into his empty plate. At that moment, the servants came in, carrying the tureens of soup, and the hostess took her annoyance with me out on them, causing the first servant in the procession to halt abruptly, and the ones behind him to trip over one another, sloshing soup onto their smocks.

We were not to begin eating, much to the chagrin of the hostess's brother, until the guest of honor arrived, and nobody knew when this would be. There was some grumbling from the male guests, some loud sighing from the female guests. The hostess reached for her brother's collar and pulled out the tucked napkin, but he defiantly tucked it back in.

I hovered uncomfortably, then went back to my seat, which was now occupied by Fräulein Agata.

Osip was telling her about the labor camp in Siberia, how the grizzly bears had gotten into the graves and developed a taste for human flesh. You could see buttons frozen in their scat.

"Thank God you got out," she said, touching his elbow. Fräulein Agata switched her allegiances easily. An imperial general, a Socialist revolutionary, it was all equally exciting.

Osip looked at me but I felt suddenly shy, so I drifted my gaze over to the hostess's brother, watching him go into the kitchen and come back with a bowl of soup just for himself. He sat down and slurped it loudly as the rest of the table watched. I could feel Osip's eyes on me, but I couldn't look away.

This soup dispute probably would have escalated further, but then the door blew open, and the guest of honor arrived. The perfumer's nostrils quivered, though it didn't take a special nose to smell him. The man who came in stank like a goat. He had a long beard that hung to his belly button. He was laughing as he entered. He'd opened all of the birdcages in the other room, and now the little canaries were flying in desperate circles around the dining room. One flew right into the window behind me. Another was perched on this man's shoulder, edging its way toward his beard, which was thick and long and seemed to contain food.

This man was Rasputin, the "holy man" who fucked his way through town. He was the tsarina's favorite charlatan. Everyone at the table was standing and clapping in confusion as they batted away birds. The servants quickly returned and laid all the food out now upon the table. Blintzes and piroshkis, caviar in all colors, pigs stuffed with lambs, lambs stuffed with pigs. I don't know. Everything. I had never seen such a spread.

The hostess was babbling about what an honor it was to have him in her home. Even her brother stood up a bit as he kept eating. Rasputin was flanked by an entourage, some dressed like him in peasant clothes, others in elegant suits. Bird shit was landing periodically on the tablecloth, which everyone was pretending was not unusual in the least.

My teacher stared at Rasputin, mesmerized. He was a gross old goat, and yet, I felt something too. A pull as erotic as quicksand.

Rasputin took the hostess by the shoulders and embraced her warmly. "Thank you," he said, "for inviting me into your home."

He stared out at the table of food before him. Then he stuck his dirty thumb into the raspberry jam. For some reason we were all still clapping, even as he stuffed that thumb into the hostess's mouth. Her eyes went round. Fräulein Agata opened her own mouth, ready for a similar sacrament.

Before taking his seat, he had me stand and twirl around. I felt his gaze like a wind blowing through me. "No, dear heart, that won't do," he said, and made me switch seats with my cousin. It was embarrassing, me in her dress from last season, being scrutinized and rejected in this way.

The French perfumer was disappointed in this outcome as well. He tried to protest, at which point he was ejected from the party and his seat was taken by a man in Rasputin's entourage. A nervous-looking type who must have been hired by the tsar to monitor things. He took no interest in me at all. His eyes were locked on his charge.

We all watched a canary disappear into Rasputin's beard and thrash around in there.

"He's found something, the little one," Rasputin said. "Let's give him some cake!"

The servants immediately brought out cake.

"Let them eat cake!" I heard Fräulein Agata shout, louder than she had probably meant to, but then Olga and I took it up as a chant. The call from the French Revolution. We were feeling rowdy and things seemed to quickly devolve.

Rasputin had his hands on both of Hanna's shoulders and was murmuring some sort of gibberish and she was looking down, smiling bashfully and twisting the end of his beard around her finger. I got up and went over to them, not sure how to put an end to it. He was used to getting his chicken cooked a certain way and Hanna seemed more than happy to oblige. Fräulein Agata got up and joined me, and then Osip did too, all of us trying to pull Hanna away from this madman. By then the hostess finally had enough of us and kicked us out.

My cousin made a scene. She went half limp and we had to drag her out the front door. The servants threw our bicycles down the stairs, and we walked them along the river, taking turns getting on once in a while to show off in front of Osip. It was unusual back then for anyone to have a bicycle.

Hanna was glum. She kept dragging her feet.

"Oh, Hanna," Fräulein Agata comforted her as we walked along the Neva. "There will be more parties. It was enough to have been picked." If Rasputin had picked my teacher, I'm sure we never would have left the party. But now that we were gone, her allegiances were with the revolutionary and Rasputin was a dirty old goat.

In the blue light of the afternoon, snowflakes began falling into the river and disappearing. It was a few days away still from freezing. When I was still little, Osip had been there for the bloody massacre. Unarmed protestors were slaughtered by the Imperial Guard in front of him. Shot on the ice and chopped up to bits just for asking for better working conditions. This led to the revolution in 1905, the one that ultimately didn't take. But the next one would. I had no inkling yet that I would be a part of it.

The vision I had seen when looking at the hostess's palm—where had it come from? I don't think I had any talents in clairvoyance, but it wasn't that far off from what did happen. Now that I'm on the other side, I can see the way time is not a line, it's more like a spiral, and that I was young and porous enough to stumble on the knowledge swirling around me.

"Excuse me," Paul interrupts, talking with his mouth open like he's at the dentist. "The name you kept saying . . . was it Rasputin? Are you talking about Rasputin?"

She has been holding his jaw with her little hands, talking animatedly into his shining mouth. She lets go now and dabs at his damp chin.

"Yes," she says, and places her hands on his shoulders. They stand there, like two girls teaching each other how to dance, swaying slightly in the damp breeze.

"What was he like?" Paul wants to know. Whenever he conducted past-life regressions with his clients in New York, they all inevitably ended up in the body of Cleopatra or Joan of Arc or Rasputin. Literal-minded people saw this as proof that it was a scam—"How is it possible that everybody was Napoleon? Everybody was Cleopatra? Nobody was a beggar who died of hunger and exposure or a clerk who died of loneliness?" But this was a misunderstanding about how all of it worked. The energy coursing through people like Cleopatra and Napoleon was so intense, it seeded many people. There were plenty of linkage points between these energetic forefathers, but it took some vision to see them and it was usually less interesting.

"Is it true what people said about Rasputin's dancing?" Paul wants to know. He'd heard about this ecstatic dancing that put people in an altered state and that Rasputin had used it to hypnotize the tsarina and gain power in the imperial court, or maybe he had used it to cure the hemophiliac son of hers?

"His dancing?" the girl says, and strokes his cheek.

This man is the only person whom she's seen cross to this world, and yet she isn't sure whether he's up to the task of hearing her story. "Why does everyone talk about his dancing? It was very stupid. It doesn't interest me at all. I'm telling you about him only because it's the beginning of my own story."

The cloud descends on them and Paul is suddenly immersed in a deep fog, dampness with voices coming from every direction:

—*She's talking about Rasputin. Doesn't like his dancing.*

—*She probably never saw it. Everybody liked his dancing.*

—*Forget dancing. Rasputin taught me a thing or two about fucking. I'll give him that.*

—*You, me, and half of Russia!*

—*Liars. All of you. He taught you nothing. What could he have taught you?*

Paul rubbed his face. His jaw hurt and his throat felt ticklish. The girl was gone. The cloud had reabsorbed her.

He cleared his throat. "Hello," he said into the phone he was holding in his hand back on earth. "I hope you got all that. Send me a photo when you can."

He hung up the phone without waiting for an answer. His ears were ringing and his hands were numb and clumsy. He went to the cabinet and got some hydrogen peroxide to gargle with. He wanted to get ahead of the comedown. It had taken him hours last time to get warm. His boyfriend, Sergio, had lain on top of him naked like one does for hypothermia. Sergio had found the whole thing arousing, but Paul felt exhausted. All of Paul's energy, erotic and otherwise, had gone into suspending himself on the other side.

LATER THAT EVENING, Paul puzzled out the messy notes Zhenia had sent him over email. Being on the other side with Irina, he could feel her desire for something merge into him, and it was strange now to read the transcribed specifics attached to the feelings she'd given him.

The stuff about the party, that giddiness, he supposed that was something he recognized. It's how he'd felt after moving to New York in the 1980s. He'd start each night not knowing with whom or where he'd end up: Andy Warhol's factory, the kitchen of a spaghetti restaurant, the basement of a university library, a bridge, a tunnel, a bathroom in the Empire State Building. It was so freeing and exciting until everyone started dying. Friends, strangers, lovers, his first boyfriend. It was after this that he'd gone away to the Institute to study. He'd wanted to see those people again.

Paul shivered. Reading her words somehow brought back the coldness. Maybe he would walk over to the Y and sit in the sauna. It used to be he'd meet men there to fuck, or at least wrestle with a little. Maybe he'd find a reason to stick his thumb into a stranger's mouth.

CHAPTER 8

That night, Zhenia was woken up by the sound of a man singing. She'd fallen asleep with the door to the balcony open, and the man's voice came in clearly. She sat up. The bed next to her was empty. Ben was still out with his new friends from his show.

Half-asleep, she dragged herself out onto the balcony. The singing was so strange, a voice that felt like it was calling to her. It was not any sort of song she recognized.

She threw on a leather jacket that one of Ben's friends must have forgotten at their apartment and found herself moments later on Fountain Avenue, walking toward the sound. She wanted to see the face of the person singing. She walked and walked and the singing did not get any closer or any farther. Could it be, she wondered, coming from inside of her somehow? Could it be the voice of the baby? She stopped walking finally when she got to the elementary school.

At night there were always cars parked out front with people in them. On cold nights the car windows would be fogged up. People were sleeping or maybe cruising. The singing had stopped by then. Was it singing even? she wondered. Maybe it had been more like a long wail, a howl. She was so tired. She started walking back home.

Right as she rounded the corner to her building, she saw Ben. She could tell immediately that he had to adjust something about himself when he saw her. He'd been caught off guard.

"Where've you been? Why are you wearing that jacket?" he asked, holding open the front gate for her.

She told him she'd been sleepwalking, which maybe she had. She wasn't sure where the singing had fallen on the spectrum of reality, and explaining this felt impossible. It was definitely the kind of thing Ben would not understand.

ZHENIA CALLED PAUL the next morning, lying flat on her back, not even bothering to sit up. Ben was snoring next to her.

Paul answered the phone midsentence, talking to someone else in the room.

"Hi," he said finally.

She told him about what had happened with the singing man the night before. "Was that connected to the ghost?" she asked him, her voice still groggy.

Paul sounded distracted, maybe a little impatient. "Was it a dream?" he said.

She sat up and looked at Ben's suitcase, packed and ready by the door. He wasn't leaving for a few more days. The eagerness of that gesture! "Not a dream. No. Do you think the ghost was communicating with me?"

"I don't know," he said. "I'm not with her."

"Can you be? I have some questions for her."

The sound of rustling over the mouthpiece of the phone, the voice of someone in the background. Zhenia pictured a much younger man on roller skates.

"I don't know," Paul said. "It's not really a good time."

"It's a good time for me." She looked up at the popcorn ceiling and didn't blink.

More muffled stuff, the young man's protests, and then Paul was back on the line.

"That's fair, but get a pen and write it all down, okay?" he said. Zhenia picked up the pen and notebook from her bedside table. "What do you want to ask her? If she came to you in a dream?"

"I want to ask her what kind of person leaves their kid in an orphanage." Her grandmother's abandonment was something Zhenia had carried around and inhabited like it was her own. "Who keeps a kid until they're old enough to know what's happening and then decides she doesn't want them?" Zhenia's voice quivered. "Aren't mothers supposed to sacrifice everything for their children?" Though, even as she said this, it felt obviously not true. Not that her own mother hadn't sacrificed for her, she had—demonstrably and resentfully—but not in the grand sense that Zhenia imagined she would for her own child. Not with love.

Paul made some sighing, snuffling sounds, grunts. He repeated her questions into the air and began to shiver. The response came in English. The voice not his, but made using his vocal cords.

"What kind of person? I don't want to generalize. But, probably a desperate one? Verochka was four when I left her. Talkative, always hungry, always demanding my attention. I would eat in secret or else she would reach into my mouth and pull the food out. I'm not blaming her. You have to understand, after the February Revolution we were so hopeful, but then once the Bolsheviks took over, there was no way forward for us. Osip and I had gotten out of Russia, but then we came back, and there we were. Stuck. He was sent away. And what do you think they would've done with me?

"Vera was going to end up in an orphanage regardless. I could try to get out and survive, or I could stay and die. I know that in the stories, everyone always does the honorable thing and dies, but tell me, how would that help Vera? Not to mention myself."

Zhenia looked at these words written in her hand on the page. She wanted to argue about these facts but she didn't know the shifts in history well enough. She listened to Paul continue in a high, strange voice.

"I put her in the best orphanage. The children in the neighborhood were going hungry, but there she was fed and clothed better than anywhere else. The ideas back then were so rosy—a breakdown of the nuclear family was an opportunity to build a more perfect society. The new generation wouldn't be encumbered by the baggage of their ancestors. No strong and unreasonable attachments to people such as myself, who did not deserve these attachments. Vera was little. I thought she would forget me."

"You thought she would forget you? You lie like a rug!" This was her grandmother's favorite idiomatic expression in English. "We tracked down your new family in America. A smug bunch. For them you weren't such a revolutionary."

"For them, I wasn't."

"Your other two sons and that daughter, they didn't know who you really were."

"People under terrible conditions—Hanna and I thought this was the clearest way to see a person's essence. Their true self. I believed that for a long time. My true self was cowardly, I suppose, because I was not willing to die. Well, I built another life for myself. In my other life, I did all the actions that were necessary to make me a decent person, even if my heart was hollow."

"Her whole life, my grandmother wanted to meet you so she could spit on you."

"Spit on me? I doubt that is what she really wanted."

Paul made some choking sounds in his throat.

"If I could spit on you for her, I would," Zhenia said quietly.

"You think that this hurts my feelings? No. I know that what she really wanted was not to spit on me, but to fall on her knees in front of me and beg for forgiveness for whatever it was she had done as a child to deserve being abandoned by me."

Paul coughed.

Another man got on the line. "Paul will have to call you back," the voice said.

"No, it's okay," Paul said after taking some small sips of water. "I'm okay. Sergio, give me back the phone."

"I don't like this," Sergio said into the phone to Zhenia before handing the receiver back to Paul.

Zhenia didn't like it either. Picturing her grandmother begging on her knees for love made Zhenia feel physically ill. Her grandmother's soft old knees bruised by the kitchen floor.

"Zhenia," Paul said, panting slightly. "Interesting stuff! Will you send it to me? I think the more of this I can show my agent, the better."

CHAPTER 9

Paul's friend from the Institute was in town giving a lecture at the John Jay College of Criminal Justice on the use of psychics in investigations and forensics. She'd found dead children in some highly publicized cases and now traveled the world talking about it. They'd both attended the Institute in the 1980s. Back then you learned about paranormal things by mailing away for pamphlets advertised in specialty magazines. Paul had always been interested in the occult. From a young age he could feel things swirling around him, and he hoped the Institute would give his contact with the other side some order, so that he might learn the protocols and create a structure and hierarchy, and that way he wouldn't disappear into it. When so many of his friends were wasting away in front of him from AIDS, the Institute was an escape—trading the dying for the dead.

Paul's friend came to the Institute because she'd lost her mother at a young age and hoped that she could learn how to find her.

"I've talked to everyone but her," the psychic said sadly, peeling the wrapper off her beer bottle. It was the lunch rush and they were crowded at the bar, too close to the dartboard. "As is often the case, the things you want the most are impossible because they are warped by your desire. Desire is so strong it blinds you. Cupid was blind, the incarnation of desire." She took a swig of her beer and watched a dart sail by them and land nowhere near the bull's-eye. "Sorry," she said. "I'm in lecture mode. Do you want to get out of here?"

They went to an exhibit nearby at the Met. They bought tickets to see Monet and the Impressionists, but ended up in the Egyptian room instead, looking at the shriveled mummies.

Paul, walking among the glass cases, tried to tell his friend about his new book—he was already beginning to think of the channeling project with Irina as a future bestseller. It seemed inevitable! The true story, told through him, of a revolutionary! How could this not be of interest to everyone who lived through the Cold War, i.e., the demographic who spent the most money on books? He didn't know the full story yet, but it was sure to be big! The woman had killed people, after all! It was certainly a departure from his previous, more saccharine collaborations, and his subspecialty of pets, which he had fallen into years ago, and which was lucrative enough, though a bit limiting.

Paul's companion did not seem very interested in his story. She kept interrupting him to wander off and converse with ghosts that he could not sense or discern. It was disorienting. Was she faking it, or was it merely that the two of them were on different frequencies, hearing different kinds of spirits?

He asked her this when they ended up at another bar. She had ordered them both martinis, but he was sipping his water. He didn't drink anymore. It interfered with his "instrument"—that's what he called his body.

"The mummies always stay around, I mean that's their thing, and they hate to be alone. But there are always too many cats in there," she said, scrunching up her nose. Paul had not been aware of any cats.

"Don't you want to stay sharp for your talk?" Paul asked as she took a long gulp of her drink. Seeing her this way made him nervous. Back when Paul used to drink, he'd find himself in the dark in-between places, and sometimes he'd had trouble getting out. He'd ended up in the hospital even, getting his stomach pumped, choking on the charcoal they'd filled him with, his parallel self still crawling through endless interconnected burrows, but he was finally jolted back into his body by all the vomiting.

She shrugged and chewed the olive. "Don't you miss living?" She pushed the other martini toward him. "Living like we did before the Institute, when our obligations were not to a world that isn't here." She stabbed her finger into the table for emphasis, and the drinks sloshed slightly but didn't tip.

"Sure, I do. My boyfriend complains that I'm like a monk," Paul said. It was difficult to be in two worlds at once. He thought of Irina's icy breath, somewhere on the other side but not far at all.

"High priest and high priestess," his friend said, clinking her glass against his, which he held only so that she wouldn't knock it over.

Paul looked at his watch. John Jay College was across town, and he felt responsible for getting his friend there on time and not so drunk that she couldn't stand to give her talk.

"We should probably go," he said, signaling to the bartender.

"It's fine. I can bend time." She waved her hand dismissively.

It's not that Paul didn't think bending time was possible. He thought it was, in theory, but this woman, he was becoming increasingly convinced, had vacated the space-time continuum and was perhaps what other people might call insane.

"She just sounds like she drank too much," Sergio said later when Paul was telling him about his day. Sergio had moved all the furniture in their living room off to the side and was practicing roller-skating backward in front of the mirror.

Paul was sitting on the floor, leaning up against the wall, and every time his boyfriend would skate by, Paul would extend his arms weakly toward Sergio.

"Do you think I'm like a monk?"

"What?" Sergio said, laughing. "No."

"You said that."

"No, I didn't!" Sergio laughed as Paul grabbed for him. Sergio allowed himself to be caught and rolled closer. He held the wall lightly with his fingers, let Paul pull down his shorts, and leaned into Paul's mouth.

"See, not a monk," Sergio said, his forehead resting on the wall, "you just work too much."

Paul felt for a moment with his boyfriend's cock halfway down his throat that he too could bend time. The way he had to relax fully to keep his throat from spasming and himself from gagging wasn't that different from what he had to do when he talked to Irina.

CHAPTER 10

After we got kicked out of the luncheon, Osip was walking us home, but none of us wanted the evening to end. We were laughing and picking bird shit out of each other's hair.

"It's good luck in Russia, bird shit, yes?" Fräulein Agata said. "They taught us all the superstitions in the academy. They told us Russians are dark swamp people who believed in all of them."

"Starting with God," Olga said drily. I, myself, had never given God much thought one way or the other. Jews were Jews whether we believed in God or not, but Olga had the zeal of a recent defector. Her uncle was a priest and she'd grown up pious, praying secretly in between classes for hours a day. Now she had a new holy text—a book that once belonged to her brother. It had a faded yellow cover and she kept it under her dormitory pillow.

She lent it to me once. It was called *What Is to Be Done?*—a novel about a girl who starts a sewing cooperative and utopian commune to free herself from an arranged marriage. It was written half a century earlier by a political prisoner.

"It's awful drivel, isn't it?" Fräulein Agata had said, pacing on her balcony as I read her the book out loud. I agreed, but I was in fact quite taken with it. One character, the revolutionary named Rakhmetov, slept on a bed of nails, training himself to survive any interrogation. He hauled barges to build strength, ate only meat and black bread, and didn't let himself fall in love. He was dreamy, what else is there to say?

We stopped under a bridge to watch a blind man play the accordion and a couple dance. Hanna dropped her bike and started running toward the couple and I had to catch her sleeve to pull her back. She thought the man was choking the woman, but Fräulein Agata assured us it was just part of the performance.

It was true though that when the man moved his hands down to the woman's waist there were red marks on her throat. She hung sideways in his arms like a wilted flower. Then slowly she lifted a leg and wrapped it around his waist to pull herself up and bit his ear.

The couple must have known we were watching, but they didn't acknowledge us. They looked only into each other's eyes as they slapped and bit each other. The Tango of Death, this is what that dance was called. Who told me that? I don't know, Elsie maybe, if she was there. Or Olga— she always knew things that I didn't.

A dirty-looking girl, ten or eleven, was sitting not too far away. Fräulein Agata made a show of taking a bread roll that she'd stolen from the party out of her sleeve and offering it to the child. Rather than taking it, the girl ate it straight from my teacher's hand like an animal. Eating with no interest in concealing her hunger. How different was this girl from me in my teacher's eyes?

This was humiliating. My teacher must have thought she'd have to chew Osip up herself and spit him into my mouth for me to be able to do anything with him.

"You should ask Irina to dance," Fräulein Agata whispered loudly, and pushed me and Osip together. Hanna swayed in place, unpaired. She was the good dancer. She enjoyed her own body like nobody else I knew.

Osip did not know how to dance at all, so Fräulein Agata began to teach him—an arm around his waist, guiding him forward and back—with me jammed awkwardly between them, trying not to step on all their feet.

"It's getting late," he said finally, pulling away and hiding his hands in his pockets. I felt I'd done something wrong to cause him to lose interest in us.

"Tell him you don't want the night to end," Fräulein Agata hissed into my ear. She probably did not want to go home to her lonely dormitory with its unpleasant surprises. Who could blame her?

But I could see where Osip's attention was now. A figure standing in the doorway across the street, watching us—an elegantly dressed hunchbacked woman. When she saw that we were all looking, she raised her hand and waved.

"Good night," Osip said, kissing everybody's gloved hands.

Then, when he got to me, he leaned his forehead against mine.

"You're a lovely kid," he said. And before I could protest that I was not a kid, he kissed me wetly on the mouth.

I'd never been kissed before by a man. I did not particularly like it. But it was exciting, because I seemed to have arrived there without my teacher's prompting. I had won a game without quite understanding the rules.

My teacher stared at him when he was done. "Well, I better get these girls home before they turn into pumpkins and rats," she said.

She was silent our entire walk back. I saw then that it hadn't been the victory I thought and that Fräulein Agata would make me pay for this betrayal.

"Fräulein whatever-her-name-is sounds like a monster," Zhenia said, yawning. She was sitting up in bed, propped by several pillows.

"Well, if she does, it's only because I am making her sound this way," Irina answered. "She wasn't a monster at all. She just had needs like anybody else. You're an actress in Los Angeles, are you trying to tell me that you don't care about attention?"

"How do you know what I do?" Zhenia said, feeling uneasy. "Do you watch me?"

"Watch you? No. I'm an interdimensional being. I live in a cloud of ancestral grief. I contain knowledge the way your internet does, but I don't see anything other than what's in front of me."

"Well, I'm not an actress," Zhenia said.

"Zhenichka, you're not a good actress, this much is obvious. But my point is still the same, no? Some people need the attention of men like they need air."

Air was overstating it. But, yes, Zhenia occasionally needed attention from men. An erection pressed against her leg at a bar or in a supply closet. A tangible talisman of her desirability. All the more potent if the men were spoken for, driven to do things to Zhenia by a compulsive force and against their better judgment. With the Tin Man, for example, however complicated his feelings may have been about Zhenia and his marriage, in the animal sense, his feelings had not seemed very complicated at all.

Comparing her to the manipulative German teacher, though, this was a stretch.

"Who are you talking to?" Ben asked, sitting up in bed, his hair hanging forward over his face in long, greasy strands.

Zhenia felt the irritation sparking off her. "Family," she answered, and held her flip phone for a moment in her hand, Paul's voice coming through tinny and small, before she snapped it shut.

"Do you think if I had kept at it longer I could've been an actress?"

Ben shrugged and yawned. "I don't know. I thought you were relieved not to be?"

Zhenia nodded, since this was factually correct, but not a satisfying answer. "Are you coming with me to my OB appointment?" she asked, tucking a strand of hair behind his ear.

"If you want me to," Ben said, moving her hand away from his face.

CHAPTER 11

Zhenia drove because it gave her something to focus on. Being a passenger now only made her carsick. Ben looked out the window and didn't say anything. Occasionally, he'd run a plastic comb through his slicked-back hair. A new tic.

At the red light she stopped and watched him. Neither of them was talking. His hair had the texture of a vinyl record, shiny and ridged. She imagined placing his head on a turntable, dropping down the needle, and playing it. A slow, deep voice at warped speed would speak out loud all of his secret thoughts:

"I don't want to have a child with you. I don't want to be with you. I don't want you. I don't want you. I should have picked Naomi when I had the chance."

Ben turned to her and opened his mouth, and for a second she thought she had summoned him to speak. But he was just telling her to go because the light had changed.

The OB, a middle-aged woman with a tortoiseshell headband in her frizzy white hair, walked into the room, flung her arms up, and then walked right out without acknowledging either of them. For a second, Ben and Zhenia forgot that they were upset and bulged their eyes at each other. Maybe synchronized eye bulging would sustain their marriage. Weren't there studies that showed people bonded better over negative things than positive ones?

Zhenia put her feet up in the stirrups and leaned back on the exam table. Ben rolled the little stool he was sitting on over to her so he could place his head beside hers. They stared up at the pictures of lambs in a field that were Scotch-taped to the ceiling. This was their first appointment. By Zhenia's calculations it was twelve weeks since her last period.

"How much time do we have to decide?" Ben asked her, in a voice that was meant to be reasonable and soothing. He stroked her head.

Zhenia focused on the lambs. She had told Ben she "wasn't sure" what she wanted to do. It had seemed like a way to ease him into the idea of parenthood.

The OB was back with the medical assistant, who was rolling in the ultrasound machine. Ben got up and gave the doctor back her seat.

The doctor introduced herself without acknowledging her previous entrance. She remembered Zhenia from when she'd come in as a translator. There'd been an incident with a Russian girl, a model who had probably been sex trafficked, though Zhenia didn't know this for sure, and maybe this was just her assumption about models.

Zhenia lay back down. She could see a halo of the doctor's frizzy hair over her knee.

She thought about the way her grandmother had shoved the protestors in front of the abortion clinic in Brookline, swinging her plastic bag full of snacks to smack anyone on the sidewalk. "You're in my way!" she'd cried out in her thickly accented English.

When the protestors tried to engage Zhenia with their fun facts about fetuses and fingernails, her grandmother began to bark at them like a dog and hiss at them like a cat.

"Surprise," she'd told Zhenia as she guided her through the clinic's front doors. "With people like that, always employ an element of surprise."

Her grandmother was the one who took care of Zhenia after the abortion she'd had in high school. She fed her soupchik and played cards with her and read Gogol's *Dead Souls* out loud in an effort to cheer Zhenia up or at least distract her.

The doctor squeezed some clear blue lubricant onto a dildo-type wand and inserted it gently into Zhenia. It felt cold and strange pressing against her cervix. Zhenia bleated, looking up at the lambs. An element of surprise that nobody acknowledged. On the black screen, they saw the snow turn into a fetus. Ben's face was unchanged by the little floating sac.

Then the doctor flipped some switch and they heard the machine-gun fire of the heartbeat.

"Very fast. That's normal," the doctor said jovially as Ben's face twitched.

"I had a vasectomy," Ben said into the room.

"Well, the proof is in the pudding," the doctor said, and slid out the wand. The word "pudding" made Zhenia gag.

The doctor looked at Ben's face more carefully now, as if he were the one who had made the gagging sound.

"There are ways of verifying the paternity in utero?" the doctor suggested, snapping off her gloves.

Ben pretended to hem and haw about how he didn't think it was necessary, but he obviously did. They worked out the logistics of the blood work as if Zhenia weren't there, naked from the waist down on a table between them.

After the doctor left, Zhenia got dressed in silence. The nurse came back into the room and Ben clenched his jaw a little dramatically as she drew his blood. Zhenia could feel the gel slide out into her underwear in a gloppy deposit.

Zhenia and Ben walked out of the office, both of them stiff and wooden, but perversely arm in arm. It was in this configuration that they bumped into the Tin Man walking into the OB's office with a blond woman.

He nodded at Zhenia, and Zhenia nodded back but kept moving, not stopping to introduce him to Ben.

"Congratulations!" the Tin Man called at them, and it took everything in her not to turn around and give him the finger.

"Who was that?" Ben asked.

Zhenia waved away the question. She was upset with Ben for having questioned his paternity. It bothered her, his implication that she could be capable of being unfaithful, though at the same time she knew factually that she was capable, that she had been unfaithful many times, just not in this particular instance.

She gave Ben the car keys. "I'm going to stay here and fill out some paperwork," she said. She had a growing pile of forms she needed to go through and send to insurance. He would be back to pick her up for their date at the Magic Castle, a members-only club for magicians in the Hollywood Hills.

Zhenia nursed her bad mood in the little office the translators had in the back of the hospital. There was a lady there named Dee who ran all the administrative stuff and rarely left that room. Dee was a calming presence. She rested her large breasts on the desk and hummed to herself, and always reminded Zhenia to take breaks.

During her lunch, Zhenia ran into the Tin Man again in the cafeteria.

"I'm having my uterus taken out," she whispered, standing too close by the soft-serve machine.

For a second the smug expression on his face melted.

"Or, I could have been," she continued. "Don't congratulate me."

He nodded. "Okay," he said. "So you *are* pregnant."

"For now. Yes." Zhenia felt herself deflating. "It's kind of a Schrödinger's cat situation."

"Okay," he said, and pressed down the lever to swirl chocolate and vanilla into a cake cone. "I don't think you are using that correctly. But okay. Was that your husband?"

He used the hand holding the ice cream to press the lever again as he filled a second cone.

"Why am I not using that correctly?" Zhenia asked him, ignoring the other question. "The cat's existence depends on other people's observation of it."

He had an ice cream cone in each hand.

"I've got to get back to work," he said, and squeezed around her to get to the cashier, who took the lanyard from around his neck and scanned it.

Zhenia trailed behind him, trying to use the internet on her flip phone to look up Schrödinger's cat so she could prove him wrong, but by the time she found it and looked up to tell him, he and the blond woman from earlier were already standing by the elevator, licking each other's ice cream cones.

Back in her cramped office as Dee hummed, Zhenia daydreamed about the curve of the Tin Man's cock, the way it had felt in her hand, like a weapon—which one was it that curved up? A scimitar. She'd stroked it and his eyes had rolled back into his head. Eyelashes fluttering over white crescents.

"Yes?" She answered the phone, blinking several times to erase the feeling of the ghost cock in her hand.

It was Paul.

CHAPTER 12

Hanna was walking me to school the next morning in the dark. The thin layer of snow had turned icy. I usually got a ride from the coachman but my aunt had somewhere she needed to be, probably the tailor's to buy herself another ball gown to wear around the house, since nobody invited her anywhere.

Hanna and I were taking turns sliding on the ice, holding on to each other so we didn't fall down. She kept asking me about the kiss, and though erotically it was a baffling nonevent and interesting to me mainly in how it shifted my relationship with my teacher, I made up some nonsense as though I were a heroine of a Romantic novel. We were almost at the school when a very strange-looking carriage pulled up beside us. It was gilded and ornate, with the two-headed eagle coat of arms carved into the door, but it looked very old, in that narrow style from a century earlier. It must have come from a museum. Or some back room of the palace where they kept obsolete things.

The door to the carriage flew open and the horses slowed but didn't quite stop. There was Rasputin again with an entourage of men. One was passed out with a lantern on his lap. Shadowed chaos in the velvet red upholstery. How many of them were in there, I don't know.

"My little bird!" Rasputin shouted, leaning his torso out of the carriage. He seemed out of his mind. "There she is! My little swallow!"

I dragged Hanna toward school, pretending not to hear him.

"Come, come!" In his stupor, who knows what he thought was happening.

Hanna pulled away from me. I tried to grab her hand back but she let her muff drop to the ground, and while I leaned over to pick it up, she climbed up into the moving carriage.

It seemed impossible to me that she could have gotten into his carriage by choice. He must have hypnotized her in that moment when I'd been looking down.

The coachman gave the horses a lashing and they broke into a trot. I ran after them, waving both muffs and shouting, trying not to fall. But it was no use. I slipped and they turned at the roundabout and were gone.

I got up, avoiding the gaze of the people who I imagined were watching this whole scene from their bedroom windows. I was scared. We never went anywhere unchaperoned. If my aunt found out, she'd be sure to blame me. She would kick me out of their home and I would have nowhere to go. What was that maniac going to do with her? He could've done anything he wanted. He had the power of the imperial court behind him, he had the tsar by his whiskers, and my cousin was a nobody, just some Jewish girl without any of the rights you, Zhenichka, take for granted.

I ran to school, straight to Fräulein Agata's classroom. She was in the middle of regaling the younger girls with an inspiring speech about our world's inevitable march toward progress. I stood in the doorway, out of breath, looking a fright, still in my galoshes, the bottom of my skirt soaked up to the knee, clutching a muff in each hand.

She tried to ignore me, but when I wouldn't leave she finally came over. I was terrified, but in some way I was relieved to have bigger news to distract from my own transgression.

When I told her about Hanna she was furious. "You idiot, why did you let her go?" My teacher's own life could be ruined now too—the school would hear of her extracurricular activities, her lack of judgment. They wouldn't want the scandal. They'd send her back to whatever hell it was she'd escaped, back to a country that was being torn apart by war.

To you, maybe this seems overblown—you probably get into cars with strange men all the time. But back then it wasn't done. And Hanna, she was innocent, coddled. She only saw the good in people, to a fault. That disgusting old goat could hurt her in ways I didn't fully understand.

I don't know how I got through the rest of the day. My heart beat so loudly I thought everyone would be able to hear it. I missed all the questions asked by my history teacher, spilled an entire pot of ink on my desk, and got my knuckles rapped with a ruler. After school I couldn't go home and face my aunt, so I walked down Nevsky Prospect. I walked in circles, a muff on each arm, trying not to think about what that goat was doing to my cousin's body at that very moment.

It got cold and dark early so I wandered into the Astoria, the grand hotel where my future would ultimately be decided. Back then it was a popular spot for diplomats, Allied officers, and journalists to lunch. I sat in the lobby and pretended I was waiting for someone, making a big gesture of looking at the large clock and affecting an air of impatience anytime the hotel's concierge looked my way.

"Young lady, how can I help you?" he asked, and I looked down at the two muffs in my lap and pretended not to speak Russian, though I'm sure my school uniform gave me away. To avoid unpleasantness, I wandered off to the restaurant, where there was a din of people drinking and scraping their forks.

I was surprised to see my teacher's general there, eating some elaborate dessert with a young woman who was probably not his wife. The young woman had hair the same red color as Fräulein Agata's, and this fact alone gave me an unpleasant feeling. I felt pity for my teacher, which I knew was unforgivable. How easy all of us were to replace!

The bellboy was asking me now, in all the languages he could muster, what business I had in the hotel. I got out of there before the general noticed me, though what difference would it have made?

Outside again it was even darker and colder. The gas streetlamps were shivering. After a few more blocks, it was finally too cold for me to stay out, so I went home.

I came in through the back door into the kitchen. My teeth were chattering. I thought I might try to sneak past my aunt and the servant and hide in my room. I wanted to put off for as long as possible having to tell my aunt that my cousin was missing. But then I heard voices coming from the drawing room.

It was Hanna. She was home and safe. I pressed my face into a corner and cried into the wallpaper from relief.

"Irina, is that you?" my aunt called from the other room. "Where have you been?"

There was Hanna, sitting by the fire, embroidering flowers onto a handkerchief. She tied the thread and passed me her project so I could blow my nose. I turned away from them and stood facing the fire, trembling.

"I told you, Mother, the teacher let me study with them today and then she kept Irina after school to help with tutoring the younger ones."

"Yes," I lied. "I helped them prepare."

My aunt scolded me for being late, for ruining my clothes. Why was I soaking wet? She didn't understand. My cousin pet my hand mildly. I thought I was losing my mind, she was so convincing.

"I'm sorry I spoiled your handkerchief," I said, wiping my nose again with a particularly dainty flower. What had she done all day and why did lying come so easily to her?

Later, after I was in bed, she came into my room. I couldn't sit up without banging my head on the sloped ceiling. I had a hot-water bottle on my feet, but still I was shivering. She sat on the edge of the bed and stroked my hair.

"You scared me half to death," I whispered. I could feel the buzz of excitement in her fingers.

"It was marvelous," she whispered back.

This infuriated me. "What could have possibly been marvelous?" I snapped, sitting up too quickly and hitting my head.

She looked down at her toes and wiggled them inside her slippers. "What he did to me felt so good."

I thought of myself as the bad one, capable of surprising those around me. I'd been the one to be kissed. And Hanna had always been bland. Bland and good. This transformation of hers was incomprehensible. And the total absence of remorse or shame. Had she done these kinds of things before? I clearly would have been none the wiser.

The next day, when Hanna walked me to school, Fräulein Agata looked at her with a newfound curiosity. I was allowed to skip calisthenics on account of being slightly feverish. While the other girls stretched and jumped, I sat with Fräulein Agata on her small balcony and sniffled as she smoked her prohibited cigarettes. She was still mad at me, but she wanted to talk about Hanna.

"Your cousin," she told me, blowing smoke out her nostrils. "We've misjudged her. We thought she was a rock, but she's an egg."

And that was exactly it. She was an egg, and she was starting to hatch.

Paul was sitting on the floor by the windowsill, wrapped in the duvet he'd pulled off the bed. Outside, a pigeon was pacing on the fire escape. Somebody was buzzing at the door.

A client.

He'd lost track of time. He stood up too quickly and this made him dizzy. He grabbed hold of the wall, waiting for the spinning to stop. He had a weekly appointment with an elderly heiress to a shipping fortune who liked to talk to her dead cat.

The cat was, Paul suspected, not really a cat, but her dead sister pretending to be the cat. He'd expressed this early on, but it didn't seem to make a difference. It was easier for his client to accept love from the cat than from her sister, with whom, according to all the tabloids many years ago, she'd had a complicated and litigious relationship.

Paul buzzed in the heiress and ate a marzipan rose, a gift from another client. He didn't allow himself to hover over his email, waiting for Zhenia to send photos of her notes, even though he wanted to know what it was he'd just channeled. He could hear the heiress huffing and puffing as she came up the stairs, but he waited to open the apartment door until he was done chewing. It was important to give himself time to come back to earth fully before departing again. There was a level of showmanship that was expected from him with his wealthier clients, and he didn't want to disappoint.

CHAPTER 13

"Do you think I'm a rock or an egg?" Zhenia asked Ben as they waited in line to go through the rotating bookcase to get into the Magic Castle. Getting in was basically impossible unless you were a professional magician and a member, but Ben's friend worked there as a bartender and had gotten them on a list.

"Is that a BuzzFeed quiz? Are you a rock, an egg, a Carrie, or a Samantha?"

Zhenia wobbled in her high heels, leaned on Ben's shoulder. "I worry I'm a rock," she said.

"You're my rock," Ben said automatically, eyes on the moving line.

What did people mean when they said that? Zhenia was tied around his ankles, sinking him? He couldn't dig through her, he couldn't build on top of her? She was made of millions of fossilized dead things but she herself had never been alive?

"Jesus," Ben said, noticing that she was crying.

She wiped her face on his shoulder. "It's the hormones," she said.

When they were first together Ben would act like it was a miracle when Zhenia cried. Maybe it amazed him that he could cause such feelings in another person, because he'd been terribly shy in high school and hadn't had much luck with girls. But as they stayed together longer, and Zhenia cried more and more often, it must have become clear to him that this wellspring of feeling was related to him only tenuously.

THE SADNESS IN her and festering wounds came from something in her childhood or even earlier. She dabbled with antidepressants, but she never stayed on them long enough to change because they all had side effects that made her feel sluggish and dead, much like this pregnancy. When she cried now she could see Ben's jaw begin to clench, the rounded muscle ball protruding under his stubbled cheeks. Just like when the nurse had been drawing his blood, but now it was Zhenia's turn.

"Were you very into magic tricks as a kid?" Zhenia asked him.

"Wasn't every little kid?"

"I can see it," she said, reaching up and smushing his cheeks. "Little Ben with some dumb haircut sending away cereal boxtops for magic trick wands."

Her tone was objectively a bit nasty, but she did find the image of shy little Ben trying to get mastery over some pointless sleight of hand genuinely touching. His barely suppressed hope as he shuffled cards or cups that this would awe people and gain him respect.

He took his hand out of hers and put it in his pocket. She knew that he'd been looking forward to this evening and now Zhenia was trying to ruin it for him. Their pattern was that Zhenia would feel sad about something, then she'd lash out at him and this would make Ben more withdrawn, which in turn would make Zhenia more self-pitying.

Zhenia looked at the other people in line. A man with embroidered jeans tried to catch her eye. She stared back at him without blinking. Why were all the men here wearing those stupid fedoras? She'd saved Ben from that at least. So he can't say she didn't give him anything.

"Come on," she said, slipping her hand back into the crook of his elbow. "I'm sorry! It's cultural! It's how we joke. Sorry if I don't come from a farm in the Middle West where everybody is nice to each other! After *you*, after *you*, after *you*, after *you*," she said in a mock meek voice to invisible people, and walked through the bookcase-cum-turnstile, smack into Naomi, who was standing in the gilded hall with the castmates from her show, one of whom was a founding member of this place.

Zhenia froze for a moment, blindsided, embarrassed to be caught publicly in her rituals of meanness. She was just feeling her way into the rhythm of their argument, and to suddenly have a witness who knew both of them diminished any pleasure Zhenia could take in riding the fight's familiar grooves.

"Hey!" Naomi said to Ben, and hugged him. "Congrats on the show. Isn't Will amazing? He directed a couple of episodes for us."

Zhenia stood there wobbling in her high heels, staring at them. The jealousy she felt was almost like a balm, a plastic bag over her head. They were meant for each other. They always had been. Zhenia had merely been a detour. Ben had been dealt a bad card, but see, this is where that sleight of hand can finally be put to good use.

"You're here," Naomi finally said to Zhenia, and Zhenia nodded, avoiding eye contact, not wanting Naomi to bring up the breakup that Zhenia had fabricated when visiting her house.

Maybe it was not so much a fabrication as a premonition?

The hall had many rooms going off it, with many acts happening simultaneously in each little theater.

They followed Naomi and her group toward the room with a red diamond over the door.

Ben was very excited to be with Naomi, Zhenia noticed. Of course, she knew all the best acts to see, blah blah blah.

"Are you in the film business too?" Naomi's castmate asked Zhenia politely.

"She could be your stand-in," another castmate said to Naomi. "I guess you don't look alike exactly, but you guys have such a similar vibe!"

Zhenia smiled tightly. Her stand-in, yes. That's what Naomi had always wanted Zhenia to be. A friend for her shadow. Or no, Naomi didn't care about that. She just wanted Zhenia to keep Ben warm, so Naomi could slip in when she was ready.

"No," Zhenia said, "I'm not an actress." She said it with a protracted hiss.

"What do you do then?" the small elfin blond asked after the others had already turned away in discomfort. What was that dog whose jaws clamped shut on something, and there was no opening them? This blond pit bull.

"I'm a geneticist," Zhenia asserted loudly.

Ben stopped his conversation and looked over at her.

"The only thing that can save us from replicating the bodies, thoughts, and patterns of our ancestors is a mutation, an act of grace. We can wait for nature to do this, or we can make it happen ourselves," Zhenia said.

Naomi tried to hold back a laugh, but it came out as a snort. Zhenia in a corner always came up with something interesting. That is why this cushioned basement she'd chosen to lock herself into with Ben, and now populate with babies, was especially, in the words of Naomi's TV alter ego, a bummer.

Ben didn't even know what to say.

"What the fuck?" he finally whispered as the house lights dimmed. He didn't wait for an answer, already entranced by the woman onstage Hula-Hooping. The lady danced, spinning in circles. Every time she did a full rotation, she would turn back, wearing a different-colored outfit.

Zhenia kept watching Ben watching the magic show. When she noticed herself doing this she became annoyed, at herself but also at Ben. Why couldn't she just watch the show directly? Why couldn't she be awed by this woman's gifts at illusion instead of bifurcating her vision with Ben's, and feeling his awe but not her own?

The lady onstage was now in a bikini, and then, a few rotations on the Hula-Hoop later, somehow in a full-length gown. Everybody clapped. Then the main act came on, a magician in a space suit. He had volunteers from the audience pick cards, and then whichever card they picked would appear inside the plastic dome of his helmet.

Everybody gasped and clapped.

"How do you think the Hula-Hoop girl did that?" Ben wondered as they filed out of the room. "She must have had something hidden in her mouth. Like a button she was pressing or something. And the magician in a helmet," he gushed. "What was the trick there?"

Zhenia was mildly curious about how they did it, but mostly curious about why they would bother.

"It's magic," Zhenia said. "Why are you ruining it?" What kind of magic was she talking about now? Not tricks. No. More like the inexplicable magic of existence that Ben had no interest in engaging with on those terms. She was steering them back into the fight.

Ben kept smiling and didn't go for the bait. Naomi and her friends drifted away from them to the next room, and he wanted to follow, but Zhenia held him in place.

Zhenia's lipstick was smudged outside the border of her mouth, and he didn't say anything, just looked at it. A man with little scissors and a card came up to them and offered to make their silhouette portraits. He positioned them facing each other, almost nose to nose, like the optical illusion where you see either a vase or two profiles depending on how you look at it.

"You guys are the perfect height for this," the guy with the scissors said as he snipped a black piece of card stock.

Zhenia and Ben breathed on each other as the man worked. Ben smiled and adjusted a strand of Zhenia's hair behind her ear.

She often thought Ben hated her or was glaring at her, and then she would look at his face and he'd be smiling.

"Hold still," the man with the scissors said. "Just one more minute."

"Do you believe in magic?" she asked the man without moving her head.

He made eye contact with her without slowing the snipping he was doing with the scissors. "Abso-fucking-lutely."

"Can you make things disappear?" she asked.

"Depends on the things."

These feelings of dread and loss that she woke up with.

"Pregnancies?" Ben joked.

"Don't know about that," the man said, not engaging. He took the last snip, letting the extra paper fall away, then placed the cutout on a jumbo playing card and handed it to them. It was the sort of object one found in the belongings of a dead aunt. An object so clearly trying to have sentimental value, like the sand-art trinket her grandmother had brought with her from Russia. The layers of colored sand faded, but if you looked at it closely you could see the image of a sailboat in shades of tan.

Ben had the stamina to watch endless magic tricks. They went from table to table, little theater to little theater.

Zhenia was exhausted, and every time she would try to sit down some-where to escape the onslaught of magic, a magician would come up to her and start pulling things from her own purse, pulling her driver's license out of her bangs, pulling her car keys with their rabbit-foot key chain out of her ear. Zhenia finally lost it when a smug, portly man had somehow managed to take her grandmother's opal bracelet off her wrist and pull it out of his own gross mouth.

He wiped it on his shirt and returned it to her.

She gagged dramatically, overdoing it a bit, until the magician backed away from her.

Then she went and found Ben at the bar, talking to Naomi and his bartender friend.

She told him she would be napping in the car.

"Are you sure you don't want a drink?" the bartender offered.

Zhenia shook her head. "I'm taking him to the airport," she said. "And, I'm pregnant," she added, making it official.

"Oh shit," the bartender said, assuming it was good news and clapping Ben on the shoulder. "Well, more for you then! Congrats!"

ZHENIA CALLED HER mom as she waited for the valet to bring out her car. Her mom was not sleeping yet. She was in bed watching a show about a no-nonsense British detective with a short haircut who solved murders.

"Nathaniel probably already told you," Zhenia said.

"Told me what?"

Zhenia didn't know whether her stepdad really hadn't said anything or if her mother wanted to pretend that he hadn't. Maybe she just wanted to hear her daughter tell her herself.

"I'm going to have a baby," Zhenia said.

"Oh!"

By her mother's reaction, Zhenia could tell that Nathaniel really hadn't told her.

Zhenia did not remember ever telling her mother anything that seemed to elicit this sort of joy.

"So you're going to move back to us, then?" Marina said as though this was the only reasonable thing to do. Was she anticipating already the end of Zhenia's marriage?

"When is your due date?"

"April twelfth."

"Good. Better than a summer baby. I was so hot the last two months."

Zhenia's mother was acting as if this was something she had been waiting for patiently and silently.

"It must be too early, then," she said, "for you to know if it's a boy or a girl. I hope it's a boy. For your sake. They're easier."

"Thanks, Mom," Zhenia said drily, her nose twitching in a rabbity way that made her grandma call her *Zaika*, the Russian word for "bunny."

"Do you think Babushka will know what's going on?"

Her mother went quiet. "Zhenichka. Who knows. I think she's been gone for a while."

This wasn't the first time her mother said this to Zhenia, but for some reason it was the first time that Zhenia actually heard her.

"Okay," Zhenia said. "I think I'm going to come visit very soon then."

She could tell that her mother was covering the receiver and talking to someone in the room. Nathaniel, probably.

"Did you know anything about Babushka's mother?"

"Babushka's mother?" her mom said, getting back on the phone. "She was a spy. Or something. You know all the same things I know."

"This guy called me and has been telling me her story."

"I don't know what you mean by that, Zhenichka. But come home quickly. You have the future inside of you and all you want to do is talk about the past."

Then Zhenia saw Paul's New York number on her caller ID, which she'd saved in her phone as, simply, Pra-Babushka. Great-Grandma.

If Ben knew about these calls, he would probably try to dismantle them like the magic tricks. He would want to figure out what Paul had in his mouth, what buttons he was pressing, in her, or in the universe. The only thing about magic that interested him was proving that it wasn't magic, and probably hoping in some distant, hidden place inside himself that he was wrong.

CHAPTER 14

When Paul gets to the place where they usually meet, Irina is already there, leaning against a papier-mâché-looking rock, waiting for him. She skips toward him, uncharacteristically hitching her skirt up over her knees. As she gets closer, Paul can see she has garish circles of rouge on her cheeks, blue eye shadow.

"I missed you," she says, puckering her lips. Her voice is hers but there is almost another voice inside of it. "I've been thinking about you."

"Would you like to continue with your story?" Paul asks, leaning back from her slightly, and trying to sound neutral.

"Yes, yes, of course!" She takes his hand and clears her throat. "My whole life I was mistreated terribly and did nothing wrong myself. I always behaved very honorably even though I never paid people back the money I borrowed and I was a stupid whore."

Then she takes one of Paul's glowing fingers and puts it in her dry little ghost mouth.

As Paul tries to pull it out, she bites him and smiles. Paul feels terror wash over him. The fingertip pierced with what feels like ice. Then she lets go and his finger makes a suctioning pop as he pulls it from her mouth.

She begins laughing, her mouth wider and wider, and then she explodes into a dark, powdery cloud. The smell gets stuck in Paul's nose. Dusty books, stale cigarettes, vodka sweat, and cat dander.

THE SMELL, IT turned out later, belonged to a man who ran some hole-in-the-wall bookstore in Petrograd and then another one in Paris, an émigré who hated Russia and France by equal measure, and Irina especially, though she never even knew who he was—she just bought her newspapers from him, and apparently had at some point borrowed money. Paul had heard that spirits could take on the form of whomever they wanted, but he had never come across an impersonator before. The spirits he talked to were lingering obsessions, too absorbed in their own sorrows to have any interests outside themselves.

PAUL WRAPPED HIS finger in a mustard bandage. It throbbed for days. A snakebite, he told his other clients—even though there were no visible marks under the bandage and where would he have been bitten by a snake? Sergio didn't ask.

Sergio had seen Paul get unreasonably attached to spirits on the other side. A year earlier, Paul had talked with some lady once or twice and when she suddenly disappeared he'd mourned that loss more than he'd mourned the deaths of people he had known in real life. The man who'd hired Paul to make contact had taken it all in stride, but Paul couldn't let go of the feeling that he'd failed to convey some important message. Sergio had nursed him through all that and now trouble was brewing all over again. Sergio could see it from a mile away, but Paul could not. It was like he was being hypnotized by the very snake that bit him.

They were going that night to Sergio's work party—he was a fundraiser for the local NPR station and a donor was throwing a party at a mansion in the Hudson Valley. They took Paul's scooter, even though it was cold and windy and quite a long drive, but at least this way Sergio didn't have to listen to Paul complaining about having to go to the party the whole ride up.

The mansion was grand and overlooked the river. The mood of everybody at the party was festive because Obama had just won the week prior and people finally felt like they had something to celebrate. The mansion itself had a storied political history. According to the host, it had been occupied by the Roosevelts at one time or another.

"I can feel them here." Paul nodded patronizingly and ate some hors d'oeuvres.

Sergio took the tour of the grounds and was mid-banter with some people from work when the host rushed over to him.

"I think your father isn't feeling well," the host told him. It took Sergio a moment to realize that of course he must've been talking about Paul.

A caterer had found him slumped in some back stairway doing the thing he did.

"He needs his medicine!" Sergio lied. "That's all." He was sure that his co-workers thought his elderly boyfriend was a junkie, but this honestly seemed preferable to the truth: he was ditching Sergio to commune with a spirit named Irina. His co-workers of course would have lapped that up (*Oh, do me next! I think I used to be a French prostitute in a past life! Ooh-la-la*), and Sergio didn't want to encourage him.

"Does he need to lie down?" the host offered. So, Sergio and the caterer heaved Paul under the armpits and carried him to a bedroom that had once belonged to a child and still had a shelf of basketball trophies more than two decades old.

In revenge, Sergio went outside and smoked cigarettes, which he'd quit, with a guy from the IT department. They flirted a bit until the host of *All Things Considered* joined them, and then a bunch of other people did too, and everybody was in a very good mood, but Sergio started to feel shy so he went back inside to check on Paul and found him sitting up in bed on the phone with that girl.

WHEN PAUL FINALLY manages to track down the real Irina, she staggers out of the cloud and collapses. He comes over to her and helps her up. Holds her like a baby or a pietà across his golden lap. A horizon line appears and disappears in the darkness around them.

"Verochka is somewhere close," she tells him. "Very close. A mother knows these things."

He tries to tell her about the impersonator, shows his finger, but she waves his hand away and closes her eyes. She won't look.

"And the other one, the one growing in Zhenichka, we've had some words as well. I've been preparing it for what's to come."

She looks up into Paul's face. "Ask Zhenichka, will you, if she will name her baby after me. Tell her I would be honored. The baby and I already have an understanding, I feel."

Paul does as he's asked, but he looks uncertain.

"She says she does not like the idea. And anyway, she thinks she's having a boy. She can feel it."

Irina reaches up and takes Paul by the ears like they are handles and uses them to pull herself up. "A boy? I don't think so. It will be a girl. She'll need protection. Well, name her Vera then. By then Verochka should be dead-dead and out of this half-state. Or maybe name her Hanna, my cousin, she had a lot of good qualities: she was kind and brave and good at enjoying life. A name, I see now, means a lot. The Russians understood this with patron saints, and us Jews, we understand that there are no saints, only relatives, to help guide us."

Paul says, "Please, let go of my ears." He feels hurt that she is treating him suddenly like one of those lamps at the dentist.

Irina lets go and slides her hands down his neck. The light emanating from him feels strangely porous. They look at each other. A quiver of tenderness. He realizes how scared he was when the other ghost was impersonating her. Looking into her gray eyes is giving him a vertiginous feeling, so he takes her hands off his neck and places them back onto his ears and says: "She's ready now. We can continue." He opens his mouth.

CHAPTER 15

I had become Fräulein Agata's little pet since the beginning of the previous year when a letter for me arrived by special post delivered to her classroom. It was from my stupid mother, telling me that my oldest brother had died "bravely and in battle" fighting in the pointless war that our incompetent and delusional tsar, who truly believed he'd been handpicked by God, had dragged us into. Then she wrote that my middle brother would be fulfilling his "duty to the crown" by enlisting in the same infantry unit.

Fräulein Agata made all the girls move their desks and sit on the floor while she held me. The girls squatted awkwardly in a circle and recited their conjugations as Olga squeezed my hand and Fräulein Agata stroked my hair. Olga cried quietly too, thinking, no doubt, of her own dead brother.

My brother had died at the hands of Fräulein Agata's Germans, and yet here I was, learning her language and sobbing into her lap.

"German is very adaptable," she always told us. "We can make new words out of old bricks."

I'd heard Yiddish from my mother's family growing up, so German came easily to me. I collected the words that resonated:

Fremdschämen—secondhand shame.

Fernweh—far sickness. The opposite of homesickness, and something I felt constantly.

Treppenwitz—staircase joke. A phrase that comes to you too late, as you're already walking down the stairs.

Innerer Schweinehund—inner pig dog.

Their individual units of meaning formed something greater, expressed things I felt but didn't know I felt until I heard them. The same was true, at first, for Fräulein Agata's opinions. I did not know I believed these ideas until she expressed them, and then I immediately took them on as my own. Of course the tsar was an idiot! Of course the war was pointless and terrible! Of course workers deserved rights, and women deserved work, and the luck of where you were born should not determine your fortune in life!

AT LUNCH, INSTEAD of eating with the other teachers, Fräulein Agata often let us come to her room and pull chairs up around her desk. One afternoon, she served us hard-boiled eggs she must have stolen from the cook. The eggs had been boiled in beet juice, dyed pink for Easter. Was it spring already? No, no, impossible. It was still 1916. By Easter the Revolution would be in full swing, Rasputin and a lot of other people would be dead, Tsar Nikolai and his German wife, who ordered all their furniture from a department store catalog, would be on the run and my teacher long gone.

We were eating, but there were many awkward silences. Fräulein Agata was glum. She'd recently been dumped, unceremoniously, by the general. I hadn't dared tell her about seeing him at the hotel. Without the general's protection she was in a precarious position at the school. The general had probably also been giving her money, which she had relied on to buy clothes and perfume and feel like a woman in her prime and not a hag foreigner, softened and bruised on the vine, unpicked and forgotten.

Olga thought it was for the best. The general was, after all, an imperialist monarchist pig, so wouldn't this have made him, by Fräulein Agata's own definition, the enemy? Also, he was ugly and disgusting. But when we'd tried to say as much, Fräulein Agata snapped at us: "You'll understand when you're older. You can't marry a character from a book, Olga."

Olga's nostrils flared in annoyance as she got up from the table and went to study the topographical map of Germany hanging on the wall.

My teacher was talking about Rakhmetov, the revolutionary in *What Is to Be Done?* But my teacher had misunderstood. Olga didn't aspire to marry Rakhmetov, she aspired to *be* him.

Our teacher's hypocrisy put Olga in a foul mood. To me, Fräulein Agata's flightiness had seemed part of her charm; there was a tingle of excitement in not knowing where things would land, but Olga was so staunch and rigid, she had no patience for this. She scowled at the map and chewed her yolk.

My attempts at conversation were rejected by Fräulein Agata as well. She was still punishing me and I was crawling out of my skin to get back to the way things were before the kiss, when I was still eating out of her hand. To fill the silence, my teacher made Elsie play the piano.

Poor Elsie. She just wanted to sit with us and eat her eggs, but she dutifully went over to the piano and began to plink the keys as she tried to figure out the song Fräulein Agata was humming, the tango from the other night. But Elsie wasn't getting it right, so Fräulein Agata waved at her to stop. Elsie looked down at the keys, reprimanded, and began to rise.

"Maybe some Chopin," Fräulein Agata said to the room, and Elsie sat back down and played, stopping only occasionally to cough that wet, tubercular cough of hers. She provided our teacher with a portable accompaniment. As long as the room had a piano, Fräulein Agata could have Elsie set the mood.

When my cousin appeared, and I saw that she was holding another letter to me, I went white as a sheet. Who writes with good news? This one was from my middle brother, which meant, at least, that he wasn't dead. He was writing to tell me that he was planning to visit Petrograd on his way to the front. My brothers and I were never close. This was how my mother wanted it. But I had not seen Lev in some time and I suppose I missed him.

Fräulein Agata perked up at the news of his visit. She wanted to know what he looked like, whether he was handsome. We plotted all the places we would show him, and I naively imagined that maybe Fräulein Agata could marry him and then she wouldn't leave me because she'd be like my sister.

I was wrapped up in this fantasy, and I didn't notice at first the way my teacher was staring at Hanna.

"What do you think it was that Rasputin saw in you?" she asked Hanna out of nowhere.

Hanna smiled sweetly. It was no mystery what he saw.

"Weakness maybe," Fräulein Agata said to herself.

It embarrassed me, this cruelty, especially since I didn't think Hanna could defend herself, and I wasn't going to defend her either.

"And you're young, of course. That helps. Blanker canvas."

Because there was no back-and-forth, no parrying, my teacher's insults sounded like rocks landing in a pail.

She said these cruel things and yet with her body she drew Hanna closer and kept her voice light. The effect was disorienting.

"Tell me about yourself, Hanna," my teacher said, and by then Hanna was sitting in her lap.

My cousin was so guileless. She did not try to be clever at all, which for me was a sin in itself. About her family Hanna just said that she loved her mother very much and that her father was a very kind man who worked hard.

I tried to interject, prod her to say something that sounded more interesting or mysterious, but this only irritated my teacher.

"She doesn't need a translator, Irina."

My teacher turned her back in such a way that I could no longer participate in the conversation. And then, Hanna began to talk of physical pleasure—something I knew little about. My teacher's interest transformed from mocking to genuine. I tried to squeeze my way back into the conversation, but this only caused my teacher to blink her eyes closed in irritation. Elsie had switched to a more dramatic song, pounding on the keys.

I got up and stood by Olga facing the map on the wall, letting my face quiver there. I had been the favored one, and now my cousin was taking this from me. Without meaning to, but still. This was too much to bear. Without Fräulein Agata, I had nothing. I'd become a shopgirl at my uncle's feed store, selling grain to chickens. My mother's idiotic worldview would be lying in wait for me and soon I'd be married and breeding and sending my sons off to wars, having not a thought in my stupid head except the style of my next dress and which new war I should send my sons off to.

"Ugh," Olga said, taking one look at my face.

Olga had a concreteness that made it difficult for her to go along with commonly accepted social niceties. She passed me a handkerchief. "Don't be stupid. She's just trying to get a rise out of you." She traced a mountain range on the map with her finger. After Fräulein Agata had taken an interest in Olga they decided that Olga's dream would be to go to Switzerland, where women were allowed to attend medical school. But then Olga's brother was hanged by a military tribunal for terrorist activities and Olga's ideas evolved. Being a doctor did not interest her. She was a talented science student, but she was not a healer. She wanted to slice open the country and pull out every bone.

Fräulein Agata wasn't the only teacher Olga was close with. The chemistry teacher was also a fan of Olga's. She was his brightest pupil and he provided her with all the supplies she would need for making bombs, without asking any questions. He must have assumed that she was above reproach. She seemed so rigid then and ostensibly such a rule-follower, even if the rules she was following were not those of the school or normal society.

"I hope your cousin hasn't gotten pregnant," Olga said.

I nodded knowingly, but I had only a rudimentary idea of how that all worked. I had been relieved when Hanna came back; it hadn't occurred to me that there was another shoe that could still drop.

I listened to Hanna going on dreamily about a summer she had spent at my estate, about a cake she had eaten, about a flower she had seen. Fräulein Agata was nodding as if what my cousin was saying interested her, even though there was a sense of growing impatience in the room, but perhaps this was just the skittering of the keys in Chopin's mazurkas.

"See," said Olga. "You have no reason to worry. Fräulein is already growing tired of her."

I moved away along the wall, annoyed that my fears were so transparent, but Olga grabbed me by the braid. "Oh, come on," she said. This was her version of a peace offering. "Come with me after school this week. I'll take you to someone you might want to see again." It took me a moment to realize who she was talking about.

"Why don't we all go?" Fräulein Agata said, appearing suddenly in our conversation. Of course she had been keeping track of us all along, even when she'd seemed entirely absorbed in whatever my poor cousin was rambling about. "A little outing will be nice. Maybe we'll discover something new to show your brother."

"Did you?" Zhenia interrupted.

"Did I what?"

"Take your brother there? Was he impressed with this city version of you?" Zhenia thought of the time her own brother visited her in L.A. when he was touring colleges. A trip without adults, which had made Zhenia feel grown-up. She drove Greg to his campus visits and went on the tours with him, and at night Ben boiled them pasta dinners. It had irritated her that Greg kept going out onto the balcony to call their mother and report back to her.

"My brother never came. I spent a whole day sitting at the table laid out with food, shooing away flies and waiting for him. I got so angry. I was sure he'd found something more entertaining along the way to amuse himself with. But the truth was he'd never been allowed off the train. Something about his papers. We only heard about this later, when he was already at the front line, and he was killed not long after that."

"Oh." Zhenia's voice across the chasm. "That's sad."

Irina's form quivers. "Sad, not sad, what difference does it make?"

Paul doesn't know what they're talking about, but he feels the gravitational pull of sadness get stronger. It suctions Irina to him for a moment, but as he reaches for her she swats his hand away and goes on talking.

Olga had invited me mostly to pique Fräulein Agata's interest and it obviously worked. Olga glanced around the room, pausing as though pretending to consider it.

"You can all come," she said. "But don't make a scene."

Hanna and Fräulein Agata had their hands on each other's faces. They were playing the game we called "Mirror." I was surprised that Hanna was very good at it. Much better than I was.

"What scene?" Fräulein Agata said, raising her eyebrows in exaggeration.

"What scene?" Hanna repeated, trying not to laugh.

Elsie's playing ended abruptly with her coughing and coughing. We looked over at her and there was blood on the keys of the piano.

There was so much blood to come, it often blurred together. How to explain the months and months of violence that followed, what they did to me? But then, blood on ivory was still a shock, and I suppose that is why I remember it so clearly.

Sergio had to wait for Paul to fully come back to reality before they could leave the party. They were the last ones there and it was very awkward. The hostess had already taken off her shoes and her earrings, and the host had offered to call them a cab, but then what would they have done with Paul's scooter? So instead, despite barely knowing how, Sergio drove them back, stuck the whole time in second gear so it took twice as long. By the time they finally got home, they were too exhausted to fight about what had happened.

They lay next to each other in bed and Sergio watched Paul's chest rise and fall. "Tell me something about her?" he said, and put his hand over Paul's heart, which was still beating very quickly.

"She was alive at the time of the Russian Revolution," Paul said without opening his eyes. "She came under the influence of a strange woman, a teacher. I don't know what happened yet, but I think something terrible."

"The Revolution. Interesting. Which side was she on?" Sergio liked to watch history documentaries. "Was she a Bolshevik?"

"I don't know the details, but she was against the tsar. She seemed part of the elite, but also sort of an outsider."

"Hmm"—Sergio scratched his cheek—"I feel like those are the ones who get the angriest. Wasn't Lenin like a count or something?"

"No, I think you're thinking of Dracula." Paul smiled at his own dumb joke without opening his eyes.

"Har, har." Sergio squinted at Paul. "And the girl? The one you talk to on the phone. What about her?"

Sergio had seen Paul poring over printouts of the girl's notes. Their process seemed overly complicated. Inefficient.

Paul reached his hand up and groped around until he found Sergio's arm and gave it a little squeeze. "The girl," he said. "I don't know. She's walled off. She's angry. She's fighting all of it on some level. She doesn't want to receive the other one's . . ." Paul was drifting off to sleep. "Wisdom," he finally finished after a long pause.

Was wisdom a thing that could really be received? Sergio wondered. In his experience, it could only be taken. This whole project, it made him think of a Halloween costume where Irina was the horse's head and Paul was the horse's ass, and so was the girl, which maybe made it not a horse but a centipede.

CHAPTER 16

Zhenia had fallen into some kind of trance listening to the story. She was going through the motions, driving Ben to the airport and arguing with him, but inwardly she couldn't stop thinking about the blood on the piano keys, the feeling of imminent violence that hovered over their games—it was pressing into something inside her, making it hard for her to catch her breath. She came back to herself midsentence. Her voice shrill with a Russian accent that came out only when she was very tired or upset. She was criticizing Ben for something. She trailed off and focused her attention on the road. A light rain had begun to fall, the first one in months, and the roads were slippery.

Ben was sputtering. "You're on me for trying to 'dismantle' the magic and ruin it for you? Because I wanted to know how they did the tricks I 'dismantle' everything? You are insane."

Zhenia thought Ben made a good point and started laughing in a way that made him nervous. He hovered his hands over the steering wheel, ready to take over.

When her laughter finally faded, she looked over at him and he looked earnest and sad.

"I don't want a child," he said. "I've never wanted a child. You know this. And yet, still you've made this decision unilaterally."

"Don't you think you'll come around?" she said hopefully.

"I don't have a choice, so . . . it's not fair for me to take it out on the kid." Ben had a very good relationship with his own father. He couldn't imagine being a bad parent. It seemed outside the realm of possibility to do to this baby what Zhenia's father had seemingly done without too much difficulty—rejected her existence completely and totally, and disappeared before he even appeared.

"Well, do you want to break up?" Zhenia went to the extreme, saying it and not believing at all that he might say yes. Their relationship for the past six years had been predicated on his pursuit of her and her mild acquiescence.

WHEN HER GRANDMOTHER, still occasionally lucid half a year ago, asked Zhenia if she loved Ben, Zhenia had said that he treated her really well.

Her grandmother had wanted more than anything for Zhenia to get out into the world, to get away, and only now did it dimly occur to Vera Osipovna that maybe there was no getting away. This listlessness and strange inertia had followed her granddaughter out west. It was not, it appeared, something that could be outrun. Zhenia had chosen to marry a person whom she held at arm's length, whom she herself did not love, and maybe in all of the upheaval of her childhood, she had not learned how to love or what that even meant. How could she know about loving a man properly? Whom did she have as a model? A math professor with his own family in Russia who had refused to even meet her, or this pale, ugly Nathaniel, with a nervous hesitation around anything that could displease Zhenia's tyrannical mother?

Of course, all of these things were excuses. Vera had no role models either in the orphanage, and yet the love she found when she married Grisha took her away from all that. Their love was such pleasure, it had often felt taboo. That she could, in a totalitarian state, where everything was monitored and warped, be permitted to have this pleasure, a pleasure that untethered her from everything on earth but him.

I don't think it's a good idea," her grandmother said gently. "Did you already do it?"

It might not have been a good idea, but it was Zhenia's only idea, and they had. They'd married that morning in the East L.A. courthouse. Their witness had been a complete stranger. Ben had wanted to ask Naomi, but Zhenia had flown into a jealous rage. She didn't want Naomi anywhere near this day. The cat that drops a mouse out of its mouth long enough for Zhenia to marry it.

"I'm very happy," Zhenia said to her grandmother, and though she wouldn't have said this was false, self-conscious under her grandmother's scrutiny, it sounded false.

But her grandmother didn't probe further; she was already asking what time Zhenia would be there to visit, saying things in her confusion about space and time that made no sense at all. When she'd been lucid, her grandmother had made Zhenia promise she wouldn't visit. To have Zhenichka witness the humiliations of her failing body and mind . . . this was awful. Not what she wanted at all. She wanted Zhenia to be free, to lead a rich, interesting, and unburdened life.

Anyway, because her grandmother's momentary lucidity was overwritten by her confusion, Zhenia didn't let herself dwell on this disapproval of her marriage.

It had not seemed like a remote possibility to Zhenia that Ben would want their marriage to end. Yes, she'd said that it ended to Naomi, but she hadn't meant it! She had really only suggested it now in the car to be reaffirmed in his love, to hear him say that she was being ridiculous.

She felt her cheeks burning. Ben was looking out at the road. There was an accident up ahead, a rainy-day inevitability, and they were now crawling along amid the red taillights reflecting off the wet pavement.

She wanted very much to take back what she'd said, to have the words, like a silk scarf that had emerged dry from the magician's mouth, be shoved back in.

Months later, in what felt like an entirely different life, Zhenia would tell the Tin Man's wife, Chloe, about the dissolution of her marriage.

"The last few months of it felt," Zhenia said, "like we were always fighting and I was always taking him to the airport."

"That makes sense." Chloe nodded. "He was leaving you, so that's how you'd remember it."

"Was he leaving me? I don't know," Zhenia said stubbornly.

Chloe blinked a few times, confused. "Well, he left you, no?"

"I think in articulating it, I created it."

Chloe was looking down at her baby, rubbing her back in a circle to get a burp out. "You don't think you said it because you thought it? You think you said it and *then* you thought it?"

Zhenia leaned back on Chloe's couch and looked up at the ceiling.

"I thought a lot of contradictory things simultaneously. Maybe in that moment, if I had said that they would figure it out . . ."

"That *they* would?" Chloe repeated with a smirk. "Who's *they?*"

"That *we* would. Whatever. I misspoke."

Chloe didn't say anything about this kind of dissociation and magical thinking, just patted and patted the baby's back until finally a stream of clotted milk came pouring out of the corner of the baby's mouth.

"Though," Zhenia continued, smiling despite herself, "I guess it was appropriate that my marriage ended after visiting a clubhouse for magicians. The stability of marriage was an illusion. A purgatory. All of it had a temporary clapboard feeling."

"Well, that's all life, isn't it?" Chloe said, wiping the baby's mouth. "Temporary."

And the women nodded at each other and at their babies, but neither of them in that moment believed it in their hearts.

BEN HADN'T ANSWERED Zhenia right away, and this silence was unbearable. The rest of the breakup, though, felt like a ride on a rail. Zhenia found herself saying: "Is it someone else?" and then more shrilly, "Is it Naomi?"

It wasn't Naomi. It hadn't occurred to Zhenia that there could be someone other than Naomi. Not a handpicked successor, not an approximation of herself, but someone completely different. Someone he'd met in Atlanta on the set of the show. She did makeup. She'd given him nice little chin massages after she'd peel off his fake beard at the end of each shooting day. Her face had been so close to his face, he supposed there was some sort of circuit jump of intimacy that happened just by having this person, even in a professional setting, be so close to his face, touching him so gently. One day she told him that she was developing feelings for him, and it felt very good to be desired in this way. He realized he could no longer say no to himself.

Zhenia couldn't believe any of this was happening to her, even though of course part of her had been longing for it. Why else would she have told Naomi about it ahead of time? Ben got out of the car and got his packed suitcase from the trunk.

"I desire you," Zhenia said in a small voice that would not have been audible to him. Did she, though?

He crawled back into the front seat and, leaning over the center console, hugged her tightly and quickly and then hurried off to his new life in Atlanta.

ZHENIA FOUND HERSELF driving again in the rain, looping on highways. She was looking for the canyon roads where the man had taken her and Naomi in the convertible. She thought, maybe if she would drive them herself, that feeling of being a helpless passenger in her own life would be gone. But it was dark and she couldn't find the right exit. She kept having to get back on the highway and circle back, at one point narrowly avoiding a small mudslide.

Eventually, she gave up and drove home. She had a sudden and very strong craving for a dessert called Gogol-mogel that her grandmother used to make for her. She stood in the kitchen, mixing egg yolks, sugar, and cocoa powder in a mug with a fork. The balcony door was open, letting in the cold night air. She had always loved the sound the fork made beating against the side of the mug, like a desperate bird. Zhenia tasted the concoction. The sugar didn't dissolve fully, but this was how the mousse was supposed to be, grainy on the tongue—objectively maybe a flaw, but also Zhenia's favorite part.

She thought about Irina getting that sad letter from her brother and suddenly had a strong urge to call Greg, who was maybe the only other person in America who liked Gogol-mogel. It was late, but he'd become nocturnal in college.

"Congratulations!" he said as soon as he answered the phone. "Mom told me about the baby.

"I hope it wasn't a secret," he added when Zhenia didn't say anything. "Oh shit. I probably shouldn't have said anything."

He had a niceness that Zhenia lacked and a desire to make the people around him comfortable—in short, he wasn't very Russian.

"No. It's fine. It's true. Thank you," she finally said. "You're going to be an uncle."

She could hear that someone was in his room, talking in the background, but she didn't ask him if it was a bad time to talk because she didn't want to get off the phone.

"What else did Mom tell you?"

"I don't know. Don't be mad at her. She just was very excited."

"Did she say anything about Babushka?"

"Nothing new. Taking care of her has been hard."

Zhenia was sure that being taken care of by her mother was no picnic for Babushka either, but she knew that Greg would parrot back whatever her mother had said, and she didn't feel like talking to her mother, so she changed the subject.

She started telling him about the conversations she'd been having with Irina through Paul the medium. She was talking about it in a sort of cynical and snarky way, like wasn't this whole thing just cuckoo-bananas? Wasn't it just a visit-to-Absurdistan?

And when Greg started laughing along, responding in exactly the way she had set the story up to be responded to, she started to cry.

Greg immediately got flustered. "Are you okay?" he asked.

Her body could feel suddenly what had happened with Ben, even if her mind was a disconnected stupid thing that understood nothing. How would Zhenia raise this baby? How would she feed it and take care of it? Wake up with it in the middle of the night? Ben and this makeup girl were probably stroking each other's faces, fucking in the moonlight, and she was completely alone.

"I'm fine, I'm fine," she said, and hung up the phone.

CHAPTER 17

Since getting bitten, Paul became more careful. He started to bring gifts—lumps of sugar and a pile of tea that he burned in a hot pot set up next to the altar on the windowsill overlooking the fire escape. It was loose Russian tea he'd gotten at a deli a few blocks away and it smelled to him like it was already full of other people's memories.

The tea makes us wetter and denser. We feel agitated and sentimental. It reminds us of delightful things, burnt tongues and the way sugar once crunched against our teeth, when we had teeth.

We become dusk and dawn and the air after it rains. We're inclined to forgive the man his ridiculous preferences. Let the girl go and talk to him. What do we care? Her woes are our woes in the end. All of our suffering is communal. All of us had our own Fräuleins, our own Olgas and Elsies, and in the end we have all ended up in the same place.

Elsie was soon shipped away to Baden-Baden or somewhere else to deal with her TB. To us she was as good as dead, and Fräulein Agata had to rely on other methods for setting the mood. In truth, things sped up rather quickly after Olga took us to a party at Osip's apartment.

There were quite a few people packed in, smoking and barefoot, dressed theatrically, speaking in a quick code of inside jokes that I was too dumb to decipher. They were about a decade older than Hanna, Olga, and me, Fräulein Agata's age but not beholden to the bourgeois social conventions of grown-ups, so they seemed outside time. They knew one another from their days together in the SRs; this was the group responsible for the Revolution of 1905, "The Great Dress Rehearsal," as Lenin called it.

I was looking for Osip in the smoky room, but he wasn't there. I tried to gauge Fräulein Agata's feelings about this but she was glancing around like a crocodile, a condescending smile plastered on her face. "Well, well, well," it seemed to say, "which of you shall I eat first?"

But this look began to waver the longer we stood there waiting to be introduced and offered a seat. The rugs and old furniture had been painted white, like props on a set, and were occupied with past and future terrorists, none of whom seemed interested in us. Fräulein Agata watched a volley of remarks between Boris—Osip's childhood friend and houseguest who was staying in the city illegally—and Osip's sister, who lived in the apartment as well. Boris had served time for a failed assassination attempt on a grand duke and was always finding ways to bring it up.

I couldn't tell whether my teacher was following what they were saying or just looking for an opening in the conversation. She cleared her throat strategically, but they ignored her. She didn't know how to position herself and her own eccentricity within all the existing eccentricity in the room.

Osip's sister was raising her voice, talking louder and louder over Boris's braying.

"Are they laughing or arguing?" I asked Olga, who seemed to know a surprising number of the people present on account of her older brother.

"Showing off," Olga answered dismissively.

I could feel an impatience building in Fräulein Agata and it made me nervous. I never quite knew what she'd be capable of. If she wasn't up on a pedestal she felt short.

Hanna sucked on a strand of hair, turning to look at an oil painting in a gold frame hanging on the wall over Boris's head. It was a naked girl, a mythological creature, with a broad frame and breasts like rocks, holding a carafe of water on her shoulder.

"You're not ideologically superior just because you were punished!" Osip's sister suddenly exclaimed. Then she dumped the contents of an entire ashtray onto his chest before storming out. After this, the attention in the room finally seemed to settle on us.

Boris sat up, the burnt matchsticks and cigarette butts scattering around him. His eyes lingered on our uniforms.

"Are these Osip's schoolgirls? What's Lara going to say?"

"Why should I say anything?" the hunchbacked woman from the other night said from a cloud of smoke.

Fräulein Agata observed all this with a stiffly ironic expression on her face. "Why should she? Is she his lovvver?" she whispered loudly, not really believing this was a possibility. It didn't occur to us to think of this hunchbacked woman as competition in our pursuit of Osip, and I suppose Lara never was competition. *I* was the footnote in their love story, not the other way around.

"But I thought you married him," Zhenia interrupted, confused.

"Yes. So? I would think in the context of your own marriage you would understand perfectly."

Zhenia's nose twitched. "Understand what?"

"That marriage means as little or as much as you make it mean."

Zhenia felt a rebuke in this. She'd let her own marriage mean plenty. And, even if it hadn't, it wasn't as though she let anything else mean more, and wasn't everything relative? She began to scrape out the dried remnants of the night's Gogol-mogel with a spoon, and Irina waited pointedly until she was done to continue with her story.

Hanna was not paying attention to my teacher or Lara. She was oblivious as usual, staring at the painting and trying to hold an imaginary carafe of water on her shoulder and tilt her head in the same way as the naked girl.

She turned to Boris and smiled, dropping the strand of hair out of her mouth. "She looks like me, doesn't she? I've never seen a painting like this.

It's so odd." She fell back into the couch into the spot where Osip's sister had been.

"Looks like you? I wouldn't know," Boris said, brushing the cigarette butts and ashes off his lap and onto the floor. "It bears further study . . ." He smiled at her and wiggled his eyebrows, which made her giggle.

"Your cousin sounds like a real ditz," Irina hears Zhenia mutter.

"I don't know this word," Irina says to Paul. "What is this 'ditz'?"

"It means not very bright. Kind of stupid," Paul clarifies.

"Well, I did think she was a little stupid! I had to feel superior to her in some way or I wouldn't have been able to stand it! I was jealous of her ease in the world—I loved her, but at night I would pace in that slope-ceilinged room of mine and feel rage over the injustice of my situation. My cousin had a keen intelligence, actually, when it came to the physical realm, to the world of the body, things I didn't understand at all. But she wasn't an intellectual, and she was sort of dreamy, so it was easy to think she wasn't smart."

Fräulein Agata certainly didn't see her as very bright. They were quite different.

"Your cousin could stand to be a little choosier. Is there anyone she won't accept attention from?" Fräulein Agata now didn't bother to lower her voice. Who knows where this would have escalated if somebody hadn't given my teacher the attention she felt herself entitled to.

It was Lara, asking something to be polite. The question had been innocuous, but Fräulein Agata found a way to open it up. She began to speak about Marx. Oh, how she spread her feathers! Oh, how clever she was! I couldn't understand some of the finer points, but I could tell from the way the other adults had stopped talking and were listening to her monologue that she was saying all the right things. And, having read *Das Kapital* in its original German, she was able to quibble over some of the smaller points of its translation that people at this party seemed to find genuinely interesting. Even Olga was nodding, probably because she was relieved someone she brought was making a good impression.

Guests, in fact, seemed to be so rapt listening to Fräulein Agata that they didn't notice when Osip came in through the front door. His shirt was torn and he was pressing an icicle to his bloody lip. It was exciting to see him with the air of the outside world still clinging to him, bruised so handsomely. He came right over to us, and I could sense Fräulein Agata was pleased that he'd caught her speaking.

He apologized for his lateness.

"What happened to your face?" Fräulein Agata moved his hand away from his lip.

"Joined the factory fight club?" Boris laughed, lighting one cigarette with the end of another. Lara started fussing around his injuries. She had on a cream-colored blouse with a silk bow around the neck, and Fräulein Agata reached over and yanked on one end, untying it. She apologized but it was strange. My teacher had these impulses sometimes where she couldn't keep her hands to herself.

The party went on from there, but for some reason that moment felt for me like something stuck in my eye.

The cloud is aquiver. We pour ourselves into the space between the girl and the man. We've been eavesdropping.

—That sounds like a nice party.

—Once I was at a party where a girl jumped out of a cake.

—Once I was at a party on a boat where we played cards all night and drank champagne, and when we found out the host was cheating we threw him overboard.

—The girl didn't have a stitch of clothing on. Not a stitch.

—Oh, how the champagne sparkled in the moonlight.

—I miss parties!

—*I'd even take a bad party. The kind where the hostess gets too drunk and people say nasty things to each other.*

—*Where somebody plays footsy with your husband or pinches your rear.*

—*What about this place? Isn't this a bad party?*

—*The worst. The worst kind of party.*

—*A terrible party. I just want to go home.*

—*I want to go hoooome.*

Several voices begin to wail at once. More of us join. A howl that turns into a wind. It blows the man's cap right off his head. We watch it stutter over the ground. He catches it eventually, pulls it back down over his bald pate.

—*Home. Home. Hoooome.*

But there is no home, of course. Inside or out. This realization shuts some of us up.

CHAPTER 18

I wondered later whether Olga had brought Fräulein Agata there as a trap. She wanted to show us that our teacher's words were nothing. Olga could not stand hypocrisy, though in the end Olga was the biggest hypocrite of all.

"Well, *aren't* words nothing?" Zhenia interrupted. "Isn't it our actions that ultimately reveal the truth of who we are?" She was sitting on the balcony, watching the sun glint off the windshields of the cars below, and thinking, of course, of Ben, of his words, and then of his actions with the makeup girl.

"Words are not 'nothing,' Zhenia! Before Fräulein Agata's words, it had not occurred to me to think of myself as part of a larger system of exploitation. And then I saw my own circumstances—my dead father, my stupid mother, my slope-ceilinged room, the anti-Semitic masses—all of this was no longer my tragic fate but an opportunity.

"There was no justice—that much was clear. There was the rotting corpse of the feudal system and a group of corrupt men, blinded by their own greed and stupidity, leading us into more wars and toward an inevitable breaking point. There were stampedes crushing each other to get a commemorative cup and a bread roll on the tsar's coronation day. There were gray-faced bureaucrats writing in ledgers while Jews were being gutted and raped by gangs the tsar was supporting. How could people really think that despite serfs being emancipated two generations earlier, anybody was free? The tsar truly believed that he was father to the people and that his power came directly from God. Well, my father was dead, and I didn't believe in the tsar's God. I believed in Man. By the time I sailed to America, I lost my faith in Man as well."

"And now?" Paul interrupts. "What do you believe now?"

Irina looks at him strangely. It takes them both a moment to realize what has just happened.

"I seem to understand you suddenly," Paul says, surprised. "It's strange. I seem to have learned Russian. I thought it would be like learning French in high school, slow and incomplete. But it wasn't like that at all. I'm speaking Russian right now, aren't I? To you? I just know it fully all of a sudden?! Knowledge by osmosis?"

She pats his cheek. "Why not?" She does not seem the least bit surprised by this. Why shouldn't knowledge from her be flowing into him and altering his brain?

"As for what I believe now . . ." she continues, answering his original question, "I believe that in order to survive, I betrayed everybody who was ever dear to me, including myself. Now I survive and survive and survive. It's fitting that I cannot disappear. I keep living on. Here and in you, Zhenia. Do you really think you will ever be rid of me?"

A shiver went up Zhenia's arm and then she felt the baby move inside of her for the first time. The quickening. A flinchy, fluttery feeling.

MY IDEAS WERE probably as muddled as your own. If you'd asked me that afternoon what it was that I believed, I wouldn't have been able to give a coherent answer, but if you'd asked me how fervently I believed it, or how willing I was to act on it, I wouldn't have hesitated even for a moment. I wanted very much to be someone important.

Boris was waiting for us around the corner from school, leaning on a lamppost, his hands deep in the pockets of his leather trench coat. When Hanna saw him, they embraced in front of everybody. They had a definite gravitational pull. He kissed her on the tip of her nose. She kissed him all over his eyelids. They were shrouded in the steam from their own breath. It was really something brazen, in the middle of the sidewalk! Even Fräulein Agata, though she pretended not to be, was a bit scandalized. She pulled them apart and walked between them.

"I'm surprised to see you," Fräulein Agata said stiffly to Boris. "I didn't know you were a doctor." She pointed to the leather doctor's case under his arm. He looked at her curiously but didn't respond. I think before his first arrest he'd been studying at the University to be a doctor.

"How is your friend Osip?" she asked. She must have been waiting for Osip to visit us and been disappointed to instead be seeing Boris.

Boris shrugged off the question. "He's good. Busy."

"And what about that hunchback? Was that his wife?"

"They're not married," Boris said, and grasped Hanna's hand behind Fräulein Agata's back.

"Where did he find her? In Siberia?"

We were walking down the street toward the end with the larger houses.

"No. She came with him to Siberia though. Abandoned all her organizing here to go with him, which frankly put the rest of us in a bind."

"So, her organizing work was for nothing?" Olga said with distaste, adjusting her pince-nez and looking at the larger houses at the end of the block. "To abandon the cause . . . and for what?"

"Love," Fräulein Agata said with some satisfaction. The word out of her mouth seemed to shimmer.

"You'd think because somebody is ugly they'd be more noble. That they'd have more sense," Boris said, pulling on his beard.

Fräulein Agata bugged her eyes out. "I don't think that! How stupid."

"No. You wouldn't. You surround yourself with beauty." He ducked behind my teacher's shoulder and kissed Hanna's gloved hand.

In truth, there were far more beautiful girls in our class that Fräulein Agata could have surrounded herself with but they were not as pliable. My teacher was very good at sensing need. Some of those beautiful girls did not have this need at all; they were complete as they were. Fräulein Agata and I would gossip about them on walks we would take along the river when I was supposed to be in my other classes.

"Their lack of curiosity! Their boring lives!" she would exclaim, her mouth hanging open in mock horror. "I fear that this is the direction that the general's daughters are heading in without me there. Will you check on them for me?"

She had me do this more and more since the general ended things, and of course, I always did. My curiosity was bottomless, and for a while so was my willingness to please her.

Fräulein Agata slowed her walk and squinted at Boris. "Who I surround myself with is none of your business," she said. She looked at Olga. "Perhaps it's who *you* surround yourself with that's questionable." She turned to me, and then beyond me to her ever-faithful audience, who, she must have imagined, were watching her from their windows. "With my girls, their beauty is just a part of it. They are evolved," she continued, raising her voice. I noticed Olga exchange a look with Boris as poor Fräulein continued like a dumb rooster. "If we are to believe Darwin and his discoveries, people are evolving, with each generation more and more. They were not always like they are now, their bodies were hairier, their souls too must have been different. Even a few years ago, people owned other people. It only goes to follow that society can evolve just as individual people can. Who is to say that the world can't be different from how it is?"

I was still taken with these words, but I could tell suddenly that Boris and Olga were not. Boris sighed and lifted his hat to scratch his bald spot.

"The world becomes different when we make it so," Olga said, scanning the buildings up ahead.

"Well, certainly . . ." Fräulein Agata seemed to grow vaguer. "I suppose I should get you girls home."

"No, not yet," Olga said, stopping suddenly in front of the stairs that led down to the dock on the river. We were not far now from where the luncheon had been that had started everything. "You talked and talked so beautifully to us, teacher. I wanted to give you the opportunity to finally act on it."

The cloud inches closer. Sighs. Drizzles. Moves past. We want more tea. We have heard this all before. Either heard it or lived it. In one form or another, all of us have betrayed people we once loved.

CHAPTER 19

Boris and Olga led us toward a houseboat, parked on the Moyka canal. I don't think I'd been on a boat before. I thought, finally, an adventure! Robinson Crusoe! We'll sail off to the Seven Seas, except this boat did not seem very seaworthy and was probably frozen into place. Fräulein Agata hesitated on the dock, but she eventually allowed Olga to give her a hand and pull her up the ladder onto the deck.

"Whose boat is this?" my teacher wanted to know, eyeing the men's long underwear, red-and-white-striped, strung up on ropes instead of a pirate flag. "Not yours." She looked at Boris. They looked much too small.

"Don't worry about it," Boris told her.

I understood then how he saw her: an annoying woman who blushed too easily and spoke with an ungainly German accent, asking too many questions and talking too much in general. After I saw this, I couldn't unsee it.

He led us through the door into the boat's interior room, where an old woman was sitting next to the blazing woodstove, a needle and thread laid out on the table beside her. She stood up when she saw us, and bowed to Boris.

"Who is that?" My teacher's voice sounded loud in this small, cozy room.

Olga took her hand, I'm not sure why. Probably just to get her to shut up. We watched quietly as Boris opened up his doctor's bag and pulled out several foreign newspapers, a sheaf of letters, a gun, and three bullets and laid them on the little table.

Boris took the gun apart using a small metal tool. His hands, I noticed, had a quickness and intelligence to them. Competence under his affected manner. When Boris was done, he lit a cigarette off the candle on the table and then apologized since this was considered bad luck. He said he would wait for us outside.

After he stepped out, the seamstress had us take off our dresses and stand in our petticoats. My teacher hesitated, but Olga pushed her forward. It was cold in the room. We stood huddled together, shivering, all of us trying to get close to Hanna, whose body gave off heat like a fresh loaf. Fräulein Agata was breathing strangely.

We watched the seamstress use the knife to cut the stitches in the linings of our uniforms. Then she began to twist the paper into thin white ropes and sew them into the hems.

"What am I transporting exactly? I should have a right to know, I think." Fräulein Agata was trying to keep her voice calm.

The seamstress raised her eyebrow and looked at Olga.

"I want to know that I agree with whatever I'm doing." Fräulein Agata's chest and neck were splotched with red. "You're asking me to trust you, but I know nothing about this." I felt deeply embarrassed for my teacher then, even though I suppose it was not unreasonable. Just cowardly.

Fear has such a strong smell. Before, when people would say dogs can smell fear, I thought this was an abstraction, but anybody who lived through the Revolution can tell you that it doesn't take a dog's nose to smell it. Anybody can smell fear.

The seamstress was holding three bullets in her hand.

"Those bullets are meant for someone. Tell me what good will all this do? Change happens slowly through education, otherwise you shoot one and another pops up in his place." She was pleading with the old woman, whose face was impassive. "We'll get caught."

"Sew it into mine," I said. "I don't mind."

I looked at Fräulein Agata. I was giving her an opportunity to contradict me.

Instead, she turned to Olga. "That stupid book has filled your head with nonsense. As your teacher I carry a certain responsibility to your parents, who have already tragically lost a son because of his involvement in unsavory—" She didn't finish her sentence because Olga slapped her across the face. Olga slapped her again, with the back of her hand, her knuckle cracking against our teacher's tooth.

"Olga." Hanna grabbed Olga's elbow, and this got Olga to stop.

The sound of the slaps seemed to hang in the room as Fräulein Agata got dressed quickly without looking at us, a thin line of blood dribbling from her nostril. It was so sudden, all of it, that I didn't have a chance to react. I stood there with my mouth hanging open.

To Olga, people were cowards or not. Rats or not. In a revolution, how else can you think?

"Following orders and not asking questions. Is this what I've taught you?" Fräulein Agata whispered to me from the doorway. I closed my mouth and didn't look at her. I felt ashamed on her behalf.

Boris was waiting outside, and I heard my teacher hiss at him, "Let go of me, I don't need your help getting down." The boat rocked as she disembarked, and once she was gone, I felt relieved. That I could see somebody so suddenly for who they really were—this filled me with wonder.

Hanna said, "Well, that's a shame," but she did not seem particularly fazed.

"What if she tells on us?" I asked.

"She'd never tell." Olga shrugged. "Telling would only dig her own hole deeper."

None of us said anything more about it.

The seamstress sewed the bullets into my bodice. The barrel went into Hanna's hair. The rest of it was sewn into Olga's dress. Hanna was the most likely to be groped, so it made sense to put the least on her.

"History is too slow," Olga said. She wiped her pince-nez on her petticoat and looked at me with those little myopic gray eyes.

"I can barely feel the bullets," Hanna said, running her hands over the stitching under my breasts.

That evening when Paul went to the piano bar for the sing-along, he got a good spot right by the piano, but then, for some reason, he kept picturing the shadowy girl from Irina's story, coughing blood all over the keys, so he let the crowd push him toward the back. His friends were there and they noticed that he seemed out of sorts. His friend sang him "I Dreamed a Dream," because, "Paul, you seem *Les Misérables*."

"Work problems," Sergio shouted over the crowd as an explanation, and Paul mixed his ice and his soda water.

"So what's going on?" his friends asked between songs.

"He's writing a book again!"

"My agent passed on it," Paul said, feeling the disappointment of this very acutely. "She said it wasn't right for my brand." A tear dripped out of his eye. "Too political."

Without the container of the book, even if it was a pretext, he didn't know if he could go on with the project. But could he really give up the feeling it gave him—being her conduit, her vessel, letting her stretch out something in him with her little ghost hands? He wasn't sure he could walk away from it even though the Institute always hammered home the importance of a financial exchange, or else boundaries could erode and things could get messy. What's the saying about prostitutes? You don't pay them to have sex with you, you pay them to go home.

"Oh." Sergio rubbed the tear in with his thumb. "Does that mean you won't be on the phone all the time with that girl?"

Paul shrugged. He wasn't sure what it meant. He reached over and took a sip of Sergio's drink, then a gulp. The others in the group exchanged looks or looked down at the ground. They'd heard stories about when Paul used to drink.

"I think 'meaning,'" Paul said, setting the empty glass down on the crowded table, "will present itself when I'm ready for it." He wiped his mouth with the back of his hand and waved to get the bartender's attention. There was a creeping sense of dread, but very quiet, and actually, as the alcohol hit him, everything began to feel like it might fall back into place.

"In other news . . . I'm learning Russian," he said, brightening. "Well, I've learned it, I think."

CHAPTER 20

Boris walked us over the bridge to the Peter and Paul Fortress. Its golden spire punctured the gray sky. I could feel the bullets pressing into my heart. We waited for the cannon to fire over the river, which it did every day at noon, then Boris told us which guard to look for and gave us a bottle of vodka to bribe him with and a package of soap for the one who worked beside him. How he knew to do this and where he received the instructions, I don't know. Boris was our go-between, connecting us to a larger network. The fewer people we knew, the safer it was for everyone.

Each metal door we went through sent us deeper into the underground catacomb illuminated by lanterns. I expected to see skeletons hanging on the walls. There were distant groans of men, the sounds of chains. But the man we were led to had a napkin tucked into his collar, and he was sitting in his cell eating something that left his lips shiny and which smelled quite appetizing. A fatty-looking meat soup. He wiped his greasy lips. The guards seemed to be working for him. So, why have us schoolgirls do the smuggling? Maybe to see if we would. Or maybe he really did need what we brought him.

Immediately, I liked this man's face. I thought he must have been very brave if he did something to warrant getting imprisoned there. He had a gray goatee and round wire spectacles perched on a nose that looked like it had been broken more than once. How is it that some people look intelligent and humane, that their faces reflect these qualities? This man would look at you, and you'd feel deeply understood. The glasses helped. He did end up being quite intelligent, though not at all humane, and I suppose he understood me enough for his purposes.

He wiped his fork on a napkin and used it to rip the stitches in our dresses to get everything we brought him. I remember dropping the bullets in his hand.

It was really quick, and felt like a big deal, like we'd committed a brave act. But it also felt like a game with no real consequences. It took a few moments. We knew nothing about what was in the letters or what the gun was used for.

Years later, when Osip and I were in exile, after your grandmother was born, I saw this man again at the sanatorium. He and I had an affair. He brought me back to myself at a point when I was very lost. Maybe this affair saved my life, or more likely it destroyed it.

—*An "affair" is elevating it. It was nothing.*
—*Brief and inconsequential.*
—*Not even worth discussing.*
—*Yet she discusses it.*
—*Well, he did screw her in more ways than one.*
—*I liked the part where they were slapping each other.*
—*Very satisfying to slap another person.*
—*The most natural thing. A baby comes out and you give it a good slap.*
—*She could use a slap. That's for sure.*

When we came out of the jail, we were euphoric. We blinked in the daylight and vibrated with our own sense of power. A joyous blankness. We looked into each other's faces and started laughing. Unity and annihilation.

Boris wasn't waiting for us, so Olga, Hanna, and I ran home holding hands through the Summer Garden, where the marble statues were in wooden crates for winter—a path lined with upright coffins.

Schoolgirls, schoolgirls.

For us, the objects we'd delivered to this man had only been symbols. A trinity of bullets for the tsar: one in the forehead of his God, one in the forehead of his Son, and one in the forehead of his Holy Ghost.

PART 2

CHAPTER 21

Zhenia got the call early in the morning from her mother.

"Zhenia, Zhenichka, she's dead."

Zhenia swung her feet around the side of the bed and sat up. There was a glass with dusty water that had been sitting on her bedside table and she chugged it. She was sure that if something like this had happened, she would have felt it. She would have woken up in the middle of the night clutching her heart. But she had slept well. She hadn't even gotten up to pee.

"When did it happen?"

"Yesterday evening. The funeral's this afternoon."

"What do you mean?!" Even if Zhenia drove straight to the airport and got on the first flight, she still wouldn't make it. "Why didn't you tell me last night? How am I supposed to get there in time?"

"It's all just a formality, Zhenichka. She's dead. And really she's been dead for a while. We're only burying her body. What difference does it make if you're here for the funeral or not."

To Zhenia, though, it made a difference, and the fact that her mother didn't understand this baffled her. They argued, and finally her mother agreed to push it back a day, so that Zhenia could get on the first plane and Nathaniel could pick her up.

"Did you tell Greg yet?"

"I'm about to."

Zhenia called Paul. She wanted to know if her grandmother was with Irina now, and if this meant that Zhenia would finally be able to talk to her. The phone rang and rang, but nobody answered.

Zhenia texted the Tin Man as she stood in line to go through airport security—*my Babushka died*, she wrote. She added a frowny face, then erased it because it seemed so trite and stupid, and instead just asked him to talk to his Russian anti-Semitic patient himself, since Zhenia wouldn't be there today. This would be awkward, since he'd pretended not to speak Russian before, but this wasn't her problem.

She hesitated at the full-body scanner—she'd heard the X-rays could hurt the baby. "I'm pregnant," she had to repeat to several TSA agents before she was taken aside for a pat-down.

"Ow," Zhenia yelped dramatically when the woman slid her gloved hands over her crotch. The woman in the blue uniform froze and looked at her, but Zhenia wouldn't make eye contact.

She was so angry with herself for not having been there. Whether Baba Vera had wanted it or not. She didn't even know what kind of funeral her grandmother would have wanted. When her grandmother had been lucid enough to discuss it, it had seemed too morbid to ask.

She called her mom as she boarded the plane. "Do you think we should tell her other family?"

Her mother was in the funeral home, changing the arrangements.

"What other family?" Marina said. "She has no other family. If she did, they would be the ones picking out her burial plot and not me."

"Is it going to be open casket?" Zhenia asked, shoving her rolling suitcase in the overhead bin.

"No, Zhenia. How ghoulish. Why. You're curious? You want to see what a dead person looks like?"

"I want to see *her*."

"Well, she won't be there. She's dead!" Her mother lost her cool. "If you want to see her, then look at a picture of her from when she was alive." She hung up.

Zhenia called her back, but Marina didn't answer. She called Nathaniel as the flight attendant was going down the aisles telling everyone to turn off their cell phones.

"Is it because it costs more?" she asked Nathaniel, and didn't let him answer. "I'll pay the difference!" Nathaniel, unlike her mother, wasn't going to point out that since they paid most of her bills, this was essentially the same thing.

It wasn't about the money, though. Hours later, when Nathaniel had picked Zhenia up and taken her to the funeral home for the viewing, Zhenia realized that her mother had been right.

Zhenia had never seen a dead body up close before, not of someone she'd known very intimately. The mortician had done Vera's makeup in a way that made her face look completely unfamiliar. This was enough to make Zhenia release a wail. She spat on her cuff and tried to wipe off some of the lipstick and rouge. Her grandmother used to keep a tube of lipstick by the front hall mirror and a brush, and on her way out of the house she'd always stop and roll the lipstick up (pink) and dab it on and brush out her short curls into a nice gray pouf. As Zhenia tried to make adjustments, a worker from the funeral home descended on her. The cotton batting that they used inside the mouth to keep her grandmother's face in position had begun to slide around, and the funeral director, wearing the same kind of purple latex glove as the TSA agent, discreetly readjusted the batting and moved Zhenia's hands away. The results were not great. The face looked crooked now, but also more like Zhenia's grandmother than the taut-faced, rouged person they'd created. Still, her mother had a point. This doll Zhenia had insisted they make out of her grandmother's body was not a source of comfort at all.

"*Nu*." *Welll* . . . her mother said, sitting on the bench in the main room, filling out paperwork. "I always let you get your way and then we both regret it." She took Zhenia's hand and petted it as Zhenia cried wetly.

ZHENIA'S ROOM HAD been converted into Nathaniel's home office. Her grandmother's room in the attic was full of cardboard boxes. There was a foldout couch in the living room where Zhenia could sleep, or Greg's bed, though her brother was on his way home for the funeral with his girlfriend, whom Zhenia had not known about but apparently everyone else in the family had met many times.

Life had flowed on here without Zhenia. For the last two years she'd gone to Ben's house for Christmases and Thanksgivings. She truly had believed that her grandmother did not want her coming home and so she'd stayed away. She'd lived in exile, but now she couldn't help wondering whether it had been a terrible misunderstanding. Was this a test that she had failed?

During Zhenia's absence, her grandmother got sicker and could no longer climb the stairs and so was moved into the dining room. Instead of a table, under the low-hanging chandelier there'd been a hospital bed, but by the time Zhenia stood there, it had already been taken out by hospice. In its place stood two exposed slippers and a bedpan. The slippers must have been a formality—it had been a while since her grandmother had been able to get out of bed and walk.

What had it been like for her grandmother to lie under the chandelier like a goose upon a table? Trapped still in her body. Half in, half out. The last time Zhenia saw her in this room had been over Skype. Nathaniel had set up the laptop and Babushka had been talkative but not very lucid. She was recounting childhood slights. Something about a cabbage, a rope, not wanting to dance, spilled lilac perfume. Vera kept trailing off and looking at something out of frame. "What is she looking at? Is someone else in the room? Is it Greg?" Zhenia had asked Nathaniel, but Nathaniel spun the laptop around in a full circle to show that nobody else was there. Could that have been Irina visiting then?

And was she here now, fluttering the curtain?

"Irina?" Zhenia said out loud.

No, it wasn't her. The window was open to air out the smell of mentholated creams and the body's slow decay. Outside, Nathaniel, in a fleece vest, was raking leaves. The home health aide who'd sat with her grandmother had left a stack of romance novels on the windowsill. They felt like an intrusive presence, so Zhenia lifted up the screen and pushed the books out into the yard below.

Vera's own books had been moved to the room's built-in bookshelves. Zhenia ran her hands over them. Goethe, Pushkin, Chekhov, Mandelstam,

Nabokov. They smelled like her even when the rest of the room smelled like her death. Between two volumes were some folded papers—drawings Zhenia had made when she was little. Princesses with millipede eyes and extravagant gowns. A play, written in pencil—"Little Red Riding Hood," in which the Wolf/Mom is slayed heroically not by the Woodcutter but by the Grandmother. In the corner of it, in her grandmother's palsied hand, the date. Next to this, a plastic bin with medicines. A device for measuring blood sugar. Zhenia took it out and put her finger in it. Poke, a drop of blood.

Zhenia had loved, as a child, watching her grandmother do this. It reminded her of a fairy tale transposed onto mundane life. Prick your finger on a spindle, let the drop of blood fall onto the snow, and get a baby. She had been her grandmother's child, a baby made elsewhere from snow and blood. So much of her grandmother's life was like a fairy tale. The Grimm kind, not the Disney version. The stories about the orphanage, all prefaced with: "It was not all bad. It could have been a lot worse."

Zhenia sucked her finger. *Blood of my blood*, she thought.

Marina came in holding a stack of bedding for Zhenia. Zhenia picked up a trinket off the shelf—the little glass container full of sand—and brought it up to her eye. She'd been sure that if she looked closely enough, there'd be an image of a sailboat, but it just looked like regular sand now. Had it faded completely? She knew her grandmother had gotten it on a trip to the Black Sea, but she didn't really know why it was special enough to bring to America when they'd only been allowed two suitcases each.

"What's the story with this?" Zhenia asked Marina. "Why did she have this keepsake?"

"It's from when she made my father go on vacation without me. This was something she wanted to remember."

To point out that it probably wasn't about Marina seemed pointless. Zhenia squinted at the sand. "I thought it looked different."

Marina bit her cheek. Had Marina done something to it? Zhenia wondered. Shaken it? Replaced the sand? Zhenia set it back down on the shelf.

And there, behind it, was the leather doctor's bag that as a child Zhenia knew not to touch. It felt strange taking it now in her hands, in front of her mother, and flipping the brass clasp at the top. Her grandmother always included Zhenia in her secrets, her private life, but the leather case was forbidden. Zhenia remembered her grandmother taking it out occasionally and brooding.

"Have you looked through this already?" Zhenia asked her mother.

"Why would I look through it? If there was anything in there she wanted me to have, she would have given it to me."

"But aren't you curious? Don't you want to understand?"

"What do you imagine I don't understand?" Marina turned and left mid-phrase. "I'll leave the sheets for you on the couch," she called, already in the other room.

One time in elementary school, Zhenia remembered, her grandmother had this doctor's bag open on her lap and was looking through it. They were on the couch, her mother with baby Greg, her grandmother, and Zhenia. It was a plaid couch that had been given to them by some charitable organization and which they'd long since gotten rid of. They were sitting together, watching the news—a segment on the Biosphere 2 project, the failed experiment in Arizona where people had tried to create a closed ecological system in a glassed-in greenhouse.

Zhenia's mother had a Hobbesian view of humanity. Put eight people in a glass house and of course they would fight. "That blonde one," she said, pointing Greg's rattle at the woman on TV in the navy space suit, "she will suck up all the oxygen."

Zhenia had tried to argue, the coziness of the experiment, they could all grow together! Couldn't an outcome of something be positive for once? Her grandmother was just clutching the leather case and staring at the TV worriedly. When Marina noticed, she finally turned it off.

Zhenia started to protest, but her mother cut her off:

"Enough, none of it is science. Rich men playing pretend. Those stupid space suits."

Her grandmother finally was back. "It's true," she said. "Everyone keeps trying to re-create the Garden of Eden. But we all know how the Garden of Eden ended."

"How did it end?" Zhenia asked. Her sock had a hole in the toe and she was picking at it. Her grandmother grabbed her foot and covered this bare toe with her soft, warm hand.

"With knowledge!" she said.

With knowledge, Zhenia thought, and opened the case.

CHAPTER 22

But what new knowledge could Zhenia really get about a person who has lived inside her, telling her to put on mittens when it was cold, to eat something, to make herself some tea? First the external grandmother took care of her and then the internal one. It was her grandmother's voice that kept her functioning in this world—even after her grandmother had stopped making sense or being able to speak.

Zhenia pulled out a black-and-white photograph from the case. Marina, twelve and skinny, with two braids, leaning into the body of her father. Baba Vera, turned toward him, midsentence, gesticulating with a blurred hand. They formed a wobbly triangle. Deda Grisha looked tired, holding them both. The peacekeeper in the family. He was dead before Zhenia got to meet him, but his sainthood was the only thing that Zhenia's mother and grandmother were able to agree on.

Then under this, old identity papers with a photo of Vera when she was a young woman. Her face was too thin. She was looking into the camera, but her gaze was vacant. It was taken in 1953, before Marina was born, when Deda Grisha was at a labor camp. He was gone for six years over nothing. A joke about the regime that someone in the engineering group had told and which he had not reported. Their apartment in Leningrad was confiscated, and Baba Vera had been forced to survive on her own, not knowing when, or if, he would come back.

And under this document, a scrap of paper. A portrait done in pencil of her grandmother as a teenager. Head tilted to the side with a slight smile, eyes locked and bright. The pose and expression were familiar to Zhenia and yet the face wasn't. Who had drawn it? Probably her grandfather. "To my love," it said underneath.

And under this, an empty envelope addressed to Vera at their apartment where they'd lived when they first came to America, before Marina had met Nathaniel. And the return address: Irina Horowitz, her second husband's last name, her address on Long Island. Zhenia didn't know there'd been a correspondence. She thought her grandmother had only tracked down the other family after Irina died. What had Irina written? Zhenia searched through the rest of the bag for a folded letter but there was nothing. It must have been too painful to keep.

The rest of the papers in the bag were loose pages addressed to Grisha, but if they were meant as letters, they were never folded or sent. Maybe this was more like a journal, or something she gave him in person? These letters were mostly full of things Zhenia did not know about, but there were a handful of references to events from her grandmother's life that Zhenia recognized.

"And how the men who turned us into orphans clapped and clapped."

This was probably referring to a concert that happened every year, when the children in the orphanage were brought to the palace to sing about brotherhood and the new world order. Her grandmother had told her about this many times—the way they'd be trotted out in starched and ironed white shirts, bows in their hair, pleated skirts and dun-colored tights that were manufactured in the Soviet Union but were in short supply. Zhenia imagined little Vera, her clothes stiff and new, her cheeks hollow from hunger, her face flushed from the cold of the walk and the heat of the room. Her voice must have been so thin as she sang in a large, echoey chamber, in a palace that had recently belonged to a tsar and now belonged, ostensibly, to the people. The children's voices would have bounced off the stone walls and floor. The candles in their sweating hands would have dripped hot wax onto their wrists. Her grandmother had shaken with rage as she described to Zhenia the fat faces of the functionaries, red from vodka, jowls hanging over their collars, and the wives with fluttery nervous expressions and hats that came from abroad. All of these monsters had clapped and clapped and Vera had been forced to curtsy.

Or: *"I shuffle and reshuffle the same worn memories trying to imagine what I could have done to get a different outcome. Are the memories even true? Was it actually sunny? Did I have a lollipop? Had I behaved poorly that morning spilling my mother's perfume or was that a different morning entirely and to make sense of things that could not make sense to me, I created causes and effects that were not there?"*

The morning that Vera was referring to was, Zhenia knew, the central rupture in her grandmother's life. Irina had taken Vera on two trollies, given her a lollipop, and left her in an orphanage. Once on the other side of the gates, Vera had tried to break away from the groundskeeper and run back to her mother. What if she'd tried harder? Would her mother have changed her mind? Vera never stopped waiting for Irina to come back because what child wouldn't? And when, months later, Irina's aunt Gittel showed up to check on her, Vera had been so excited by the visit that she bragged to all the girls who slept near her that she would be leaving any day now. Her great-aunt had come and was making arrangements to take her home.

But after that first visit, Irina's aunt never returned. Maybe Vera had done something to offend her without realizing it? The woman had seemed so grim, dressed in black, wincing at the sound of all the children's voices. Vera thought about their encounter very hard and often, she'd told Zhenia. It was many years later when Grisha reassured her that there had been nothing she could have done. For political reasons, the children in this orphanage did not get "adopted out." As children of enemies of the people, they were simultaneously tainted and symbols of the regime's generosity. Even though the parents couldn't be rehabilitated, the regime was willing to give their progeny a chance.

"The same loops, enough to make me dizzy, but I have to remember that a different outcome would have also meant no you."

Ultimately, Vera had told Zhenia, it had all happened for the best. How else would she have met Grisha? He was the kind headmistress's son.

Skinny, malnourished, but growing still like a weed. He'd come help his mother sometimes and hungrily watch the kids eat, but he was not allowed to eat their food.

After the orphanage Vera went to the university, where she studied chemical engineering. She would have preferred to study literature, but there was no way forward for her in the humanities, not with her family background. There were many men at the university who took an interest in her. They thought she was beautiful and mysterious. She didn't talk about the orphanage, and omission after omission made it impossible for her to be herself. Swiss cheese. Even if she didn't lie, she still created a circumstance in which the other person had to lie to fill those holes. They assumed her upbringing was like their own. She played games with these men but never felt comfortable. Then, one day, in the student cafeteria, there was Grisha!

She was so excited. "Why are you eating here?" She thought he must have been looking for her. But he, it turned out, was also a student, discharged from the army after injuring his foot. They talked about his mother, who'd passed away from heart failure. Vera said that the headmistress's kindness had rescued them all, her ability to stay human even when this was dangerous.

Grisha had filled out a bit since she'd seen him last, broad-shouldered now, the Adam's apple protruding not quite so painfully.

"You're my home. You're my only home."

Zhenia loved when her grandmother would talk about being in love. It always seemed very romantic, even when it made Marina's eyes roll out of her head.

But reading things like: *"Your hands inside of me, on me, and in me. I want you to devour me. First, feast on my breasts, then my ass. I need you to turn me inside out. I need you or I will die. I need you to fill . . ."*—this was too much. The explicitness, the appetite, the lust. Her grandmother was unrecognizable and Zhenia felt lost. Is this what people were really like behind closed doors? She had never felt this kind of hunger toward Ben or anyone else.

And the way her grandmother wrote about Marina also took Zhenia aback. Vera was so openly jealous of her own daughter.

"You spoil her. I heard her sitting on your lap and whispering, 'Let's leave her. Let's run away.' And you did nothing. You let her sit there. You patted her hand."

It was perverse, of course, after living through her mother's abandonment, to have her child threaten to abandon her again.

"You don't make love to me. You say she can hear us. I don't care who hears us. I could care less. When you touch me it's the only time I feel like I'm alive in this constant nightmare of my life."

They all lived together in one room. She and Grisha had been together many years and she hadn't been able to get pregnant. She had not particularly wanted to, though Grisha really wanted a child. But after Grisha came back from the labor camp, part of him had been broken and hollowed out. And when Vera got pregnant, it felt like a miracle.

"Her growing in me is what brought you back to life. I did not have the power to do this, but she did. Of course this is very painful. She took you from me. She took you."

Zhenia's grandmother thought that Grisha spoiled their daughter. She hit Marina. She spanked her and smacked her on the head. Of course, this was common back then. Discipline. In America, once Vera was completely dependent, Marina would recount all these slights tearfully to Nathaniel over dinner. Marina would hold her ears like they were ringing, remembering the way Vera had boxed them. And Vera would sit at the other end of the table, chewing her food and acting as though she weren't hearing any of this, telling Zhenia, "Eat, eat, why aren't you eating?" or pouring Greg milk.

"So dramatic. Your mother is the one who should've been the actress," Baba Vera said after one of these performances the last time Zhenia had come home for Christmas. And Zhenia did feel annoyed with her mother, probably because she couldn't connect the villainess from these stories with her grandmother, the person she loved most. The person who had shown Zhenia more love and affection than anyone else ever had.

Zhenia was relieved when Paul called and she had a reason to stop looking at the letters. She put them back into their leather case, the clasp clicking back into place.

CHAPTER 23

"Paul," Zhenia said before he could speak. "She died. My grandmother. I'm in Boston."

"I'm sorry to hear that," Paul said. "I'm sorry for your loss."

"Does Irina know already? She must. Are they together now?"

Paul stares for a moment at Irina. A slight breeze forms around them, then the air grows still.

"No," he says. "Your grandmother is not here."

"Is she still on earth?"

"Do you feel her near you?"

"I'm with all her things but . . . no, I don't feel her really. I didn't feel her when I saw the body. I thought I would, but I didn't."

Paul can hear Zhenia start to cry. He makes some sympathetic sounds. "It's a different process for everybody as far as I can tell. Where they end up and how they end up there."

"So, can you bring her back?" Zhenia squeaks.

"Sorry, what?"

"Can you . . . sort of herd her spirit into me? I'm four months pregnant. I feel like I have this receptacle inside me, waiting for her."

"No," Paul says. "No. I wouldn't know how to do that, nor does that sound like a good idea." It's one thing to talk to the dead, and another to bring them back to life. Not that it's even possible in the way she means it. "People are not whole beings. That is completely an illusion created by our brains. Think about how many dead Irinas there must be, for example. The Irina that came to America is not the same one as the one we're talking to."

"Stop talking about me as if I'm not here," Irina says. "Tell her that you can't sweep a soul into someone like it's a dust pile. What an idea. As if Vera would even have wanted that. She's free now of her body, shattered into parts. The baby will have shards of all of us in it, whether Zhenichka likes it or not. This is a genetic fact."

Zhenia's crying is wet and long and Paul and Irina sway together in the soft darkness, listening to her choke and hiccup.

"What did you tell her in that letter?" Zhenia finally manages to say.

"She didn't tell you?"

"No."

"I told her not to contact me." The cloud behind Irina moves closer. "I didn't want her to hurt my family. Her existence would have contradicted the person they believed me to be, the person I had become. I thought, what good would seeing me do her now? She'd lived most of her life already, and I had lived mine."

Paul looks at Irina and she is dense with our condensation.

"Tell her something about her grandmother," Paul says gently. "Tell her something that you remember."

Irina pauses.

"I remember her chapped round cheeks. They looked like red apples in the cold. And how she would pat my face with her chubby hand and say things under her nose in her deep little voice, repeating back to me my own mannerisms and inflections . . ." Irina blurs around the edges.

"She thought maybe you wouldn't be able to abandon your own reflection." Zhenia begins to cry again.

"Zhenichka," Irina says into Paul's mouth, growing impatient, "stop it with your crying. Vera has been suspended between your world and what comes next for a long time. I don't know where she is now, but she has finally gotten out of that in-between state and that's something to celebrate. In-between states are very difficult. I should know. Be glad she isn't with me. Be glad she's somewhere else. Maybe most of her is free."

"Shall we keep going?" Zhenia heard Paul's regular voice say in the phone. "Do you have a pen?"

And in a daze, she wiped her nose with her sleeve and got a pen off her grandmother's bookshelf.

The day they came for Fräulein Agata, I was sitting in her class. She had the windows cracked open to let in the cold air because she was worried about aging and everyone knows that meat sweats and spoils faster at warm temperatures. While a girl with a nasal voice read Goethe's *Faust* in halting German, Fräulein Agata was pacing in the front of the room, pirouetting for my amusement. After her humiliation, she tried to win me back in various ways. I was her last remaining disciple. Olga had switched to French. Fräulein Agata told me that with Olga she'd miscalculated and created a monster. She'd wanted to give Olga the tools to think for herself, but the problem was that the things Olga was thinking were not right. She needed to be stopped. People like Olga, who had no appreciation for beauty, who wanted to become like machines and had no feeling for the human condition or sentimentality, they were the most dangerous. I think on this account she was wrong: sentimental people could be just as dangerous. For example, the man who tortured me later had talked with a tremor in his voice, a tear in his eye about some fat childhood pony, and yet none of this depth of feeling was extended to the people whose lives he destroyed.

My teacher pantomimed being dipped by an invisible partner. The Tango of Death. Our inside joke. She looked possessed, ridiculous, and this made me pity her, but to cover this, I clapped and grinned, rubbed my hands together for warmth. She pressed the side of her face to the chalkboard seductively and slid down. The door to her classroom opened behind her. The headmaster and a group of police officers in black-and-green uniforms stood in the doorway. She straightened up, her back to them, a streak of chalk on her face.

The reading girl trailed off and we all stared dumbly. I could see that Fräulein Agata's hand trembled as she wiped her cheek. She locked eyes with me for a moment and then they took her away. We all sat very still in our seats.

Someone started reading again, because they didn't know what else to do. Someone else got up and closed all the windows. I waited for Fräulein Agata to come back even though I understood that she wouldn't. I got up to follow her, then sat down again, worrying I'd draw attention to myself.

Then I decided that I didn't care, and walked quickly down the hall to the principal's office. I stood outside the office, trying to hear what was being said, but it was quiet. I pushed open the heavy door and there was the secretary, sitting with crumbs around her mouth, eating a tin of cookies. No one else was there.

"Where did they go?" I asked her.

Fräulein Agata had been fired immediately. I watched through the window as one of the groundskeepers dragged her steamer trunk down the driveway toward the waiting carriage. My teacher's nose was red, like she'd been crying. I knocked on the glass to try to get her attention, but she didn't look up. I ran outside without my coat, but by the time I got down the winding hallways and out the door, the carriage had left. The officers had left with her. Only the headmaster was still there, looking glum.

Oh, my teacher, with her beautiful red hair! She had enjoyed poking at the status quo, flicking her tail at it here and there, nudging all of us toward the edge, but I don't think she ever thought we'd go over. It was an erotic game. Nothing was supposed to actually give.

After she was gone, I went to her room to see if she had left me a letter or trinket of something to remember her by. There was nothing. The room was completely empty. I never saw her again.

Zhenia was sitting on the floor, next to her grandmother's slippers.

"So, Olga was the one who told on her?" Zhenia sniffled, looking at her notes to see if she had written this somewhere.

"No," Irina says, looking at Paul. "It was me."

"You?" he asks. Paul had not seen this coming.

"What do you mean? You've been going on about how she inspired you and taught you how to think," Zhenia says.

"Yes, she had good qualities, but I had no choice. I'd come to believe that the only way to cure the evils of the unjust economic order was through active warfare. My teacher would have sat back and pontificated endlessly, until the point where it would have been more expedient for her to turn on us and snitch."

—*This is how they operate, you see.*

—*Exactly, exactly. They imagine YOU capable of doing to them what they end up doing to you.*

—*"Look at what you made me do!"*

—*Well, she probably would have snitched though. We were all snitches.*

—*The police could find ways to make you talk.*

—*The police were remarkably stupid. Chasing me through the streets! Slipping and falling! Holding on to their hats as their pants fell down, their pants as their hats blew away.*

—*That's from a Charlie Chaplin film. That's not real life.*

—*And anyway, power doesn't have to be smart to crush you.*

—*Crush, crush, like a cockroach.*

—*Crush, crush, like a bedbug.*

—*Like a sow bug.*

—*That was good evening exercise! To stand on a chair and crush the cockroaches with a broom.*

"So, what happened to your teacher after you betrayed her?" Paul wants to know. He feels something like repulsion bubble in his throat.

"Betrayed her! Maybe I saved her life. I don't know what happened to her. She wouldn't have lasted long in the Revolution. Who would've had the patience for her tantrums?"

"You're two-faced," Zhenia said, feeling this repulsion too. "Eating from her hand and then biting it off."

"Maybe I was two-faced, but I wasn't false."

"You believe that a person can be two-faced and not be false?" Zhenia asked, thinking of the other version of her grandmother she saw in the brown leather bag.

"Oh, Zhenia, why are you asking me questions that we both know the answer to? I suppose there were people who really did exist rigidly with only one face. Osip, for example. Maybe Olga. But to imagine that someone like Olga was morally superior for being consistent seems foolhardy.

"This reminds me of the story about a revolutionary I'd met at Osip's. They'd been part of the same network. She'd been caught making a bomb and was sent away to a labor camp until the February Revolution, when all political prisoners were released.

"While imprisoned, she'd gotten typhus or maybe some vitamin deficiency and it left her blind. When Osip introduced us, he placed her hands on my face and she felt around. Her eyes were open and blank. She touched my nose, which was on the larger side, and smiled.

"I watched her closely: when she stood up, she walked with her hands in front of her, then ran into a wall, which she followed sideways to the doorway. She bumped into furniture. People always stare at a blind person because you can stare with no repercussions. Her eyes had been so blank when she was touching my face. I didn't think that was something a person could fake.

"Then, a few months later, I saw her in the park reading a book. She looked up and watched a bird flutter down and peck at something in the path.

"Had she been cured? Or had she just believed herself to be blind until she was? She left for Moscow, and I didn't see her after that, though I did come across a photograph of her in the paper because she tried to assassinate Lenin. She shot him several times outside of a factory."

"Why?"

"Because he betrayed us and the Revolution. As soon as he gained power he turned on all of us. But that's not my point. My point is that I was blind in much the same way—selectively. Do you see what I mean?"

Zhenia felt the baby inside of her shift. Of course she knew what Irina meant. The cat was in the box and not in the box at the same time. Anton licking an ice cream cone, and bringing the other for his wife, but also fucking Zhenia in the closet. Zhenia's grandmother dead but alive, lying under the chandelier for months and months, and Zhenia not visiting, not once. "Sounds like you can justify anything," Zhenia sniffed.

Paul closes his mouth and looks at Irina. His revulsion bubbles over into something else. He leans forward and kisses her.

"I'm sorry," he says, and then he kisses her again.

He feels agitated, hungry. "I want to be closer to you," he says, not quite knowing what he's saying. And somehow in this embrace he can see the German teacher, through a windowpane, more zaftig than he expected, her face obscured by a cloud of her cold breath, leaning against a large steamer trunk. Irina's giddiness from her moment of power slithers through his chest and disappears into the ground.

Kiss us again! We all vibrate. With tongue! And teeth!

He tries to kiss Irina again but she pushes him away.

"Can I visit you?" Zhenia is asking on the phone.

"What?" Paul says, panting still.

"Maybe if I'm there in person it would change something. Maybe you could help me find where my grandmother went. I want to talk to her again. I need to be with her."

CHAPTER 24

Zhenia went into the kitchen. Her eyes and nose were swollen and red. Her mother was chopping boiled potatoes for a salad she was making for the wake. Zhenia found herself putting her arms around her mother's shoulders from behind.

Marina stiffened. She stopped chopping for a moment and looked up out the window. Nathaniel had raked most of the leaves around the play structure and was gathering them into large paper bags. The play structure had been purchased for Greg almost two decades ago and was decomposing slowly in their backyard.

"Now we don't have to take it down," her mother said, gesturing out the window.

"We'll have another little one to play on it."

Zhenia nodded, letting go of her mother. It was dusk and she could see the mossy slide outside but also their reflection on the glass. She and her mother looked so much alike. Two wolves.

"Remember when you went on vacation and didn't take us?" Zhenia said. Why was she bringing up old slights? Maybe this moment of closeness made her nervous. She needed to be the one to pop it first, and remembering spring break of her junior year was an easy way to do it. It had been a cold and miserable week. Marina, Nathaniel, and Greg went to Cancún and left Zhenia and her grandmother in Boston, where it got dark at three in the afternoon and the dirty snow was grainy with ice.

"That's not true," Zhenia's mother said, shaking her head vehemently. "We bought you tickets. You were the ones who decided not to go. Out of nowhere, Babushka developed a fake phobia of flying. And you said you needed to stay home and study for exams. What should I have done?" Her mother was already raising her voice.

It was true, but it didn't feel true. It felt like Zhenia and her grandmother had been left behind. They had concocted a plan to stay so that Zhenia could get the abortion. They'd decided not to tell Marina. Why, Zhenia didn't really understand, but it had seemed easier not to complicate things further with her mother's disappointment.

When Marina, Nathaniel, and Greg had come back with sunburns and hair wraps a week later, it felt aggressive. Her mother had refused to take her hair wrap out for a week and had gone into the lab where she worked with the soggy graying thread on her head.

"I mean it, Zhenia. What should I have done?"

Zhenia stroked her mother's hair where that wrap had been. Marina tensed, then moved Zhenia's hand away.

"I don't know what you should have done," Zhenia said. "You could have asked me again. Sent me an engraved invitation."

Marina nodded. Jokes. Her difficult mother was dead and Marina felt terribly sad and relieved and sad for being relieved and sad for having a different mother than the one she'd always wanted.

"I think you were right," Zhenia said. "About the funeral. I'm not going to go. I'm going to go to New York instead."

Her mother froze, knife in her hand. "You're the one who made me turn this into a spectacle! I didn't want to. I invited her Orthodox relatives from Long Island. I'm making all these kosher salads. Now I have to think of them showing up or not," she said tearfully. "A small life and nobody shows up when it's over. You're going to leave me to wait alone at the grave site for relatives who won't come. Nobody will be there."

"People will come. The people she learned English with. Or the ones from the community college classes."

Zhenia's mother angrily blew her nose, then pushed the chopped potatoes into a large glass bowl.

"I don't know any of those people. Most of them are probably dead. She was difficult to be around. She didn't have friends. She had you, and you aren't coming. I got my hopes up for a second that you'd finally become a real person."

Zhenia was genuinely taken aback by her mother's reaction.

"You were the one telling me that funerals were meaningless rituals. That she was dead and there was nothing we could do about it."

"Nathaniel," Marina shouted. "Nathaniel, take her to the bus station. She's going to New York. I can't look at her."

Nathaniel came into the kitchen, looking confused. He had a leaf stuck to his fleece vest.

Zhenia pulled it off him. "Thank you," she said.

Before he could ask what had happened—fights like this weren't uncommon, since Marina and Zhenia did not know how to communicate and were always baffled and enraged by each other's reactions—right then, Greg and his girlfriend came in through the front door with a clatter of rolling suitcases. Zhenia was flustered. Greg hugged her, and then his girlfriend, the one Zhenia had never met, hugged her, and her mother's rage was replaced with a whirlwind of activity.

Zhenia grabbed her things from her grandmother's room, and then stood awkwardly by the door, waiting for Nathaniel to take her to the bus station.

"Where are you going?" Greg asked, looking at her strangely.

His girlfriend had barely set down her suitcase and already she had an apron on and was chopping something. Marina waved her hand dismissively in Zhenia's direction. "Let her go."

Nathaniel held the car keys but hesitated.

"Are you sure?" he asked Zhenia. "Can't it wait? A day?"

"Let her go," Marina said again, sharply enough to make Greg's girl-friend start.

WTF, Greg texted Zhenia from across the room. The phone buzzed in her hand, but she pretended not to look at it as she followed Nathaniel out to the car.

Zhenia couldn't lower the body of the person she'd loved most into the ground and throw dirt on her. Why this morning she had thought she needed to do this, Zhenia didn't know, but now this did not seem even remotely like closure. And she didn't want closure. She wanted her grandmother back.

CHAPTER 25

Zhenia had two seats to herself near the back of the Peter Pan bus that left from Riverside Station. It was still light out. Time felt strange to her. Elongated, compressed, torqued. Had it been this morning that she left L.A. and now she was on her way to New York, or was it the morning before? Her phone was buzzing in her lap. She leaned her head against the window and chewed her saltines up into a paste before swallowing, then rolled out her wrists and answered.

"Hi, Paul," she said, ready to take dictation. Several times she had to ask him to repeat himself because his speech had become slightly slurred, as though Irina were holding on to his tongue.

Petrograd was buzzing. I could feel it! It had probably been buzzing for a long time, but I was only then becoming aware of it.

I told my aunt and uncle that school wasn't for me anymore, and they didn't protest. My schooling had seemed to them like another one of my mother's pretensions. What good could it possibly do me? Olga stayed enrolled, pulling things out of the school piece by piece to destroy it from within, but I was happy to be free of it.

Hanna and I would tell my aunt Gittel that we were going down to the hospital to read to the soldiers, which we were allowed to do as long as we promised never to touch their bandages. We would ride the tram to get there and strangers would engage us in conversation because Hanna had a sweet and open face. I'd been so cloistered—to be out in the world without the filter of Fräulein Agata's irony was an entirely new experience. The suffering and hunger of the people around us was not an abstract idea. We were coming into direct contact with the things my teacher had preached about in vague terms.

At the hospital, we would wander the rows of convalescents. It was boys like my brother who'd been sent off to get mutilated in a pointless war. They would groan and reach for us. Hanna would stop and hold their hands. I'd step back and look down at the book I brought, look away from their bandaged stumps and protruding rib cages. Unlike me, Hanna was never squeamish. The men at the hospital sensed her kindness. They'd call after her like caged bears.

And then, on the way home, we'd inevitably get roped into helping some other unfortunates. We would follow strangers on wild-goose chases. Somebody would hand us a poorly printed pamphlet and we would end up in the basement of a bakery for a meeting, or filling out some illiterate factory worker's governmental forms in triplicate, or bringing some poor woman and her sick child to a doctor. To say that I wanted to be useful is maybe overstating it. But I was curious. I'd been shoved in a box for so many years, and now I was learning to straighten up, and I surprised myself the taller and taller I got. Of course, what I wanted most of all was to again feel the thrill I'd felt delivering the bullets to the man in prison. Engaging with all these people, with their squalor and their unmet needs, it was something Hanna was better at. I could play the part for a few afternoons, but then it would get tedious. A whole life could be spent that way.

"What way?" Zhenia interrupted, flipping over her notebook page. "Helping people?"

"Sure, but there are many ways to help people. And this felt like using a small spoon to try to clear a mountain. And it was dull and unpleasant and not very exciting. Listen, I have never claimed that I was noble. I think Hanna was. She didn't lose her patience with people. Though as I say it now, I see that I'm drifting her into sainthood. Maybe that's not right. Who knows what would have happened to her if she'd lived long enough to be tested by the cruelties of Soviet life."

—Oh, the cruelties! Oh, the cruelties!
—I think I was in that hospital ward.
—You were not.
—I think I was. I had gangrene. The nurses were angels with cool hands. The girls would read to us and sing.
—He does that. He inserts himself into every story! I don't even know what to call such a compulsion.

The man tries to move away from us but we don't let him. We follow him. We rub ourselves against his neck. We like the smell coming out of his pores. What a comforting smell.

—A morning/afternoon smell.
—I could use a drink. A shot of something.
—A little thimbleful.
—Vodka, moonshine, I've stooped to lower. I'm not choosy.
—Of this you don't have to convince us.

We give the man a lick, then another. He takes a deep breath and blows on us and we go tumbling down the hill. Over the zygotes, over the rabbits.

For New Year's, my aunt and uncle got a big fir tree. It was shameful, with the long breadlines, kids starving, showing off and getting such a tall tree that had to be dragged up the steps by three pale and hungry-looking men. My aunt didn't so much as offer them a glass of milk.

"But weren't you Jewish?" Zhenia interrupts again.

"So? Secular Jews in the cities all had trees and gave each other gifts on New Year's. It's how it was done."

My mother sent me a gift, a jar of honey that she'd obtained somehow from the monastery. I'm sure she didn't gather it herself, but imagining her getting stung by a swarm of bees gave me some pleasure. My aunt and uncle got Hanna a new dress and a heart-shaped locket. Hanna gave all of us thoughtful gifts. A bookmark for her father, a crocheted lace doily for her mother, and for me she got a book with a carved-out secret compartment. I did not get anybody anything and I didn't share my honey. While they put music on the new phonograph and danced, I sat in my sloped-ceiling room, eating honey until I made myself sick.

The next day it was in all the papers: Rasputin had been found in the frozen river, shot, tied, poisoned. He'd been influencing the tsar through the tsarina, filling the royal family's heads with gibberish and madness, giving advice on things he knew nothing about. Of course the people still clinging to the monarchy wanted him out. He'd been assassinated, and he didn't go down easily, but neither did the monarchy. His photograph was on the front page of the newspaper, looking much more dignified than I remembered him being at the luncheon when we'd had to pry him off Hanna. What had really happened, I wondered, in the carriage with her? What could he have done to her that she liked so much? To me that all felt like a lifetime ago.

Hanna stared at his picture and said nothing. Her father's nose was buried deep in some section of the paper related to business, and Aunt Gittel was going on about a new pattern she'd obtained that was in the style of something worn by the tsarina and about some young man (marriageable) who was coming to visit them from Rostov. My cousin's face must have given something away, because her father suddenly folded the paper and stared at us in silence.

I had few dealings with my uncle, really. He was usually mild mannered, and deferential to his wife. I rarely saw him express strong opinions, and he doted on Hanna in a way that made me long for my own father. But there was something in the way he folded the newspaper that afternoon and stared at my cousin that made me wonder whether he could sense something was changing in her.

He made her stand up and twirl around, as he squinted at her. "Enough with the dresses," he told his wife, "let's have that suitor come earlier," because it was time, he thought, to marry Hanna off.

It was abrupt. I didn't know what to make of this. Was I also to be married off? I wondered. Or, was that none of their concern? There was another cell in the monastery next to my mother. Another hole in the earth next to my father. I could go there as far as they cared.

My cousin, she never lost her temper, she never revealed her hand. She twirled in front of her daddy, then sat on his lap and kissed her new locket. He was not convinced, but he was pacified. That day it had been hard for us to go out on our usual rounds to the hospital and beyond. My cousin agreed to go with my aunt to make preparations for the arrival of this young man from Rostov, while I paced in my room, occasionally smelling my empty jar of honey and sticking my tongue into it.

At some point during all their preparations, my cousin snuck into my room and begged me to go check the fountain in the front yard. Apparently, Boris had been leaving her notes in the cherub's mouth for some time. And *she* had been leaving *him* notes at the hospital under the pillow of one of his friends. So, this was why we'd been visiting the soldiers with such frequency. Of course it upset me that I'd known nothing about it. What other things had I been oblivious to? Clearly, lots. I thought again about what Fräulein Agata had said, about Hanna hatching. How she wasn't a rock, she was an egg.

I regretted then what I had done to my teacher. I'd thought I would be out in the world, at the center of things. I had not expected in the ecstasy of administering justice, that I would be back to sitting in that sloped-ceiling room, licking an empty jar of honey, and, with sticky fingers, fondling a love letter not meant for me.

During this time, I had no contact with Osip. I hadn't seen him since the night Olga took us to his house. I remembered how I'd danced with him under the bridge under my teacher's nose and how he'd called me a child, which I suppose is what I was. A child, locked in a room, desperately waiting for something to happen to her. And then, when things did start to happen, I, of course, couldn't stop them.

Paul closes his mouth for a moment and looks at Irina. Back in the closet where he had made himself a nest, he was drinking melted margaritas from a mix. The drinking had gotten out of hand, yes, obviously. It had seemed like making the drinks sugary and festive would make it less sordid, but it did not have this effect and instead gave him a headache. Soon the girl would be here, and who knows, maybe her presence might allow him to go deeper . . . into Irina and into the afterlife, if he could just shake this headache.

Irina is staring off at the curving horizon line, thinking about something. He takes her icy fingers and presses them to his temples. Together they look out at the hologrammed darkness that surrounds them. Irina's fingers dull the pulsing in his head but also give an odd feeling of penetration, like she's merging into him. And just as he begins to sense a new dimension to the darkness, a weakness seizes him.

CHAPTER 26

Zhenia was using her purse as a pillow, lying across two seats, texting with her brother. She and Paul had been disconnected. The line had gone dead, and the sudden silence was the reprieve she didn't know she'd needed.

Zhenia's brother was upset with her for leaving, as upset as he ever got. He said that their mom was stressed out because the relatives, Irina's other children, had been calling and praying and arranging their arrival.

When Zhenia was a freshman in high school, she and her grandmother had taken a Greyhound bus to meet these relatives on Long Island. Irina had died with her secret seemingly intact. When they arrived, Irina's children went into another room and fought and then one of Irina's sons insisted on swabbing them for a DNA sample. It had been a humiliating dinner where everyone was on edge, waiting to hear what it was that Vera wanted from them. The grandchildren weren't even told who Vera and Zhenia were, just poor distant relations whom they were feeding like it was a mitzvah. When the results of the DNA tests eventually came back, the family seemed to soften. They began to call Vera, but it was like meeting them had gotten whatever she'd wanted out of her system. These were strangers, blood relations or not, and she didn't seem to have any use for them.

Seeing her grandmother's humiliation had made Zhenia so mad she'd stolen a small brass vase off a shelf, a tchotchke that sat on the living room side table for years and Marina was none the wiser, assuming Zhenia and Vera had gotten it at a yard sale.

Zhenia started typing out a text to Greg, telling him to hide the vase, but then changed her mind. Let them see it. What did it matter? All of it seemed insignificant. She'd stolen a vase but they'd stolen her grandmother's mother.

Her phone started buzzing again in her hand. Paul. She stared at it for a moment before answering. "Yes," she said. "I was wondering where you'd gone."

"Just a moment," she heard Paul croak before the deluge began.

Where could I have gone? I'm as trapped here as I felt then, pacing in my room while Hanna performed the role of an obedient child, running errands with Aunt Gittel and getting the house ready for the guest. How we managed to slip out and meet up with Olga amidst all this activity, I'm not sure.

But to be free, out in the world again! To feel it bubbling under us! It was the most intoxicating feeling. A lot had happened in our absence and Olga was starting to fill us in. I'd worried that we'd been forgotten, and I was relieved when Olga said that we had not and that, in fact, there was something very big they'd need us to do soon.

Olga snuck us into my old school's kitchen, where we stole all the rolls baked for a special dinner with the parents. Like three Robin Hoods, we walked down the boulevard with sacks slung over our shoulders, handing out rolls to people waiting in the long breadline across from the Hotel Astoria.

Business at the hotel seemed to be proceeding as usual and people like the general were probably still feasting on mutton and redheads even as the line of hungry people outside grew longer and longer.

I had not known hunger yet. But I would.

It's a dividing line, one I hope you'll never have to cross.

"It must make a person desperate," Zhenia said, thinking of how her grandmother's face would grow intense sometimes, watching Zhenia eat.

"Desperate. Sure. It would boil things down past their essence to something stickier.

"When I was at my hungriest I was at my least practical. It's a side of me that my second husband would never know. With him I was never hungry, completely removed from the person I'd been, who would dress myself and Verochka up in our torn finery and, with eyes burning, parade us down the street, refusing bread from people if the intentions behind their offers didn't strike me as pure of heart. Yes, even as my daughter cried and begged me. I had dignity, and it was not beaten out of me with hunger. With hunger I had to double down on dignity because what else did I have? Later in my life, everyone always described the other Irina as so pragmatic. The other Irina's children, they never went hungry. The only hunger they knew was fasting on Yom Kippur."

Zhenia thought of Irina's other children again and felt a sensation in her throat as though she hadn't just stolen the vase but had tried to swallow it.

"And you, have you known hunger?" Irina asks Paul conversationally.

He shakes his head. "Thirst," he says.

She traces the outline of his lips with her finger. Of course. A person who didn't understand this sort of absence and desire would not have been willing to help her.

Having something I could give people, handing out stolen bread in the street, it made me feel like a god. But when I noticed two police officers heading toward us, my heart sank. Olga shoved me forward to continue.

"Keep going," she muttered. "You'll only draw attention to yourself if you stop." And it's true. It took me a moment to realize that it wasn't me they were interested in. Rounding the corner behind us, and gathering in volume, was a group of women walking in the street. First a group, then more. Soon the entire street was filled. A demonstration pouring out of the factories and into the roads.

"A strike!" Olga said with pure delight.

The policemen were watching tensely but there were now a lot of people, and the officers were on foot. They squinted at the handmade posters. It took me a moment to understand the chanting. The factory workers were hungry.

"We want bread! Give us what you said!"

It felt like a divine sign to have people asking for something that at that very moment I was giving away.

Hanna repeated the rhyme, smiling to herself. "I like things that rhyme," she said very earnestly.

It made me think of how Fräulein Agata would always ask about Hanna—"Is she simple?"

And she was. Exactly that. But, simple doesn't mean stupid. "We want bread! Give us what you said!" Hanna shouted and waved in solidarity from across the street.

"We want the tsar dead!" Olga added, laughing.

And then we were walking with them, handing out the rest of the bread. I had never been in a crowd before. I had been at the market when it was busy, passing people on my way to somewhere else, but I had never before been inside of a crowd.

Hanna and I held hands so we wouldn't lose each other and Olga held on to the backs of our coats. The crowd carried us down the length of the street.

My whole life, honestly, I had felt so apart from people. To have this momentary sense of belonging, it was intoxicating. To shout at the top of my lungs in public!

Yes! Yes. Paul knows exactly what she means. He remembers his first Pride parade. He'd moved to New York to come out of the closet, though this was only something he understood later. He would have denied hiding any part of himself in New Jersey, there were just a lot of blank spaces, girls reaching for his crotch, and him leaving his body. And then to be standing on a street corner in New York, beaming like an idiot among the floats and glitter and assless chaps. He'd felt the euphoria of feeling safe and seen but not individually, en masse.

Paul leans in and this time, when he kisses her, she doesn't immediately push him away.

He thrusts his tongue into her mouth and he can feel the crowd holding him.

Shoulder to shoulder. Women in kerchiefs. The air is thick, damp gunpowder. It feels religious. And then being swept toward a row of men on horseback, mustached with black coats, wide sleeves, bandoliers of bullets hanging on their chests. The horses are very tall. Those men must be the Cossacks ordered by the tsar to attack the protestors. But they hold their horses absolutely still. Which direction should he go in? The crowd knows with an insect intelligence to split and form orderly lines, crouch under the horses to get across to the other end of the bridge. The horses are like coiled springs, but they don't dare move. Paul opens his mouth and out comes "The Internationale." Irina had not known it either, and yet they both sang it as though it was instinctual—like the crowd's knowledge had leaked into them. That Olga girl, eyes swimming in tears behind her strange glasses, the cousin's face shining like a lamp. To be a part of something bigger than yourself! Paul thinks, as he comes up for air.

"To be part of something bigger than yourself . . ." Zhenia writes quickly, unaware in that moment of the bus, of the road bumping below her, of her grandmother's body lying in a wooden casket.

Zhenia has never before been part of something larger than herself. She has always lacked this. It was something her mother and grandmother found repulsive after growing up in the Soviet Union—crowds, mobs, that sort of group zeal. But maybe something in Zhenia yearns for it . . . to be united with others toward a goal or purpose. To lose yourself in this way. To not always be smothered by your own stupid thoughts.

The whole afternoon we spent marching around. When we did finally get home to Aunt Gittel's house they must have known where we'd been.

Hanna's father, whom I had not imagined capable of saying a harsh word, took off his belt and began to whip us. I didn't think he had it in him. My own father had had a quick temper, he'd take his belt off and you'd run, and he'd chase you, and in the chase he'd get tired out. He'd whip that belt over you a couple of times, but never very hard, or precisely. It was just a motion that needed to be performed so we could all move on to other things. Hanna's father though, he beat us like our lives depended on it. He really must have thought that he could beat some sense into us.

I took it coldly and without tears. When it was Hanna's turn, she turned on the waterworks. I was embarrassed for her. I told her later—did it really hurt that much? I hadn't expected her to be so weak. Did you want him to feel bad for what he did? To feel regret?

"Hurt?" She looked at me like I was deranged. "Regret? No. I wanted him to feel satisfied."

"Was he satisfied?" Zhenia asked, rubbing her hands together and watching the outlines of trees blur past her window in the dark.

"No. Of course not. I'm sure he wished he'd beaten her harder or not at all. Because clearly in that amount it did not end up doing any good."

CHAPTER 27

There were clients who were waiting for Paul in the living room—on Wednesdays he gave a workshop on accessing joy. A handful of people were lying expectantly on yoga blankets. One man was in a Happy Baby Pose, clutching his feet and rocking side to side with his eyes closed. One woman was crouched over her phone, scrolling through pictures of cakes. Sergio peeked out at them through the beaded curtain in the bedroom doorway. He wasn't sure what he was supposed to do.

Paul was sitting on the floor of their bedroom closet, speaking in tongues. It reminded Sergio of his childhood in a Pentecostal church where people also spoke in tongues and an exorcism was performed on him when his parents suspected that he might be gay. When he grew up he moved to New York and met Paul, and he certainly didn't believe in any of that stuff anymore, yet here he was—sitting on the edge of the bed, listening to what definitely sounded like a demonic possession. It gave Sergio the creeps, and made him slightly jealous. His own interests didn't exclude Paul in the same way.

Finally, Paul came up for air. He staggered out of the closet and clattered through the beaded curtain into the Wednesday class, looking obviously unwell and smelling like a distillery. He handed the class a box of chalk and told them to go down to Tompkins Square Park and draw. Then he crawled back into the closet and kept going.

Sergio made Paul a sandwich and left it on a plate on the floor outside the closet door, thinking it might at least sober him up. Until recently, Sergio had not seen Paul drink, only heard stories that he'd thought were exaggerated and overblown, but he could see now that they were not. This bender had been going on for days. After a while, when Paul didn't eat the sandwich, Sergio took it away so the mice wouldn't come into their bedroom. Sergio swept aside Paul's shrine to climb out onto the fire escape, where he sat eating the sandwich and watching Paul's students below, drawing chalk outlines around one another under the streetlamps. The class kept looking at one another, pantomiming joy, and for a moment, everything felt deeply wrong.

Was Paul in love with this demon ghost? Sergio wondered. And then more broadly, by choosing a partner who had seemed completely the opposite of his own upbringing, did Sergio inadvertently choose more of the same? Is this always how it is? It was disheartening. Sergio dropped the rest of the sandwich onto the sidewalk below.

SINCE PAUL HAD begun talking to Irina his mouth had filled with tiny little canker sores that he would find himself constantly poking with the tip of his tongue. Each one a portal to her.

Sitting back on earth, on the floor of his closet, he could feel his parallel self still in the cloud, the distant sensation of night claws skittering over his face. He was waiting for Zhenia to answer the phone, only then could they continue. *He wished he'd beat her harder or not at all. Harder or not at all.*

"Yes," Zhenia said.

He digs his tongue back into the canker sore and he has the sensation that he is meeting himself on the other side. The cloud around him is suddenly so dense, it feels almost solid.

—*Beat us, Daddy!*
—*Meet us by the fountain.*
—*Harder! With a firmer grip! Like so.*
—*So, then he took his hunting rifle and pointed it right at my head!*

—I could not stand him and his wax-tipped mustaches.

—A fool if I've ever met one.

—He smelled of herring. Always of herring.

—Papochka! Is that you?

—Certainly not. Let go of me. My son would know how to use a handker-chief. Shameful.

—And what happened with the rifle? Did he shoot you in the head?

—Don't interrupt. I was just getting to that.

And there is Irina, grabbing Paul by the ears, continuing as if not a moment has passed.

The next day, my aunt and uncle locked us in the house. Stores were closed. Trollies weren't running. There weren't even any newspapers. The young man from Rostov was stuck on a train delayed somewhere between Moscow and Petrograd. There was unrest in the streets. I wanted to be down there, but I was watching from the window of my little room.

Hanna was sitting on my bed, rereading all the letters that Boris had sent her. She kept them hidden in the book she'd gotten me with a secret compartment. They filled the room with a burnt smell, because of the candle she'd used to see the invisible ink. It struck me as dumb, to put lines of love poetry and political platitudes in invisible ink. Something children would do.

"Wouldn't it make sense to burn them?" I asked her. "If they're such a secret? Otherwise why bother with the invisible ink."

Of course she wasn't going to burn them. I could tell the very idea of it brought her pain.

"Don't worry," I said, feeling bad because I didn't want to hurt her. "I'll say they're mine if anyone finds them."

And then I noticed, in the street down below, a man was walking quickly in just his undershirt. I knew it was a police officer from his pants and boots.

He must have taken off the rest of his uniform to appear less conspicuous, which was also why he wasn't running.

I struggled with the window, which was frozen in place, but in my determination I was able to pry it open.

"Hey!" I called down to him. "Hey! Pharaoh!" This is what we called those gutless tsarist toadies.

He didn't look up, just increased his speed. I took a paperweight off my desk and threw it at him. It landed in a snowbank nowhere near him.

The servant who lived in the room next door forced her way into my room and smacked me. Hanna had luckily had time to hide the letters, but the smell from them still hung in the air. The servant had been with the family for many years. Back in Kiev, during the pogroms, she'd leaned her icons outside, against the gate, to keep Hanna's family safe. She was a monarchist imperialist. Go figure. Everywhere there are people like this who believe against their best interests. Usually they think this makes them noble in spirit as opposed to idiotic.

"What was the servant's name? I don't think I caught it," Zhenia interrupted, taking a bite of a rest stop hot dog.

"Her name? What does it matter? Dussya, I think."

But before she could go on, Zhenia interrupted again. "Sorry, but weren't you also believing against your best interests? Your family was clearly well-off, bourgeois. You had servants. You didn't even mention her by name."

"She wasn't my servant. She was my cousin's. I had nobody. But yes. I'm not going to deny that I was idiotic."

Irina smooths out her skirt, her annoyance hangs over her for a moment, a physical space palpable to Paul.

"Anyway," she continues. "It was into all this that the young man from Rostov was set to arrive."

Later that night, at maybe two or three in the morning, when everybody in the house was asleep—Boris and Olga showed up.

Hanna quickly went into the kitchen and began to boil water for tea. She was nervous in a way I hadn't seen before. She stood over the samovar with her back to us, braiding and rebraiding her hair. I could see the corner of her smiling mouth. Boris stood across the room with his coat still on, staring at the back of her head, waiting for her to turn around.

Olga had brought the bread sack with her, but when I reached for it, thinking it was more food stolen from the cafeteria, she pushed me away. She'd been storing some things under my bed, some supplies, and the sack contained a jar of foul-smelling powder that she needed to combine with them. I led her up to my room, where she arranged all of the metal parts and wicks and bolts on the bed and got to work assembling them so they'd fit inside two cookie tins.

I went back downstairs and found Hanna and Boris sitting across from each other at the table, not saying much. The current between them was electric. We tried to keep our voices low so as not to wake anyone. I asked about what was happening in the city. He told us that some of the Cossacks hired to control the crowds had begun shooting at the police. Several brave protestors had been killed, but morale was high. With our help, the regime would topple and the tsar would be overthrown. It was inevitable, just a question of when and at what cost. That Hanna and I were going to play any part in this felt outlandish, but of course thrilling. We didn't have a picture of the whole, nor did he, really. It was safer that way. He talked without taking his eyes off Hanna.

Finally, Olga came down to say she was finished. The bombs were ready; they were to be stored under my bed until further notice, and I was not to bounce too much in my sleep in case this caused one to detonate by accident.

"Wait, did you say bombs?" Zhenia put down her pen.

"Yes. Where did you think I was going with this story?"

"So you threw a bomb? You really killed people?" She said this a little too loudly on the bus. Someone a few rows down turned around and squinted in her direction. "That wasn't an exaggeration?" Zhenia added more quietly, this time covering her mouth with her hand.

"Why would I be telling you exaggerations? What purpose would that serve?"

A bomb for Zhenia existed as a cartoon, a bowling ball with a wick thrown by a coyote. But this was real. What ideas could justify murdering people, probably some innocent ones in the mix? How desperate would things need to feel before such a possibility appeared on one's horizon? To overthrow something—maybe for this you needed a sense of ownership to begin with?

"Were you scared?" Paul asks Irina.

"I was agitated. Whether I was scared or excited, and whether these are one and the same, I don't know. My life had felt flabby and pointless, and then, it didn't."

Paul nods. This is something he understands. Isn't she also the bomb under his bed?

Olga stood at the other end of the table and slurped her tea as Boris told us about what we were to do with the bombs. He spoke in a quiet monotone and didn't take a breath until he got it all out. Then he looked across the table at Hanna and his face developed a rabbity twitch. He probably wanted to tell her not to do it, but also he wanted her to do it because her willingness to do it was what allowed him to justify his attraction to her.

"So," Hanna said as she ran her finger along the rim of her teacup, "are these bad men? By doing this are we preventing them from doing more harm?" She needed to say these justifications. I did not. Who were these generals to me?

"Yes, yes," Boris said in a low voice as he looked at her. "Exactly right."

And then, no longer able to resist, he reached across the table and put his large hand on her cheek and began to pet it, and she leaned over and cupped his bald spot with her palms and then slid her hands over his forehead and through his beard.

I sat and watched as they pawed at each other's faces. Hanna breathed heavily through her mouth. To be honest, I had not seen physical desire like this up close before.

But, before they even had a chance to kiss, we were startled by the sound of loud knocking. Boris froze, then carefully put his hands in his pockets. He'd chosen a life for himself that was always meant to end this way. An infinite loop of knocks on the door. I wrapped my cloak tightly around my shoulders, adjusted my face into a neutral expression. By then the servant, Dussya—is that what we decided to call her?—had come downstairs in her sleeping cap, and my aunt Gittel and her husband appeared too in their pajamas and robes but fully alert, in the way of Jews who also had survived some knocks on the door.

Everybody was surprised to see everybody else, though none of it was sorted out before your beloved Dussya opened the door. And, standing there was not an Okhrana agent or a second pogrom, but the young man from Rostov whose arrival they had all been preparing for. His train had been delayed in Novgorod, but it had finally crept into the city late that night, and he had walked all the way from the station through the roiling streets to the house.

Everybody made their introductions, and in the confusion I had the wherewithal to introduce Boris as a friend of my brother's. This didn't really assuage the air of suspicion about why we were drinking tea with him at three in the morning. Olga had managed to fade into the shadows and nobody bothered with her because they were lighting a fire in the fireplace and taking the young man from Rostov's things. They were bustling around him as he regaled them with horror stories of what he'd seen in the streets, which he assured, for the sake of the ladies in the room, he was heavily redacting. He did seem genuinely shaken by the broken store windows and the drunken fistfights.

"Revolutions are pointless," he said. "You can't change human nature.

Pointless. Pointless violence, and you just end up in the same place. Action, reaction, action, reaction."

My aunt and uncle clucked in agreement as they wrapped him in a warm blanket and sat him at the other end of the table. They shoved Hanna to go pour him some tea.

"What does it look like when everybody wins?" the young man from Rostov continued. "When everybody wins, everybody's dead."

Dussya made a fuss of crossing herself and saying, "God forbid." He was, in retrospect, probably a lot like my second husband. He had that same thick, straight hair that was hard to cut in a straight line, and a set of beliefs that were, at least on the surface, humane.

Boris, realizing that he was not going to be arrested but that this was maybe worse, stood up and put on his hat. "Of course you think it's pointless," he called down the table with a crooked grimace. "You 'practical' individualist, a product of the degeneration of the bourgeoisie, you clearly wouldn't understand what was worth fighting for. *You* certainly are not worth fighting for!"

And really before Aunt Gittel or her husband could react, Boris was out the door, and Olga slipped out behind him.

Then in that strange wake, they apologized profusely for the behavior of this man who, they kept repeating, was an absolute stranger, an absolute stranger that I had for some reason allowed into their house! I'm sure it couldn't have escaped Aunt Gittel's and her husband's notice that Hanna was staring down at the floor with an imbecilic expression on her face and soon excused herself to go to bed.

Of course, the young man from Rostov was smitten with Hanna even though she gave him very little to go on. There was a rather tedious lunch with him the next day, and a Shabbat dinner. My aunt and uncle were proceeding as if everything was as usual. The cook made kugel and we lit the candles and said the prayer and ate it, not acknowledging that half the city was starving and on fire or that their conversations about distant mutual acquaintances were punctuated by sounds of machine-gun fire and breaking glass. I had been unable to sleep the night before. Probably nobody else slept either. Everybody kept yawning with their mouths closed to be polite. Hanna was so wound up, thinking about Boris, and about what we were about to do, that she ate hardly anything and moaned quietly several times. Aunt Gittel and my uncle made every effort to cover over this and bulldoze along. They wanted to marry her off quickly to this man from Rostov and get her out of the city.

I went on Hanna's insistence several times to the fountain in front of their house, but found nothing in the mouth of the cherub and noticed that Dussya was watching me through the window. Whether she had intercepted those letters herself, I don't know.

That following night, I still couldn't sleep. The gunshots seemed to get louder. From my window I could see smoke coming from a warehouse near the river. Locked up in my house with no newspapers and no word from Olga or Boris, it was hard to know what was happening out there exactly. I felt like the experience of being with that crowd earlier had made me attuned to some larger intelligence and even though I was apart now, locked in the house, if I closed my eyes and concentrated, I thought I might be able to get a general sense of how things were going. I tried to focus on this sense as I lay on the floor, afraid that if I lay in my bed I would blow us all up. I wasn't sure if the bombs were making the ticking sound or if it was the mice in the wall.

Sometime before dawn I went downstairs to get water. I wanted to go to Hanna's room, to sit on her bed and hold her hand, but her room was right next to Aunt Gittel's and my aunt was a very light sleeper.

As I started to head back upstairs, I was startled by the figure of the young man from Rostov, blocking the doorway. I tried to pass him, but he wouldn't let me. I moved to the right, he moved to the right. I moved to the left, he moved to the left. He had some questions about Hanna. I tried to answer neutrally. She was cordial to him in front of her parents, but vacant.

He said something along the lines of how he was worried about her. His tone was condescending and unpleasant. He didn't know her at all, I pointed out. He was acting as if she was already his wife. He moved his face a little too close to mine and said that he wondered if I was a bad influence.

Sure, this was exactly what I was! I smiled at him in the dark and bit the rim of my glass. The glass broke off between my teeth and I let it drop to the floor, where it shattered. He was so taken aback that he stepped aside, and I headed up the stairs, leaving him to clean up the mess.

"Didn't that hurt?" Zhenia's hand instinctively went up to her lip. "Why did you do that?"

"I suppose it hurt. It was certainly a dramatic exit. After that I just lay on the floor and practiced spitting. I was trying unsuccessfully to hit the ceiling. Maybe the blood made the spit heavier because I couldn't get it up high enough."

"If it didn't hit the ceiling, didn't it just land on you?"

Zhenia heard Irina sigh in Paul's mouth. "Has anyone ever told you that you notice all the wrong things? Zhenichka, the way you must see your life . . . all negative space. Anyway, sometime after dawn, Olga threw a snowball at my window. This was our signal. I carefully pulled my aunt's old valise out from under my bed and Hanna and I escaped."

"You escaped," Zhenia repeated. The dark sped by the bus window. The negative space Irina was talking about.

"You know . . ." Zhenia began again, and cleared her throat. "All your words and words and words," she said, "but what is under all those words? What you did. How you abandoned my grandmother. Your words are like dust hiding your shame, and that abandonment is like a solid, black rock. I see it under all your words. And that is what you left in her, and then in my mother, and then in me."

"Well . . . the rock, the dust—I don't know. These are all metaphors and I won't debate you on them. But it is, perhaps, your own abandonment of Vera that you have not yet come to terms with."

At this, Zhenia's lips started to twitch and she hung up the phone.

CHAPTER 28

It was strange to be back in Manhattan, riding down Broadway at night, seeing the street from the awkward vantage of a big bus, like Zhenia was a tourist. Everybody below looked like they were onstage, lit by streetlamps. Hot guys on bikes. A couple arguing in front of a restaurant. Two dogs peeing on the same fire hydrant.

The bus drove slowly by a long line of people snaking outside of a theater. Zhenia used to go on open casting calls like this with Naomi, everyone in line holding eight-by-ten photos of their own face.

Zhenia still had a box of her New York headshots in a closet. Throwing them out seemed sad, but maybe holding on to them was sadder? Her face in the pictures was so embarrassing—arms crossed, glossy lips pursed, eyes looking hopefully into the camera.

"Why did you smile the Soviet way? What was the point of getting you braces?" Marina had said.

And Vera had argued, "No, she looks beautiful and mysterious. You understand nothing. You want her to smile like an American simpleton—showing her teeth like she's about to eat you."

Though Vera herself had loved showing her teeth—so much American dental work, bridge after bridge, crown after crown, a whole royal flush installed in her mouth.

Zhenia's phone died somewhere in Yonkers so she was no longer getting the constant stream of updates from her brother, pleas for her to get on a returning bus immediately. She could see that Irina had been right—that abandoning her grandmother was exactly what she did and was continuing to do, not to mention also her mother and brother—yet she couldn't bring herself to go back. No, she could not. And with Paul at least there was some hope. Something to go toward. It wasn't just . . . over.

The bus squealed to a stop inside Port Authority and Zhenia got off. She'd written down Paul's address on her hand and now had to make sure not to smudge it. He lived near her old dorm in a neighborhood that her university had slowly eaten up. Muscle memory pulled her toward the subway transfer through the long tunnels and hallways lit with flickering fluorescent lights. This was probably what lighting was like in Hell or whatever place it was Irina inhabited.

Zhenia spat on the tracks as she waited for the train to get the stale taste of hot dog out of her mouth. Then she tried spitting upward, stepping to the side. There was no way, she decided, wiping her face with her sleeve, for Irina's spit not to have landed back down onto her face.

"Nasty . . ." Zhenia heard someone behind her say.

THE PREGNANCY MADE her suddenly very hungry. Around the corner from Paul's building she stopped to get a slice of pizza. The restaurant was new but it reminded her of Sal's in Brookline, where she and her grandmother used to go when they had something to celebrate—her grandmother passing a literature class she was taking at the community college to improve her English, or Zhenia passing her swim test, or getting asked to a dance, or getting off the waitlist into NYU. The walls here were also covered in autographed headshots of famous actors. Zhenia always thought that if her photo ended up on the wall at Sal's, then she'd know that she'd truly arrived.

Ben had laughed at this when she'd told him. As a barometer of success it was so modest and so grandiose at the same time, he'd said. To be among the yellowed photos of people like Jim Carrey and Lisa Kudrow, by then you wouldn't need to know that you've arrived.

She saw his point, but it wasn't really about that. It was nice to imagine her and her grandma eating pizza under her own headshot, the earnest pinched expression looking less stupid once it had been autographed and lipstick-marked and hung in a cheap frame. It would be tangible evidence of her success hanging over them, justifying why she left and maybe even allowing her finally to come home. Anyway, the pizza place burned down and then became a Panera and her grandmother died, so some dreams you had to let go of. Zhenia shoved the rest of the pizza slice in her face and with a ball of napkins wiped the orange grease off her cheeks and from between her fingers.

THE MAN WHO answered the door at Paul's apartment was attractive and wrapped in a towel, wet hair dripping beads of water onto his shoulders.

"Sorry it's so late," Zhenia said perfunctorily. "I'm here to see Paul. I think you and I have maybe spoken on the phone. I'm Zhenia."

The man shook water out of his ear, then paused longer than comfortable before introducing himself: "Sergio."

The apartment had a strong cloying smell that made Zhenia instinctively cover her nose. When the man noticed this, it only seemed to rile him up further.

"Exactly," the man said, and cracked open a window in the living room. "It comes out of his pores. Rotting lilacs. Both of you are doing something you shouldn't be." He stared at her like he was expecting an apology. Zhenia was taken aback by his vehemence. None of this had been her idea.

When she didn't say anything, he pointed to the closet, from which the smell was emanating. She crouched down like the little mouse that Sergio had anticipated with the sandwich.

"I'm here," she said, and Sergio went into the bathroom, which was in the kitchen, and began loudly slapping on lotion.

PAUL WAS SITTING under a row of hanging shirts. He was older than Zhenia had expected. He had a large belly with white hair on it peeking out of his kimono, and a short gray beard. The photo on his website must have been taken a decade earlier, or else channeling the dead was aging him prematurely. How long had he been sitting like this in the closet?

"You look like her," he said in a daze, touching Zhenia's face like he was expecting it to give in the way that a ghost's would.

"Ow," Zhenia said, blinking but not moving.

"Did you bring your notebook?" he asked. She nodded and took it out of the purse.

"I also brought one of my grandmother's slippers. In case it's helpful to have one of her things to touch." It was a random object. A white terry-cloth slipper. Something her grandmother probably wore only a handful of times, if even. Why hadn't she taken her grandmother's ivory comb or her tube of pink lipstick or one of her books? A single slipper. How stupid.

Paul took the shoe, not really engaging, and set it aside.

It felt like there should be some ceremony, some acknowledgment that Zhenia had come here, some small talk: *How was your trip? Would you like something to drink?*

Instead, his eyes locked onto hers, and she immediately looked away. There was someone else there, she could feel it. Like a person on a landline, listening in on the call.

"You're here," he said in his weird Russian. "I feel you close. Both your heartbeats. Yours and the baby's. Finally, we can start now."

"Wait," Zhenia said. It was one thing over the phone, but seeing this man's sweating face and glistening lips. The damp smell of alcohol and flowery sweat. It was all unpleasant. Disturbing and strange. And now he was bringing her baby into it. No. She did not want to be here. She was scared. What did this Irina want to take from her? Forgiveness, forgiveness, but how would she pry it out?

Zhenia stood up in a half crouch, knocking over coat hangers. Paul took her hand. His fingers were very soft. Their softness was repulsive too, but it was like a current was passing through them into her and this had a strangely stupefying effect.

"Wait," she said again, but without really meaning it, like she used to with Ben when she knew that he could no longer hold back, that it was too late and he was already ejaculating.

Paul's jaws were moving with Irina's words.

As the sun was starting to rise, Olga walked with Hanna and me to the luxury Hotel Astoria. We walked past the Winter Palace and Hanna made us stop.

The tsar's family was away, and their palace was guarded but standing empty. A drunk was tossing rocks against the fence, but there were not many protestors around.

Olga was very specific with the timing and wanted us to keep going, but I told her not to rush Hanna. I was scared that if she did, Hanna might change her mind and go back to the man from Rostov, to the normal life that she still had available to her, and leave me alone in this.

Hanna gripped the cold wrought iron of the gates with her gloved hands as I held her muff. She closed her eyes and leaned her forehead against the fence. She whispered a psalm quietly in Hebrew. A horse peed in the nearby snow and the piss steamed in the twilight. I could feel Olga's impatience. The valise, a bag made of carpet, was heavy on my shoulder but I didn't want to set it down and disturb the bombs inside.

"What are you doing?" Olga asked.

She was praying for the enemy, Hanna told us, for the tsar's family. She was praying that Nicholas II would see the error of his ways, and that he would give the workers the things they needed and then abdicate the throne.

Olga told her it was already too late for that. I agreed. The tsar had had plenty of time to listen to the people, I said. And he had chosen not to. He had chosen to continue everybody's suffering, to encourage it. He hadn't cared in the slightest, and had probably even preferred it that way. To pray for him now seemed to me pointless. She'd be better off reciting Kaddish.

You realize after a certain point that there is a dead space between the wheels being set in motion and the event already happening. And this space is irreversible. And there might be the illusion in this space, because time seems to be going along linearly, that something can be done to alter the course of events, but it cannot.

I suppose this was the space Hanna and I were in as well. We had the bombs and we were going to throw them. We had already decided that we were the kind of people who did this and so we became the kind of people who did this and so we did this.

The air in the closet seemed to grow wetter and wetter. The clothes over them hung limp and heavy.

"Couldn't you have changed your mind?" Zhenia asked.

"No," Irina said through Paul. "Once those decisions are made cosmically, everything will lead back to them."

"That sounds like you feel it was fated?"

"It was decided. 'Fate' makes it seem entirely external."

"It just seems a little circular. You did this and therefore you are the kind of person who would do this. But people change their minds all the time." She did, didn't she, about acting, about wanting a baby? And Ben did too, about her. He had loved her and then he didn't. He had wanted to spend his whole life with her and then he didn't.

Paul wheezed strangely. "And I'm telling you they don't. If they 'change their mind,' they had never made up their mind to begin with."

Zhenia drew a circle in the air with her finger.

"Well, from your vantage with everything in retrospect, I suppose that's true, but I don't know what good this does in the moment."

"I suppose," Irina said, "that my story won't have applicable *tips* you can use in the moment. I'm not giving you advice. You want advice? Stop being a coward. Innocence is an illusion. Blood is always on your hands. Pretending otherwise is stupid and cruel. And don't waste any more of your time thinking about your marriage. There's nothing there to think about.

Just like I wish Hanna hadn't wasted her last prayers on the tsar and his stupid family."

A few blocks from the hotel, Olga took the bombs out of the valise and wound them with a little metal key that she inserted into the side of each cookie tin. She had not been able to test the bombs—it would have attracted too much attention, so she gave each of us one, so that if one didn't go off, then hopefully the other would do its job. After winding the bombs, Olga put her brother's watch on Hanna's wrist. We would have exactly seven minutes from that point on.

A small crowd of protestors had gathered in front of the hotel because this was where all the tsar's high-ranking officers were staying with their families, people like Fräulein Agata's former lover. We weaved through the loose crowd, not making eye contact with anyone. I was dressed in my school uniform and Hanna was dressed in Olga's. There were armed soldiers at the entrance, and we pretended to be the daughters of one of the generals we were about to blow up—girls who were a year below us at my school.

"Let us in," we cried. "Let us in, we're scared."

They scolded us for having left the building. It was very easy to get inside.

We went straight for the ballroom. The plan had been to detonate the bombs there, since then we'd be able to get the most impact, but the ball-room was empty. Someone had started to set the chairs up but then had been called away. A boy was lying across two of the seats, playing with a small gray cat, waving a string on a stick in front of it.

I looked at Hanna's face at seeing the boy, but she simply closed the door to the ballroom and headed for the elevator.

Boris had told us that if the man we were looking for wasn't in the ballroom, he would probably be in his suite. An elevator operator at the hotel had told him which suite and it was probably this same operator who nodded at us and pulled the lever to the top floor. The elevator was gilded and full of mirrors and without turning my head I watched as Hanna stared intensely at the operator and he ignored her. It was so cold outside, and so warm inside, and I also must have been nervous, because my hand in the muff gripping the edge of the cookie tin was very sweaty and I was worried that the bomb would slip out. When we reached the top floor, the elevator operator pulled the door open for us without a word and we got out.

I remember the flowers on the carpet. The flowers on the wallpaper. We were in a gilded Victorian field of poppies. Hanna walked slower and slower, eyeing everything and admiring it. The electric lights in the crystal chandeliers. Through the sparkling frost on the hallway windows we could see a light snow falling on the crowd outside, which had somehow grown considerably since we got there. They were watching some parade go by on Bolshaya Morskaya.

"And you were on your way to kill your teacher's lover?"

"No, not him. Someone more important and higher-ranking. Though if he had been in the room, so much the better."

"And you don't think that your cousin was slowing down because she was reconsidering it? You don't think she was changing her mind?" Zhenia asked.

"I told you. This was impossible."

—*Are you following her logic?*
—*Of course not. It's gibberish. She'll turn into a pretzel to justify anything.*
—*Like you and that submarine.*
—*Oh, let it go. What's that got to do with anything?*

To Paul, though, the idea that things are set in motion and then they have their own gravitational pull makes total sense. He requires no convincing.

His body now feels like it exists only in his wide-open mouth. It's obvious, but until this moment he had convinced himself that he was neutrally performing a service. But of course, no!

If it were up to Sergio, Paul would be using this process to integrate—to look for all the younger versions of himself and then gather them up under his skirt like the Sugarplum Fairy. But Paul wants nothing to do with the previous versions of himself. Those weaklings, those selfish little fuckers with catfish lips and whiskers. He'd barely killed them off. Let them wander in the mist alone. He can't love them. Better for him to integrate with someone like Irina, someone with no desire to please. A woman who killed. Who doesn't want to feel that? To be the eagle's claws for once and not always in the soft parts of the mouse? His mouth is so wide for her it fits her whole head.

Zhenia can hear Paul's voice changing now, coming from somewhere deeper down his throat, in his chest. She feels herself sinking deeper too. Lurching along into her great-grandmother's story.

Paul sees firsthand the painted wooden door. Brass numbers 3-2-6, the top of the "3" flat in that Art Deco way. Hanna—why, she's just a child!—walks slower and slower. Dreamy. She runs her hand along the hallway wall, then turns and strokes Irina's arm, and it sends a warmth through Paul. It feels exquisite. This must have been the only person who touched Irina with any sort of love. Hanna's cheeks are flushed red like the poppies. Time has not slowed down yet. Time is clicking along. The bomb is warm in Irina's hand from being held in the muff, feeling like another organ or appendage, an extension of herself already full of blood.

Irina looks at the watch on Hanna's wrist, breathes, breathes, and then nods, lets go of her cousin's wrist. Hanna puts her hand on the doorknob. A man's muffled voice behind the door is speaking sternly. Into a telephone? Or to another person? If someone else were in the room with him, would this change any of Irina and Hanna's calculations? No, it doesn't seem to.

Hanna looks at Irina before she knocks, then both, in the same unnatural whine:

"Papa, Papochka, let us in!"

They beat on the door and cry.

"Save us!"

The man's voice behind the door goes silent.

Everything slows down. What if the man doesn't open the door and the bombs explode in their hands?

Irina pants. Then the door opens.

There's the man they're meant to kill: in military uniform, the ends of his mustache freshly waxed, but the top of his collar not fully buttoned. His face tilts unevenly from tenderness at the idea of his daughters, to surprise at seeing instead Hanna and Irina at his door.

Behind him some other general, sitting in a chair by the velvet curtains as though posing for a portrait, makes a motion to get up.

Hanna tosses the cookie tin over this general's shoulder, then Irina tosses her tin over his head toward the other general. It happened very fast. But how is it that time slows down enough in those moments that Paul can notice the fire in the fireplace, the long, beautiful window filling the room with gray morning light?

But maybe time doesn't slow as much as Irina feels, because Hanna yanks her away from the door. They run down the hall and fling open the door to the servants' staircase. They rush down the dank stairwell. Momentarily, they slow on the landing to exchange a look. Had it gone wrong? And just as this thought forms, the whole building shakes, plaster rains down, dust. The feeling of a shove from behind, flying, flying, both girls in flight.

"So you did. You killed those men. Strangers you never met before. And you felt no remorse at all? You still don't?" Zhenia sounded disgusted.

"You overfed housecat. You want some banal performance of remorse? Who needs my remorse? Nobody. Who were these men to me? They were all interchangeable. Pillars in a system that needed to be toppled. How do you not understand that? That bomb set things in motion, it altered the course of history."

Paul feels Irina's annoyance and it combines with his own. What Zhenia was saying is beside the point. And it has yanked him out of the dark stairwell. His ears are still ringing and his insides quivering, but it is his own ass he feels on the wood floor. The pins and needles in his own foot. He is not in Irina anymore, she is again just speaking through him.

We were expelled from the servants' entrance into the smoky chaos, but despite the rush, the shoving of the crowd, everything was strangely silent. Just a distant ringing in my ears. I didn't understand at first that the explosion had left me temporarily deaf. I felt instead the way I did at home in Volohonsk, walking alone through the woods after the first snow.

The explosion caused the demonstrators to think that the officers inside were attacking them. And soon, the officers were, in fact, attacking them, shooting down into the crowd from the balconies and the roof. The demonstrators, many of them armed, shot back. Pieces of molding, smoke, ashes, and plaster were raining down on us and mixing with the dirty snow.

Hanna and I were holding hands, fighting through the crowd. In the confusion, I thought she was pulling me back in to watch the spectacle that we'd created, and since I could hear nothing, I was yanking her along.

In history books, this incident at the hotel is often the moment that's mentioned as the turning point in the February Revolution. They never mention the bomb or the girls who threw it. There was some story of a sniper on the roof, but the shooting came afterward.

By the time I finally got us to the edge of the crowd, Hanna was leaning against my shoulder and I was dragging her. Bullets were whizzing past us—I couldn't hear them, but I saw one hit the cobblestones by our feet. Then someone fell on us and knocked us over.

I crawled and pulled Hanna toward the gate of the nearest apartment building. Olga was nowhere to be found. Through the metal doors I could see a lady with a kerchief tied under her chin, crouching in terror.

She was wringing her hands and saying something to me but I couldn't hear her. She finally unlocked the gate and I was able to crawl in and lay Hanna down on her back.

Hanna stared up at the sky, opening and closing her eyes like a doll. I don't know why I didn't see it immediately, the wet red poppy blossoming on her breast. She must have been shot near the heart but it wasn't bleeding very much. She looked so strange in Olga's school uniform. A costume. Not real. Her skin was pale. I made a snowball from the ashy snow and pressed it to her wound, but of course, this did nothing. I should warm her up, not freeze her, I thought. So I wrapped my arms and legs around her, cradling her, and tried to breathe on her face to give her warmth. Her lips were moving. I don't know whether she was talking or just groaning out in pain. If she had any last words, I couldn't hear them.

We're howling now. This all seems terribly sad. Who hasn't held a doll in their lap, imagining it was a real girl, and who hasn't held a real girl, imagining she was a doll? Who among us hasn't known what it's like to be abandoned by the only person who loved us? To have nobody. For eternity to be in a crowd but to always be lonely.

CHAPTER 29

When Paul had come home from the Institute in 1986, all his friends in New York would tell him stories like this: "Zed held Desmond's hand and watched the light leave his eyes . . ." "Sasha held Larry as Larry took his last breath . . ." Death, dying, death—everywhere around him.

Paul went out to New Jersey to visit Charlie, his first boyfriend, a red-headed peach who was now dying of AIDS in the living room of his child-hood home. Charlie was emaciated—teeth, bones, sunken eyes—floating in and out of consciousness.

"He's so happy you're here," Charlie's mother said, and Paul asked dumbly, "Really? How can you tell?"

Paul tried not to recoil from this boy he used to love, whose red pubic hairs he'd once kept between the pages of a poetry book, but looking at Charlie was looking death in the face. And even though Paul understood the permeability between the two worlds, death still scared him.

He came back two more times. On the last time, Charlie's mother went out to the store to run errands, and Paul sat with Charlie's hand in his. It took him a while to even understand that Charlie was trying to speak, because Charlie's throat was so dry and he was so weak, there was no voice in the sound. He didn't know what Charlie was trying to say. He never figured it out.

He'd told Sergio the story when they were first dating, and Sergio had said: People always expect wisdom in these situations, but what is there to say? What could he possibly say that would change anything?

Sergio was not sentimental. Or maybe he was just saying that because he did not like it when Paul dwelled on the past or in any spaces that Sergio could not access.

Paul crawled out of the closet. Both his feet had fallen asleep and he pulled himself up using the corner of the bed where Sergio was sleeping. Sergio shifted but did not wake up.

Zhenia followed Paul out into the kitchen.

"Are you hungry?" Paul asked, remembering his manners. "Help yourself to whatever you find in the fridge."

She took out some of Sergio's goat-milk yogurt from the farmer's market and spooned it into a bowl. She offered some to Paul, but he waved it away, not even able to contemplate it. He took out a bottle of vodka he kept hidden under the sink.

"It's good, but it's kind of, I don't know. An unusual taste. Gamey," the girl was rambling.

Paul nodded, still blinking away thoughts of Charlie, dying, and Charlie, young and alive, and himself, young and alive.

"Please," Zhenia said suddenly. "Please, just tell me where my grandmother is. It's why I came."

PAUL LOOKED ACROSS the table at her for a moment, then closed his eyes and nodded. He made a humming sound through his nose and slowly waved his arms around in the air as though pushing aside invisible curtains. Zhenia set down her spoon and watched. To her, this all felt like a performance, not like he was really trying to make contact, just something to pacify her.

After a little bit, he opened his eyes and poured some more vodka into his glass. A splash of soda.

"So, did you see her?" Zhenia asked. "Should I go get the slipper?"

"If she wants to see you," Paul said, stirring his drink with his finger. "If she *can* see you, she will. It might not be for a long time. Maybe not until you're dead. Or maybe not ever." A spirit had to be looking for this opportunity. Paul couldn't summon a person who wasn't looking to be summoned. This wasn't a dog that waited faithfully for its owner. A medium didn't have this sort of power.

Zhenia looked down into her bowl and scraped the yogurt remnants with her spoon. Maybe she just needed to ask him again in a little while. The timing, maybe it hadn't been quite right. She could bide her time if that's what was needed.

"It's dumb to want things," he continued. "Getting them is impossible. It's never satisfying in the way that you want it to be. It never is. Desire is its own snake. Insatiable by definition . . ."

Zhenia wrinkled her nose. This sort of drunk wisdom irritated her.

". . . It can be extinguished, but not satisfied, and when it's gone it feels like a death." Paul belched quietly into his hand. "I suppose that's what death is."

Zhenia ran her finger over her bottom teeth and looked out the window. It wasn't dawn yet, but the night was loosening.

"Why do you talk to the dead? Why do you do all this?" she asked Paul.

Paul put his hand in the fruit bowl, palpated a hard peach, and put it back.

"Probably for the same reason you used to act. To become somebody else."

Zhenia nodded. She didn't know that this was really the reason she used to act. She was never good enough at it to feel like anybody but herself. What she had probably wanted, more accurately, was to be admired.

Paul looked like he was drifting off to sleep suddenly, and then like he was about to sneeze.

"I need a rest," Paul says to Irina.

"No," Irina says. "No. Let's keep going. While we're all here, before Zhenichka wanders off somewhere. Look at her, she'll be gone any moment. Let me get to the end."

"Let's begin," Paul croaked in Russian to Zhenia. She helped him back into the nest they'd made in the closet.

She shook her pen to get the ink flowing, watching his face contort and the words begin again. *I don't know how Osip found us.*

Then Zhenia put down her pen. "You're telling me about your pain, your pain, your pain. What about *my* pain?"

"You want us to sit with your pain?" Paul asked, somehow cutting off Irina's flow.

He blinked several times, and they sat in the closet in silence. Irina's presence inside Paul was palpable. It was like looking at a sack of cats. And what was it stirring inside Zhenia?

"No," Zhenia muttered. She did not want to "sit with her pain." What an insane idea. "Go on."

I don't know how Osip found us. It must have been through Olga. Hours passed. The fighting had stopped. The hotel smoldered. Dead officers were left hanging over the edges of balconies. Scattered hats. Dark pools of blood on the sidewalk like oil. A man who lived in the building had taken Hanna's pulse, then helped me carry her up the front steps into the building's vestibule. Children from the first-floor apartment kept opening their door to peek out at us, then shutting it as soon as I looked back at them. By then the silence in my ears had been replaced by a loud ringing.

Hanna's body was still warm even as it was stiffening. I thought that maybe, maybe she was still alive. There was not very much blood. I was talking to her. I don't know at what volume or what I was even saying. How could a person who was the most alive be lying like this on the floor, not alive at all?

I was so grateful when Osip arrived, because I didn't know what to do. He kneeled beside me and moved my hands off her face. It was my first time seeing him up close since he kissed me. He brought a doctor in white, and a rabbi in black. The doctor did not even open his leather bag. He helped the rabbi move Hanna onto a stretcher. The servant who had let us in stood down the hall and watched, not getting close, watching the rabbi in his wide-brimmed black hat as though he'd been the one who killed her.

Osip walked me back to my aunt's house but he didn't come inside. He left me on the doorstep. My aunt and uncle knew already when I came in. My aunt fell on me and began to pummel my chest weakly with her fists. My uncle refused to look at me.

I wanted Hanna to be buried with the other revolutionaries. I was sure she would have wanted this, but of course my aunt and uncle would not hear of it. Hanna was buried the next day in a Jewish cemetery. There are rules about burying a body. It had to happen quickly.

Zhenia stopped and drew a spiral in the margin of her notebook.

"So, do you think burials are important?" she asked.

"How can I answer that? They're important if they're important to you."

"Maybe I should have stayed for Babushka's funeral. Do you think it matters?"

"Of course it matters! But this is the trouble with you." Paul seemed to lift off the ground with Irina's irritation. "Even if you did go to the funeral, you wouldn't really be there. You find a way to go from place to place and never leave the room."

Paul opened his eyes and looked at Zhenia, offered her his hand in kindness. She took it and for a moment her eyes filled with tears. Of course it hurt, because Irina was not wrong. Zhenia lived her whole life like this. She'd thought she was being a good girl, doing what her grandmother wanted by avoiding pain, her grandmother's and her own. Swaddled tightly and moved away from anything that could hurt her but also from anything that could matter. How stupid all of it was now. Her grandmother was dead and she would never get to see her again, the baby would never get to meet her.

And here Irina was, laying out her story on a table for Zhenia, expecting her to feast. Have some of my shame, some of my selfishness, my youthful stupidity. See the world from my point of view so you can forgive the awful things I've done! Listen, translate, transcribe, try to understand—all *this* Zhenia could do. She wanted to know, after all, how it was she herself had ended up here, in this predicament. But forgiveness? Surely Paul and Irina must see that this was not something Zhenia was capable of! Even if she wanted to be, which she did not. Forgiving Irina would be the ultimate betrayal of her grandmother.

Paul looked exhausted, but his mouth stretched open unnaturally and he continued.

My aunt Gittel had always been so haughty, but now she was like a broken umbrella. Her daughter was everything to her; it mattered a lot less that over the next few years her house was taken, her husband's business looted and then "requisitioned" by the same people their daughter had helped. Aunt Gittel's shrewdness did not translate to the new world order, or perhaps she'd given up.

The man from Rostov didn't stay for the funeral—he got on the first train out of Petrograd, putting the whole shameful episode behind him. He didn't want to be associated with the family in any way. The funeral was quick and sparsely attended. My uncle was only able to get a minyan of ten Jewish men by making the people who worked for him come and carry the coffin.

I stayed in their house during the shiva. Dussya covered all the mirrors with blankets. My aunt, who usually changed her dresses several times a day, wore the same black dress, torn at the sleeve and the hem. I wore the same dress I had worn to my father's funeral, which was now much too small for me. I don't know why my aunt and uncle permitted me to stay in the house, but it didn't seem like I could leave. I sat beside them on low chairs as people trickled through to pay their respects. Not many people came. Most of their friends were scared to leave their houses because there was a lot of unrest, and not many people in their circle wanted to be associated with a revolutionary.

I was surprised when Boris showed up. He seemed unwell, with dark purple circles under his eyes, like he hadn't slept in days. I suppose none of us really had. He twitched as he pulled at his patchy beard and gave his condolences. My aunt and uncle recognized him from the middle-of-the-night tea party and suspected that he was responsible in some way for what had happened.

Boris had brought a newspaper, folded open to the page about the mass burial that was to be scheduled for those who died fighting in the February Revolution. It had a detailed diagram as to how people should march. He passed it to me, and I looked at the picture but couldn't quite understand it, and then passed it to my uncle, who didn't take it and let the paper fall to the ground.

Boris ran his hands over his recently shaved head forward and back. He was getting agitated. "It's not right. This is where she belongs. We need to dig her up."

My uncle snapped then. He got up from his low chair and chased Boris out of the house, kicked him down the front stairs. I saw Boris roll down a few steps, then get up and bow at me and limp quickly away.

I'd wanted to ask him about Osip, about the plot, about how things were brewing outside. Did my cousin giving up her life change anything? Were we winning or had it all just been for nothing? And what would winning look like exactly? Beyond the end to the tsar? Had my cowardly teacher and that suitor from Rostov been right? Would one dead general quickly get replaced with more of the same? There were no newspapers in the house, and besides, the kind of papers that my uncle read would have contained little information of value to me.

Olga came on the third day hidden inside a group of girls from the school, most of whom knew Hanna only tangentially from the days she would join us in Fräulein Agata's class. The girls had transparently come to gawk at the strange Jewish rituals and the dead Red hero. Olga used these girls as a shield. She even had the nerve to inquire about her watch, which I did not return to her, but instead smashed later with a hammer. I understood then that this was how she operated. She always emerged from things unscathed and I suppose I wanted to see her a little scathed. The girls she was with swallowed their whispers and giggles until they were out the front door, and then I could hear them belch them all out.

My aunt took to sleeping in Hanna's bed, when she slept at all. All night she'd walk through the house, wailing. She'd come into my room and put her hands around my throat.

"You should have stones and not children," she would hiss between her teeth in Yiddish. "You should crap blood and pus." "You should be transformed into a chandelier, to hang by day and to burn by night." "All your teeth shall fall out but one to make you suffer." "May the leeches drink you dry." "May all ten plagues be visited upon you, one by one." "It should have been you, not her. You."

I would lie there and gasp for breath and say that I too wished it had been me. Life was wasted on me. I did not know what to do with it. There was a seething outside, a dark energy that started with the people in the street but then took on a form of its own. Days or maybe weeks went by the same way. It seemed like penance to stay there and take the abuse. Why my aunt didn't kick me out of the house, I don't know.

Olga never came back and neither did anyone else. My only glimpses of the outside world came through my window. A group of factory workers wheeling a foreman in a wheelbarrow toward a canal. A parade of soldiers' wives stealing coats and hats off passersby.

One day, I saw a huge procession below. Coffins painted red. This was the burial Boris had been talking about. I put my coat on and left, taking nothing with me. I never returned or spoke to my aunt and uncle again.

Paul shifts and tries to get a breath in the stuffy closet. It feels like there is a heavy stone in his diaphragm. The radiator outside the closet door is clanging and hissing steam.

His East Village apartment had once been a squat. The neighbors had all remodeled and driven up the price, but Paul had kept his pretty much as it was—bathtub in the kitchen; splintery wood floor painted gray; clanging radiator. He'd acquired the apartment by staying in it and refusing to leave. Was this, he vaguely wondered, what was happening to him now with Irina? Had he been claimed? Was this inevitable?

This moment of clarity makes his throat seize up, and Irina wobbles in front of him for a moment, ceasing to exist. Then she's back. They are, he notices with a strange start, no longer where they were. Where did the cloud go? Where is the horizon line? His own light has become very dim. He has the odd sensation of falling but standing very still at the same time. He's inside her mouth now, not the other way around.

The crowd was huge but orderly and precise. Thousands marching in military columns, carrying coffins painted red and glowing against the gray day. Red like blood on snow, red like the eternal flame.

The smell of wet wool. Faces like those I've seen in paintings of religious pilgrimages, distorted with ecstasy.

I was in a strange state, marching alongside a column of blind people, their eyes rolling in their sockets, shuffling with the crowd, carrying a red casket on their shoulders. On the other side of me was a column of Armenian women dressed in embroidered headdresses, holding banners that said on red velvet, "Not Victims, but Heroes" and "Not Grief, but Envy."

Did you feel envious?

I wonder. Could I have been anticipating then how time would curdle all my principles? How I would turn on everyone in order to survive? Envious only in the sense that I was probably thinking: Oh, to be carried on people's shoulders like a bride! Oh, to be fussed over!

To be carried like a bride!

A man with a long gray beard and a fiddle squeezed in front of me and played as we marched.

The scraping bow, hair standing up on the nape of the neck.

There were a hundred, maybe two hundred coffins. The bodies could still be counted then. I regretted deeply that we hadn't done as Boris said and dug Hanna up so I could march with her.

Digging up the dead—yes, yes, it is tempting, but it has its risks.

The group I joined behind melted into a larger crowd on Sadovaya Street. We were flowing like a river toward the entrance of Mars Field, a park in the center of town where Fräulein Agata had often taken us on picnics.

Picnics! How quaint.

Now there were huge pits dug into the ground with narrow walkways between them. There were no priests or rabbis. There were no speeches. The coffins were lowered, a rifle shot, and the crowd kept moving to make space for the next group.

Eventually, it began to grow dark and the crowd dispersed. I had nowhere to go. I was getting dizzy with hunger. I couldn't go back to my aunt's house. I couldn't go back to the school. I had a vague sense of the apartment where Osip lived and I began to walk there.

People were on his stoop, celebrating. Their red velvet signs leaned up against the steps.

They're popping open bottles of champagne. Look at it foaming over that man's wrists.

They had all been at the funeral. I didn't recognize anyone until I saw the hunchbacked woman weaving through, so I grabbed her sleeve. She looked at me as though she'd been waiting for me and led me inside, up the stairs to the apartment.

I had to stop and hold on to the banister because I was overtaken with a memory.

A premonition.

An image of the luncheon hostess's head rolling down the street like a cabbage.

You're giddy.

Yes. Now it felt like an actual possibility. We would wash the streets with blood if that's what it took to make them clean. Drag them all out by the hair, drag them all out into the street. All those girls from my school and their families.

No more doubt?

I wanted blood.

Mmm.

What did I have to lose? I ask you, what did I have?

Surely you had something.

Nothing but my own blood! Which, I thought then, I would have happily shed.

Yourself.

Blood, blood, blood, blood.

CHAPTER 30

"*Krov, krov, krov,*" Paul sputtered in Russian, and keeled over.

Zhenia gasped, then shrieked.

Sergio flung open the closet door. "Shit!" he screamed. "Now you've really done it."

He pulled Paul out onto their bedroom floor. Paul's body was limp, then spasming. The kimono was bunched up, exposing his pale belly and loins.

Zhenia and Sergio hoisted him up over their shoulders and dragged him into the bathtub in the kitchen, which Sergio filled with warm water.

"What is happening?" Zhenia asked. This was freaking her out.

"This is sometimes how your sessions with him end."

She was holding Paul's head up above the water as Sergio poured in Epsom salts.

The Keith Haring wall clock over Sergio's shoulder said that it was already seven o'clock. Her grandmother's funeral was in a few hours. As usual, she felt muddled. Maybe she shouldn't have come here? What had been the point? Irina had been right. What doesn't she run away from? She ran and she ran and she never ended up anywhere.

Paul opened one eye and then closed it.

"I don't know if you can hear me," she said. "But, maybe now, whatever in-between space you're in, maybe there you can see my grandmother?"

Sergio pushed her out of the way. "Can't you see you've done enough? Look at him."

It was true, Paul did not look well.

"They are about to bury her," she said into the room. "And what if this is my last chance before they do . . ."

She trailed off.

Sergio slapped Paul gently, then less so.

"Call an ambulance," he told her, pointing to the ancient-looking phone on the wall, avocado green with a curly cord.

"I thought I should try," she said as she dialed.

Soon the paramedics were in the apartment, moving Paul onto a stretcher, doing chest compressions and breathing into his mouth.

Sergio was explaining that he had been communing with the dead when this happened.

A paramedic took an orange from the fruit bowl on the counter. "Can I have this?" he said.

That seemed highly fucked-up and unprofessional to Zhenia.

The other paramedic was holding Paul's eyes open and shining a flashlight into them.

"I think he's had a stroke," he said.

Later, Zhenia learned from Sergio that it had actually been a series of small strokes. He was in the ICU at Mount Sinai.

Sergio didn't know why he'd called the girl, since he felt her responsible in some way for all of this, but also she had been there, and he hadn't told anybody else yet. He didn't want to tell anyone. Paul was always so private about medical stuff.

"The doctor said that after a stroke sometimes people wake up speaking French, or having a new accent, new interests. I don't know if he will still feel the same way about me as he did before. It always felt when he was talking about your great-grandmother, or whoever that was, that he was a little bit in love with her. He'd never been interested in women. I mean, not sexually, but she wasn't really a woman. I don't know what she was. I guess the doctors would say she was a blood clot in his brain, but science is always so narrow."

Later, walking through Central Park in the warm afternoon sun, Zhenia called Ben. She had stopped in front of the *Alice in Wonderland* statue and tried to take a sip of her hot chocolate, but it was still too hot. Kids in uniforms with sequined backpacks were streaming in on scooters. Nannies were sitting on benches offering Tupperwarefuls of goldfish and apple slices to their charges.

"Hello?" he answered.

"I'm in New York," she said.

"I know," he said. "I got a notification from the credit card company."

The radio silence between the two of them had been so weird. It was easier for her to pretend all of it had been some kind of bad dream and continue as though the gap in communication hadn't existed between them since he left for Atlanta. To pretend he hadn't left her for someone else.

"I'm strolling through Central Park. I'm in front of that *Alice in Wonderland* statue. I was going to say: 'Remember when we used to go here?' But we never used to go here. It seems like an iconic place we would have gone, having lived here. It's good for people-watching," Zhenia continued breathlessly. "Babushka died. I flew out here for her funeral but then decided not to go and instead went and visited someone who keeled over in front of me and didn't die, but almost did."

Maybe if she talked quickly and kept her tone of voice casual, a little sad, not angry at all, then she could trick him into thinking that they were still together.

Ben cleared his throat. "I'm sorry to hear that, and about your grandma," he said. "I know you two were very close."

Was he a robot? The distance he was putting between them, like he was shoving her away with his voice. It felt like an actual shove, enough for Zhenia to sit down forcefully on the bronze mushroom next to Alice.

"I'm sorry if I was a bad wife." She started to cry self-pityingly. The children around her looked but didn't scatter. Ben said nothing so she got angry and said something mean in order to hurt him. "I never loved you," she said.

"I know," he said. "That was a big part of why I left you." He sounded like a real person again briefly. She could picture him rubbing his eyes with the heel of his hand, smearing his movie makeup.

It felt like she had dug a hole, covered it with a tarp, and fallen into it herself. Maybe thinking of conversations as being riddled with traps was juvenile. The truth was maybe pretty simple.

"I don't want to break up. How am I going to raise this baby alone?" she cried. "I hate you." She hung up the phone.

She wiped her runny nose on her coat sleeve. A nanny pulled a child off a nearby mushroom.

Through blurry vision she watched an old lady who looked nothing like her grandmother throw bread at the pigeons. Zhenia's grandmother had always made a point of feeding only the sparrows and the squirrels, and throwing rocks at the pigeons, because they didn't "need any more bread." A Soviet sense of justice.

Only then did it hit her that she wouldn't get to hear the end of Irina's story, and that this connection to her grandmother, however tenuous, had also been severed. Irina would remain in her Hell-type place, and that was that.

Ben could have canceled the credit card, but he didn't. Zhenia was able to use it to get back to L.A. How exactly she got back, though, she had only a vague sense.

PART 3

CHAPTER 31

It wasn't actually cold in Los Angeles that winter, but it was cold in Zhenia's apartment. There was a wall-mounted gas heater, but you had to press hard and turn it at the same time for it to ignite. This was an obstacle that often felt insurmountable, so Zhenia spent most of her time when she wasn't at work under blankets in bed.

"I'm gestating," she'd say to her mother or brother or anyone who called to see how she was doing. The side of the bed where Ben used to sleep was covered in empty takeout containers because Zhenia ate all her meals in bed while watching season after season of a show about a teenage girl detective, a role that she knew Naomi had auditioned for and not gotten.

The growing mess in the apartment was disgusting, but also sort of satisfying because it was an accurate external representation of how she was feeling. What was the term she had learned in her one lit class at NYU? Pathetic fallacy. She and Naomi had giggled so hard over that—pathetic! Phallus! Eeeee! Pathetic. Yes. She felt pathetic, sucking on her orange Cheeto fingers and wiping what was left on the sheets.

One day she came home from work and the apartment felt amiss. The bookshelf was missing half its teeth. Her first thought was supernatural. Irina had blown through and would be sitting in the bathtub, waiting for her atop a pile of her things. Then she thought, no, be reasonable. It must have been a burglar. Someone had climbed in through the balcony and used the sliding door, which did not lock. She'd been burglarized.

Though it was odd that whoever stole from her had also cleaned off the bed and taken out the garbage. It was only as she was calling Ben to tell him about the burglary that she put together what had happened, and hung up feeling deeply humiliated.

Had he gotten back in town and come by while she was at work so as to avoid seeing her? And since she worked irregular hours, did he stake out the apartment and wait for her to leave before going in? He hadn't left a note or anything.

It felt so harsh that Zhenia assumed he was doing it to prove to the new woman he was with that he could excise Zhenia from his life completely. Their relationship—a dead songbird he was dropping at this new woman's feet.

"Songbird" was maybe overstating, but regardless, whatever it had been, he wasn't done with Zhenia, because she was carrying his baby. A fact that had been verified for him with a genetic test, though this had not seemed to sway him at all.

This behavior, his anger, Zhenia understood it, and was willing to take it as penance, assuming of course that once the baby was born, he would come back. He could be sorry and stroke her hair like she was a dog, scratch her back, make her a sandwich. The small things of marriage that added up to comfort.

Saw you got your stuff. Are you going to be there for the birth at least? she texted. Three dots appeared and disappeared, appeared and disappeared. *Of the baby*, she added. Nothing. *I'm thinking of doing it at home.* And then, *in the tub.* She didn't really think she wanted to do this—her baby floating in her mildewed tub was an image she had to blink away. But maybe the idea of a home birth could get a rise out of him and elicit a response, but nothing.

Zhenia was finding it hard to imagine taking care of a baby alone when she barely seemed able to take care of herself. She pictured Ben timing her contractions, coaching her to breathe deeply through her nose. She was clinging still to this being a possibility. Maybe his bad behavior right now could somehow even the playing field and bring them closer. She would take him back. Of course she would. She might hesitate, just as a formality, make him work for it a little bit, but she had no doubt in her mind that she'd take him back. She could forgive him, the way he'd forgiven her many times before whenever he'd stumbled on her indiscretions.

When it became clear Ben wasn't going to respond, she thought about calling Paul. She wanted someone to tell her a story. She wanted to know how Irina's ended. Or, she knew how it ended, she supposed, but not how it got there. Every time she'd tried to call Paul, though, Sergio answered and told her Paul was in no form to talk to her. She didn't quite know why Sergio was blaming Paul's stroke on her, but she was open to being cosmically responsible.

The only person she really enjoyed communicating with was Anton, the Tin Man. He emailed her GIFs or little animal videos. Sometimes she would send him pictures of her cleavage, which was ampler from the pregnancy. These photos were grainy, taken with her flip phone and then uploaded to her computer. They were never solicited, but she assumed he appreciated them. He would usually keep things light and reply with a GIF of a raccoon saying "hubba hubba," or something else jokey, so that she wouldn't feel stupid, but nothing to encourage her to keep going either. Once, at her insistence, he sent her a picture of his penis. But she'd had to ask multiple times, and it looked like it had been taken under a blanket—an outline of something in the dark.

When Zhenia felt particularly lonely, she'd drink a Sprite and then lie on her side, and wait for the sugar to hype up the baby. She'd feel him begin to kick and swim and butt against her organs. Then she would sing him songs in Russian. The lullaby her grandmother had sung to her about a baby being dragged away into the woods by a wolf, though she could remember only the first two stanzas.

> Баю-баюшки-баю,
> Не ложися на краю!
> Придет серенький волчок,
> И ухватит за бочок.
>
> Он ухватит за бочок,
> И потащит во лесок.
> И потащит во лесок
> Под ракитовый кусток.

Ben had taken the car soon after taking his other belongings. And so, Zhenia had to take the bus and train to work, and was often late or missed her appointments across town entirely. Her mother didn't understand why she didn't find a used car, but this, like everything else, felt unmanageable. There'd be these moments in her day when she would emerge from her fog, like she'd been let out of the room for a second, and she'd look around her and think, Oh! I'm here! But then the fog would roll back in soon after that.

Dee told her that the complaints against her at work were mounting, and so Zhenia was trying to drag herself out of bed earlier. She was almost not late at all on the day she took a heavily pregnant girl to get the test for gestational diabetes.

The pregnant girl had come to the United States to work at a summer camp the year before and ended up meeting someone and staying. The girl relaxed when she saw that Zhenia was also pregnant, and seemed cheered at the thought that she had something to offer back as well—"You'll see me do it, and you'll know what to expect for yourself," she told Zhenia, like they were about to practice kissing the same boy.

Zhenia watched the girl knock back the awful-smelling sucrose like it was a shot and make a face, then offer up her arm to the nurse to have her blood drawn.

"I never had to do this with my other children," the girl said as the nurse looked for her vein.

Zhenia was surprised the girl had other children, since she looked pretty young.

"They're in Russia with my mother. I'll bring them over when I learn a trade."

The girl noticed the bracelet that Zhenia was wearing and pointed at it.

"Why are you wearing an opal?" she said.

"My grandmother gave it to me," Zhenia said, and looked at it sparkling under the hospital's fluorescent light. This wasn't entirely true. It was something she had taken without permission when she'd left for college. Not stolen, really. Just taken.

"Have you lost your mind? That is a very bad omen. Let me guess, the person who you inherited it from is already dead."

"Shut up," Zhenia said, covering her wrist protectively. "Shut up" sounded even harsher in Russian than in English.

Seeing how upset Zhenia was, the girl apologized, but Zhenia didn't say anything until smugly delivering the doctor's final verdict of elevated blood sugar.

The girl looked at Zhenia like it was Zhenia betraying her, rather than her own body. But then the girl quickly pulled up her Soviet-raised recourses and said that it was just as well. She was going to have a large American boy, that's all this blood-sugar stuff meant. He'll be big and strong, and hopefully cheerful. And here she would at least have an epidural, so what did it matter, his size?

Afterward, Zhenia felt bad about the way she'd acted. The gleefulness at delivering bad news had been very unprofessional. And telling a client to shut up. No, she had definitely not been her "best self."

When *had* she been her best self, though? In childhood? No, that was too depressing. She had to believe it was something that still lay ahead. That it was something she had procrastinated on but that it was on the horizon.

She was lost in thought about this when a man with a mustache stopped her in the hallway.

"Are you Zhenia Pisetskaya?" he asked.

Her hand went up to her hair. The first thought she had was of those Publishers Clearing House sweepstakes that she and her grandmother had loved. Ed McMahon showing up on people's porches with the big cardboard checks. Zhenia thought, *Finally, I've won something!* What she could have won when she never even applied for anything, she didn't know.

Of course, Zhenia had not won. She was being served divorce papers. She nodded at the man and signed his clipboard, then walked woozily down the hall toward the cardiology department.

She passed the receptionist, who was looking down at a book, and walked straight to Anton's office.

She knocked but didn't wait for a response to open the door.

Anton was in there with a woman. The one from the gynecologist's office. His wife. She was sitting on his desk and he was standing up and massaging her shoulders. She was as heavily pregnant as Zhenia was.

Zhenia quickly shut the door and walked back down the hallway, but then for some reason went back and opened the door again. Anton and his wife both turned and stared at her. He stopped massaging and dropped his hands to his sides.

"Oh, are you a patient?" his wife asked.

Zhenia stood there shaking her head and grinning, fanning herself with her divorce papers. She felt dumb that her first instinct was to come to Anton for comfort when Anton, she could see now, had been merely placating her. Even when they were more actively hooking up those couple of times, he never struck her as somebody who was doing this because he didn't love his wife. Infidelity was complicated, and frankly not something they'd discussed directly. It's possible it wasn't even infidelity exactly.

"No, it's Zhenia," Anton said. "She's the translator I told you about. Zhenia, this is my wife, Chloe." What had he told her? Zhenia wondered.

Chloe looked at Zhenia, then looked back at Anton. "I felt a pang of jealousy when I saw her round belly and then I remembered that I'm pregnant too."

"You are," he said, smiling and reaching around to stroke her belly in front of Zhenia.

"We've been trying for a while," Chloe explained just to be polite.

"Was there something you wanted to talk about?" Anton asked Zhenia neutrally.

Zhenia looked down at the envelope she was holding and shook her head. She had just wanted someone to pay attention to her and to say something nice. "Are Mrs. Golovach's test results in? She said she got a notification but the results weren't updated."

"What?" Anton asked. Mrs. Golovach was not a person who existed.

"Sorry," Zhenia said. She turned around and left.

ON HER BUS ride home Zhenia thought about the Revolution. How it would feel to throw a brick through a window. It would feel good. Probably amazing. If she could take apart her own home and throw each brick through other people's windows, she would. It would be worth it. The satisfaction of spite.

Tie a note around each one. Like the general's wife did to Irina's teacher. Each smug and self-satisfied fucker would get their window broken. And maybe then, in all those broken windows, she'd finally see the pattern, the organizing principle, the other people underpinning all her misery.

As she walked to transfer to the train, she texted Ben and Anton indiscriminate accusations: They would be traitors in the Revolution! They were both pigs in their own complacency! They would betray her at any turn! They already have!

Ben had taken a webinar once on abundance and manifestation and Zhenia had lurked in the background, rolling her eyes dramatically at that teacher. A brick through her window too! "Let's go through life thinking all resources are infinite!" "You can just visualize what you want and the universe will give it to you!" Ben had agreed with Zhenia that it was idiotic, and "very American," and yet, he did it anyway, and she supposed he had gotten what he wanted, hadn't he?

So, what if she did it now? She stood on the train platform and closed her eyes. If she visualized a revolution—would the universe give it to her? And is this what she wanted really? She pictured a wealthy person's severed head rolling down the subway steps. No, she didn't want this. Only metaphorically. She opened her eyes. A man with a runny nose was asking her for money. She dropped the change she had into his cup, watched him shuffle to the next person and the next, who pretended not to see or hear him as they boarded the train.

So what was it that she wanted? She tried to visualize Ben holding their baby. She couldn't though. When she tried, Ben's face was a blur, or his hands with the baby were. What she saw, really, when she closed her eyes was Anton, massaging his wife.

She almost missed her stop and had to rush off the train. She was relieved when she got home and looked at her phone to see that all of her incoherent texts about betrayal and the Revolution had not gone through. She'd been underground and so there hadn't been reception.

After Zhenia came out of the tub, which she'd guiltily sat in longer than she was technically supposed to this late in her pregnancy, she checked her email and saw that Anton had sent her several GIFs. A guy hugging a duck. An unhappy-looking long-haired cat in a bubble bath. The images were ambiguous but seemed like they were maybe on the outskirts of an apology. He had nothing to be sorry for, though. Not to her anyway. Maybe to his wife.

CHAPTER 32

The next time Zhenia saw Anton was weeks later in the hospital cafeteria. Even though Zhenia had been calling in sick to work a lot, and was probably about to be fired, Dee threw her a baby shower. There were balloons and a vanilla sheet cake with blue frosting. The nurses and doctors and other translators brought Zhenia gifts. There were even a couple of her former clients who had suffered through and recovered from enough ailments to have gotten to know Zhenia well. An old man whom she'd helped through several surgeries was diligently eating the cake.

"It's too sweet," he complained to Zhenia in Russian, then to whoever would listen.

Zhenia kept getting stuck in corners, her enormous stomach keeping her from squeezing between people as she was used to.

"It's the best diaper bag on the market," a radiologist said happily, handing her a gift bag with blue tissue paper. "It's the same one my wife had. She researched it exhaustively. She wrote about it for *Newsweek*."

"About a diaper bag? Um, thank you." She took the bag, and then, since clearly the radiologist wanted her to open the gift and admire it, she did that.

"It has a lot of compartments," she said.

"Yeah. You can wear it as a backpack or a purse and hang it on the stroller, and there's a changing pad built in that also detaches."

"Cool," Zhenia said. "Thanks."

She could not imagine getting excited about a diaper bag or really any baby products.

"Should I be researching diaper bags?" she asked Anton after she escaped from the radiologist.

"It looks like you already have the best one, so no," Anton said with a smirk, and licked the blue frosting off his fork.

"Is my lack of interest in all this stuff a sign that I'm not thinking this pregnancy through or simply that I'm resistant to the tendrils of capitalism working their way into my relationship with the baby?"

"Capitalism!" Anton waggled his fingers at her like he was the boogeyman.

"It's true, though. Baby things and camping equipment always seem to bring out the most consumerist sides of people. My ex-husband"—she noticed Anton blink—"always took such glee in buying lanterns with magnetic bases and sleeping pads that self-inflated even though we barely ever went camping. Nature and familial relationships are these pure things and seeing consumerism seep into them feels gross."

Anton snorted at the melodrama. "Shopping isn't the worst way to manage fear of the unknown. Nature is scary because it's larger than you and magnificent. And babies are scary . . . for obvious reasons. Are you going to be able to love this baby? Are you going to be able to meet its needs? Will you end up hurting it intentionally or unintentionally? Will the world? Well, that's inevitable, but maybe if you get the right stroller, you will at least have done something right."

"What kind of stroller did you get?"

"Oh, I don't know. I'm just talking," he answered in Russian.

They stared at each other for a moment, then he passed her something wrapped in a Trader Joe's paper bag. Zhenia could see two nurses exchanging looks. It was too intimate—wrapping a present so shittily. She peeled it open. Her two favorite books from childhood. *Cheburashka*, about this bearlike stuffed animal. And *Karlsson on the Roof*, about a boy who befriends an obnoxious little man with a propeller on his back who lives on the roof and is always getting them into trouble.

"Wow," Zhenia said, stunned. Her childhood summed up so neatly here. Had she told him, or was it just a staple of every Soviet childhood? She saw for a moment her grandmother's gleeful face as she read the parts where Karlsson ruins things and then tells everybody to just relax. Also, her humming along to the songs of *Cheburashka* playing on an old TV set, the tape worn down so thin it eventually ripped and got tangled in the VCR.

"Oh, cute," the Armenian translator said, picking up *Cheburashka* and showing it to someone else. "This is the one I was telling you about with the crocodile who plays the accordion."

"Did you get Chloe these books too?" It was a clumsy way for Zhenia to bring up his wife.

He smiled at her. "Did I get her your favorite childhood books? No."

"Are you guys having a boy or a girl?" she asked, avoiding his eyes.

"A girl," Anton said happily.

Zhenia nodded and drifted away. Was he torturing her on purpose? she wondered. Dee gave her a pair of booties she had knit herself. The custodian gave her a little train conductor onesie. A physical therapist gave her a nice, soft blanket.

"Thank you," she said to all of them.

Anton cornered Zhenia by the elevator banks. She had snuck off not so subtly, carrying all her gifts, even though the party wasn't over.

"Listen," he said. "There was something I've been meaning to ask you. Do you think you could spend some time with my wife?"

Zhenia bugged her eyes out at him.

"I could pay you," he continued. The elevator doors opened and he helped her bring the gifts in.

"What the fuck, Anton. What's wrong with your wife? Why would you need to pay someone to do that?"

"She's new in town. Having a baby should not be a solitary activity. I think you would like her."

She kept staring at him.

"She's prone to depression. Babies can exacerbate that."

"You're worried she might do something to the baby?"

He pressed the ground-floor button. "I'm not saying that." He turned and looked at her. He put his hand on her neck, stroking her earlobe with his thumb. It had been so long since anybody had touched her. The desire she felt was almost paralyzing. She thought of her grandmother in the letters begging Deda Grisha to touch her in this way.

"Obviously she can't know I hired you," Anton said. The elevator doors opened and someone held them and waited for Anton to help her carry all of her things out into the parking lot.

"And what, you want me to, like, report back to you?" she asked him. The ear he'd touched was still hot and tingling.

"Only if there's something to say. You'll like each other. You'll forget that you're being paid to do it."

"But won't she wonder why I'm always hanging around?"

He shrugged. "I don't think so. Where is your car?" He was carrying several bags in each hand.

"I don't have one anymore," Zhenia remembered. Her lips began to tremble.

Anton stared at her. A man who can't resist a crying pregnant woman is bad news.

"Oh wow," he said. "Okay." He looked at his watch. "I'll give you a ride."

ZHENIA RARELY SLEPT now, but a few nights after her maternity leave started she had a dream. She was in the bedroom of an old St. Petersburg apartment. She was lying on her back, fully clothed, and Anton was lying beside her, head propped up on his hand, looking at her face. He began to slowly unbutton her shirt with one hand. There were so many buttons, this went on forever. Chloe's pregnant belly had migrated to her back as a hump. She was sitting by the window smoking a cigarette, watching out of the corner of her eye. The slow deliberation of the unbuttoning, Zhenia's sense of immobility, a witness, all of this had left Zhenia gasping. She woke up and in half-sleep began to hump her pregnancy pillow that she slept with between her knees. She came, crying out, the sound strange and lonely in the empty, ransacked apartment. It had been months since she'd felt sexual. Every so often during the endless girl-detective show binges her hands would wander to her labia, pulling them apart and back together, kneading her clit, but quickly losing interest. There was a deadness there that she'd preferred to leave undisturbed. But now it was stirred up.

Afterward, she got up to get herself a glass of water, and there was Irina at the kitchen counter, sitting on a stool.

Zhenia had never seen a ghost before. She'd pictured ghosts would look like something underexposed in a black-and-white photograph. But that was not how she experienced Irina at all. Irina was just there, the feeling of movement in Zhenia's peripheral vision and a cold pocket of air. How Zhenia knew this was Irina, she wasn't sure. It was instinctual.

"Did I invoke you?" Zhenia asked. Had her loneliness created an inviting vacuum?

"Who knows who invoked who," Irina replied. "Maybe it was mutual."

Zhenia blinked, thinking of Irina's ghost not only watching her masturbate but maybe even seeding her with the material. She could sense Irina shifting in her chair.

"Did you try to kill that man?" Zhenia asked. "The medium. Paul."

"Kill him? He's alive last I checked."

"Okay, but did you do that to him?"

"I don't know," Irina said. "Maybe I did? But it wasn't my intention. There are limits to the physical body." Was she speaking out loud or was the voice in Zhenia's head? It was hard to tell. It had been several days since Zhenia had had a conversation with another person. She felt a little bit relieved to be reunited with Irina, actually.

"Are you going to hurt me?" Zhenia asked. The question was perfunctory, and yet her voice quavered when she asked. The real question she had was whether Irina was going to hurt the baby.

"Hurt you? How could I possibly hurt you? Or at least, in ways I haven't already. You know this is my first time back on earth? I waited and waited but the man never came back, so I went looking for you myself. It took me a very long time. I got lost. It was much easier with his help. I had to float through a lot of other squalid apartments past and present before I finally found this one."

Zhenia crossed her arms over her belly. She felt embarrassed that someone was seeing how she lived and calling it squalid but also perversely proud. Like when she was little and would insist on preserving her tears on her cheeks until her mother, or usually, her grandmother, acknowledged them.

Irina seemed to drift toward the stove. "Can you boil me some milk?" she asked.

Zhenia could not. The milk in the fridge had gone sour. She had soy milk, but apparently that wouldn't do.

"What's that saying, life is wasted on the living?" Irina said huffily.

It's not like Irina would have been able to drink it, so what did it matter? Zhenia didn't understand.

"So, are you going to tell me about having my grandmother?" Zhenia asked the ghost.

"Yes, and I think my story would put your," Irina seemed to be gesturing vaguely around Zhenia, "suffering into perspective."

Zhenia crossed her arms, ignoring Irina's condescension. "Well, go on then."

"Where's your pen? Where's your notebook?"

"Are we still doing that?"

Zhenia could sense a huff of exasperation. "Yes, we're still doing that! You have to write it down or you don't really listen! What's written is real. This is our arrangement. It hasn't changed. If you don't hear my story properly, then what is the point?"

Zhenia went and dug up the notebook she'd taken to New York. She didn't feel like arguing and besides, taking dictation was a concrete thing she could do to avoid the disconcerting sensation of looking at and not seeing something that was right in front of her.

"Don't use that pen. Put it in the trash can. It has no ink. I see you keep trying it, not using it, and then putting it back. Throw it away."

So she'd been watching her for some time? Zhenia threw the pen into the little metal wastebasket by her bed.

"Throw something else in there. I like that sound," Irina said.

Zhenia crumpled up a piece of paper and dropped it into the wastebasket.

"Something bigger," Irina said breathlessly. "A shoe, maybe."

Zhenia threw in a shoe. Then a boot. Then a medical dictionary. Finally she had to put a stop to this because it was the middle of the night and she was making a racket.

"Are we starting or what?" Zhenia said.

CHAPTER 33

In some ways, my teacher Fräulein Agata had been replaced by Lara—another older woman showing me how to live in the world. Lara had been Osip's lover for nearly a decade. I think maybe she'd given me as a gift to Osip, preemptively, because she knew that he and I would find our way to each other regardless. This way she could at least have some say in the matter.

"That's fucked up. You were a person."

"Oh, Zhenia, be quiet with your moralizing. You can call it something else if that makes you more comfortable. It doesn't matter."

The night I appeared on their doorstep, Lara led me up to their bedroom and acted as if they'd both been expecting me.

"You poor thing," they cooed, and undressed me. I hadn't taken off my clothes since my cousin's funeral. I had torn the collar, you know, this is the Jewish tradition, to rip your clothes in grief. I still couldn't hear fully from my right ear. The explosion had permanently damaged my eardrum.

Osip carried me to the tub and bathed me. He washed my hair, whistling. I lay there naked and blank, floating in the warm gray water. No man had ever seen me naked before, but I didn't feel shy. I didn't feel anything. He had that yellow silk scarf tied around his neck and I reached up and batted at the ends, like a kitten. Lara stood in the doorway and watched us.

She accepted our flirtation, but seeing us this way pained her. She left us alone to go heat up some soup. Then, wrapped in a towel, I sat on the edge of their bed and she spoon-fed me, as though I were a baby. I let her do that. I was so grateful. Somebody was finally taking care of me. Then I nestled between them in bed and slept like a corpse well into the afternoon.

In some ways, the dynamic was that they were like my parents. Lara was like a smarter, kinder, more nurturing mother that I never had. And Osip was like my father, in the sense that I loved him.

He shared with my father a flagrant generosity. He'd promise away everything we had. I was used to a man who took from his family, though of course there was nothing ideological about it when my father did it, just a gambler's thirst for the next win. With Osip, the patterns I was accustomed to were there, and I must have found something about this comforting, especially because now there was a high-minded point to all of them. Everybody who came to him, he tried to help. Every piece of bread he got, he shared.

Lara would sit by the window, smoking. I know you can picture it. Her face turned away from us, her hump shaking occasionally, while Osip fondled me and groaned.

"Did you like it?" Zhenia asked, not looking up from her notebook.

"Hanna would have liked it. I thought of her always stroking herself like a cat, she couldn't resist her own skin. I tried to feel as she would have, but of course, none of that was available to me. The closest I could feel, and which Osip mistook for passion, was the opening up of the jaws inside me. A release of a pent-up energy in the darkness. It was always dark because the curtains were drawn and the electricity had been shut off. We saved the candles for reading."

Lara came from a very wealthy aristocratic family. That spring, she would visit them regularly with a large purse and we lived off the things she stole from them. Her family knew she did this, but they pretended not to because, she explained to me, they felt sorry for her, and they could probably spare a silver tea service here and a fancy brooch there, considering what they'd put her through when she was younger with the doctors and the forced surgeries. Because of her affliction they believed that carrying a child could kill her, so they'd had her sterilized, and she never forgave them for this.

Having a child was the thing she wanted most, and I filled this need somewhat. When she'd come home from visiting them she'd always be in a dark mood. I'd sit beside her on the bed and pet her hump, which was bony and strange to the touch, and she would stare off silently into space, her purse between us, bulging with whatever she'd taken.

Once the October Revolution started and the Civil War began, she was no longer the only one stealing from her family. Her association with them was no longer such a boon. It's true that plenty of the higher-ups in the party came from bourgeois families like hers, but this was nothing to brag about. Her family was pretty clear-eyed about what was happening, and they came to Osip's apartment—her parents and her sisters—and begged for Lara to go with them to Paris. This was a few months before Osip and I would end up going to Switzerland. Lara's family had already gotten her documents. They talked to her like she was slow.

They stood there in our living room and begged Osip to tell her to go.

"He'll never marry you!" they told her. It was awful and it was true because by that point he'd married me.

Lara put her hand over Osip's mouth. She didn't want to hear him tell her to go or to stay. Both would have been cruel.

"Did you want her to go?" Zhenia asked.

"Yes. I wanted to get rid of her by then—so that Osip and I could have a true romance, not controlled by her and not squeezed into the sanctioned corners. But, the relationship Osip and I had, it required a lot of external buttressing. All those other people had seemed like inconveniences and breaks to our passion, but really they were structurally necessary, and when all those limitations were gone, and we were free to do as we wanted, like when we went to Switzerland, things did not go well for us at all."

"You turn on all the women who help you, don't you?" Zhenia said, flipping to the next page in her notebook.

"And you? You never rejected your own mother?" Irina asked, then continued without waiting for an answer.

I thought after throwing the bomb I had proven myself, but it would take more than this. For one thing, few people knew about it. It was kept a secret in order to protect me. The meetings of revolutionaries in Osip's apartment grew longer and more heated. We were all united against the monarchy and the Provisional Government that had been established after the February Revolution, but we did not see eye to eye on much else. There were factions and factions inside factions.

My own thoughts on the issues were primitive. I was against the Great War, which had taken my brothers, and I saw no dishonor in losing and getting out—so in this way I was aligned with the Bolsheviks, but I did not like the way they presented themselves aesthetically. Their style and rhetoric were too rough. Nor did I romanticize factory workers, and even less so, peasants. As for things like the historical interpretation of materialism and class alliances, this all felt beyond my understanding and in those matters I deferred to Osip and Lara, who had started off as SRs and then joined the Mensheviks.

Boris found these circular living room conversations and half measures disgusting and he defected, declaring himself an anarchist. He thought all of us were moving too slowly and in the wrong direction. He stopped staying in the apartment and began to stay in the Vyborg Durnovo mansion, which a group of anarchists and a bakers' union had taken over and claimed.

He slept, if he slept at all, under the table in the dining room. The Durnovo family portraits had been cut out of the heavy gold frames that still hung on the walls. The anarchists had turned the mansion's grounds and gardens into a play area for children, but the children were always getting lost in the topiary maze and crying hysterically for help. Boris had had enough of this at some point and cut holes through the bushes so they could just walk through from one side to the other. He also hung big black banners along the sides of the building that said: "Death to Capitalists"; "Bread! Peace! Land! By Any Means Necessary"; and "Loot the Looters." I thought they looked quite stylish. I visited Boris there a few times with Osip, who as his friend and co-conspirator was worried about Boris's increasingly erratic behavior.

Since he'd known him in elementary school, Boris had always been a sensitive boy, Osip was telling me on the tram ride there. I had just lost my virginity the night before and kept wanting Osip to put his hands on me. It felt a little bit like if nobody was holding me, I would float away. This was, I think, Boris's central problem as well. He had floated away, lost his mind when Hanna died. Strolling the grounds of this newly acquired mansion, I held Osip's hand with both of mine and couldn't bring myself to look at Boris.

I don't know if Boris blamed me or himself for Hanna's death, but something unpleasant always hung there between us. I wondered if maybe he talked to her, because several times on our stroll he seemed to be muttering asides to an invisible ghost. I don't know any better now than I did then if Hanna really was talking to him or not, but I could tell that the way Boris was acting disturbed Osip deeply.

Boris said that the time of the reckoning was now; whether the higher-ups felt this way or not, he could feel it in his own boiling blood. The workers felt it. The soldiers felt it. The peasants felt it. He was sick of Lenin and the rest of the Petrograd Soviet telling them it wasn't yet time.

"Who controls the time?" he shouted, his whole body vibrating with rage.

"But we're not organized," Osip said, trying to reason with him. My own understanding of these things was very tenuous, but I added what I had heard Osip and Lara say many times. "We don't have enough widespread support yet to try to take over! If we do it now, it could backfire and this would only help the Provisional Government, and God forbid bring back the monarchy. We need to get organized."

Boris waved this away as nonsense. "The streets will organize us!" he said, scaring a flock of pigeons that rose and then settled back down on the shore of the mansion's little pond where a woman was washing clothes in the greenish water.

I was hanging on to Osip, and with a stern look, he extracted his hand from mine and gently pushed me away. He placed both his hands on Boris's shoulders and begged him to come to his house, sleep in a bed, eat a meal, and then resume this very important work that he was doing. But this just provoked crazy and hysterical laughter from Boris that, this time, made the pigeons flee for good.

On the tram ride home, Osip told me it had been cruel of me to flaunt our happiness like that. This baffled me, since I did not feel the least bit happy.

"Did you ever feel happy?" Zhenia could see Irina's shape now but only if she relaxed her eyes into the middle distance.

"After Hanna died, happy moments became too painful. I would do something usually to ruin them, otherwise it was unbearable. Maybe this is just growing up?"

Zhenia supposed you could define growing up in this way, though she hoped you didn't have to. What, to be an adult was just to be miserable?

But then again, had Zhenia felt the kind of wonder or quiet joy as an adult that she did when she was a kid—lying in the park with her head in her grandmother's lap, throwing stale bread at birds, feeling the sun on her face, and listening to her grandmother read to her?

Had anything . . . Zhenia bit her lip to stop it from quivering. Would anything bring her that feeling again?

Her tears seemed to repel Irina, who floated to the other end of the apartment toward the overflowing hamper.

"Maybe this is why physical pain became what I liked," Irina continued. "It was all I could really understand. Osip was always too gentle."

CHAPTER 34

Zhenia took the call in the bathroom for privacy. Even though Irina could probably still see or perceive her through the wall, it made her feel less self-conscious. Zhenia had been calling Naomi for days, trying to see whether she'd heard anything from Ben, and now, early in the morning on her way to set, Naomi was calling her back.

"He wants a clean break from you," Naomi said. "I get it."

"I want a clean break from me too." Zhenia sighed. Obviously, with a baby this did not seem possible, but she didn't get into that with Naomi. It was hard to imagine that she and Naomi had been close since they now seemed to hate each other.

"But you're okay?" Naomi asked disingenuously.

"Sure," Zhenia said, and then, even though she had told herself she wouldn't ask, she still asked. "Did you meet the woman he left me for?"

"I don't know that it's helpful to think about it in that way," Naomi said. "He left you because he left you. I don't think it was because of Sadie."

"Okay," Zhenia said. And then, "Sadie." Since Ben had blocked Zhenia on all social media, she had only a vague sense of his new life, but the name "Sadie" was enough to fill in the blanks—braid crowns, daisy chains, picnic baskets, farmer's markets, beige tap shoes, whatever the fuck.

"Remember when we . . ." Naomi started to say, but Zhenia could feel Irina nearby, hanging up the phone for her.

"Don't be stupid," Irina said. "Your husband, this woman, none of them matter in the least. It's not what you should be occupying yourself with."

Was this kindness? Zhenia wondered. Or merely self-interest?

Regardless, Zhenia suspected that she was right and went back to her notebook.

Osip got me installed working as a typesetter for a rival faction's newspaper, but I bungled it. It was hard physical work, and I wasn't really equipped. After I was fired, my job was to stand in line for bread. It took hours, so at first I'd bring a copy of Marx and Engels, books that Osip's sister pushed on me so that I'd be slightly better informed and not a teenage ignoramus, which was simply what I was no matter how much boring Marx or Engels I stumbled through. I'd try to remember what Fräulein Agata had said about them, to repeat this to Osip's sister in the evenings, but thinking about my old teacher and my old life was unpleasant. Eventually, I left the books under the bed and used the time to observe what was going on around me.

One day I met a man with a sign around his neck announcing himself as an army deserter demanding liberation.

We were still fighting in the Great War, even though we had plenty of problems of our own at home and there were no supplies. Soldiers were deserting in huge numbers, but it was illegal. They would get sent to military prison or sent back to the front lines. It was a brutal system.

Some people waiting next to me began to heckle the man. Why those idiots thought continuing that pointless war, not to mention with no equipment, was desirable, I have no idea.

"You go ahead and march to your own deaths!" I shouted at these people. Unfortunately, our dispute came to blows, but I carried a knife with me, precisely for situations like this. The ladies backed off, and the heckler crawled away. His was a superficial wound, but the head bleeds.

For the most part, though, waiting in the breadlines was boring and slow. I felt restless. Maybe the restlessness wasn't even my own, but I was just absorbing it from around me in the lines and crowds.

Zhenia also was feeling restless. She could hear her neighbors getting ready for work and for school. Honestly, she wanted to get back to mindlessly watching her girl-detective show and feeling sorry for herself, checking to see if Ben had maybe unblocked her from social media. He had not. Or looking up this Sadie.

"You're not listening!" Irina said with some irritation. "I'm telling you all this about the months between the February Revolution and the October Revolution and you're not listening." Zhenia could feel Irina very close to her now. Up in her face.

Zhenia fought the urge to flinch by clenching her jaw as tight as she could, then letting it go slack and slamming her laptop shut. She picked up her pen. "Tell me about my grandmother then. What was she like as a baby?"

"What are babies like? I don't know. They cry, they eat, they sleep. What do you imagine could be different about your grandmother? She had reddish hair when she was born and reddish skin. A birthmark on the back of her neck. A stork bite is what it was called. Osip was immediately very fond of her. She was much better at being a child than I was."

"So you felt in competition with her?" Zhenia was thinking about the way her mother had described her own childhood.

"I *was* in competition with her. It wasn't a feeling, but a fact. Anyway, I'm getting to all that. Be patient, and listen to me."

Zhenia licked her dry lips and nodded. She turned to a fresh page of the notebook.

The police had started harassing me in the breadlines. I was having difficulties with my residency papers. The situation was becoming untenable.

One morning, Lara made us omelets from eggs she'd gotten on the black market. She was watching us eat, not eating herself, fussing. Osip put down his fork.

"What is it, Larochka?" he asked.

She smoothed and ruffled the pleats on her skirt. I could see what Osip saw in her—there was something very touching in her face when it was suffering.

She said, "Ossya, you need to marry Irina. You know the situation with her papers. It's not right. She's sacrificed so much for us, for the movement. They'll ship her off or worse."

Osip smiled mirthlessly at Lara. Neither of them looked at me. He wasn't sure, I think, if Lara was playing a game of chicken, if this was a dare, or a test.

"Yes, fine," he said.

"Quite a proposal." I pouted and went back to eating my eggs. I took the last crust of bread and demonstratively wiped my plate clean with it.

I knew I was being childish, which made the whole situation seem lighter. I was again their child. I lay down across the chair with my head in Lara's lap and my body in Osip's. I thought of the boy in the hotel, the one Hanna and I had seen playing with the cat. I closed my eyes and chewed on the crust.

LARA HAD ONE of her nicest dresses tailored to fit me. She herself wore a beige dress—as close to white as she dared. Osip's sister didn't come with us to meet my mother at the train station, but she did pin a sprig of violets to each of our lapels. Where she got them, I'm not sure, because she never seemed to leave the apartment.

Lara, Osip, and I walked arm in arm, taking up the whole sidewalk. The trams weren't running because the day before, during a demonstration, a group of sailors had overturned a tram car and it had not yet been cleared off the tracks. I had the unpleasant feeling of being watched from above. When Osip caught me squinting up at the rooftops, he pulled my sleeve, while pointedly not following my gaze. There was a network of skyline walkways and there were sharpshooters up there. It was best not to attract their attention.

I had only been able to convince my mother to come because I'd made insane promises about a church wedding and told her that Osip had been related to some count and that I wanted her to eventually come live with us. We left her luggage at the train station and took her straight to the courthouse. Because I was a minor she had to sign the paperwork for me.

The country had descended into chaos and yet the bureaucracy still needed oil for its wheels.

My mother kept asking why Lara was with us, and I lied and told her that Lara was Osip's sister. At the courthouse, a man with a mustache looked us over, pausing on Osip's yellow silk scarf tied in a bow around his neck, but then stamping our papers anyway. Afterward in the stairwell, behind my mother's back, Osip kissed Lara's eyelids, and her hump shook slightly, though she didn't cry.

It was several days before we'd be able to get rid of my mother—a cuckoo bird that we had to shove back into the clock. She was now a fire-and-brimstone anti-Semite, believing all the propaganda of the Black Hundreds, the far-right group. Everything out of her still-beautiful mouth was vile. She whispered loudly about Lara's hump, asking whether she stored water in there. When we finally got home, Lara unpinned the now-wilted violets and excused herself. My mother, on top of being stupid, was also cruel.

Osip was politic, polite; she was now his mother-in-law, after all. Of course, even Osip had his limits. He and I walked her back to the train station. She talked and talked breathlessly about all the murderers in the street and didn't seem to realize just who we were or where we were taking her. I still remember that sad look on her face as the train started moving. We waved at her from the platform and she was gone, thank God. It was the last time I saw her.

The next morning, when Osip was shaving, I asked him if he was worried that I'd become like my mother in my old age.

"What honorable revolutionary lives into old age," he joked. His cheek was bleeding where he'd cut it.

"You sound like Boris," Lara said from the hallway.

The door was ajar and she could see me in the mirror lick the drop of blood off his cheek with the tip of my tongue.

CHAPTER 35

Zhenia got up and went out onto the balcony. She watched the kids below, with their large backpacks, being walked to school. Irina was calling to her from inside, but Zhenia pretended not to hear. She stretched, squatted, knocked something over by accident with her stomach. There was something about Irina's demand for attention that was starting to make Zhenia feel unwell. The actual words she was writing down were maybe a distraction, the surface texture of the water instead of the wave itself. Irina was standing right in front of her now, nose to nose, and Zhenia stepped back inside to put some space between them, and somehow found herself sitting at the counter again in front of her notebook, pen in hand.

As Irina started to talk, Zhenia felt vaguely like the wave was pulling her, pulling her somewhere she shouldn't go, detaching her from herself in a way that was maybe dangerous? Or was she just being paranoid? As her hand moved fluidly over the page of the notebook, she tried to push away this feeling.

The Revolution in February had felt like such a triumph and I had been a brave hero, attuned to the crowds. More than attuned, they carried me and I carried them inside myself. But the crowds began to splinter.

One day Lara came home bloody. The factory workers whom she'd been teaching how to read turned on her and began screaming that she was a German spy and pummeling her with nuts and bolts from the assembly line.

"It wasn't their fault," Lara said protectively, as I tore up Osip's old shirt into strips to make bandages. "They'd been fed lies."

The Bolsheviks had come in the day before and told the factory workers God knows what kind of nonsense about Lara. We'd been working with the Bolsheviks and other revolutionary factions to overthrow the tsar and the Provisional Government, but it was not a unified front and we were always turning on each other.

"This is precisely why nobody in my family ever let me get a dog," I said as I bandaged her wounds. "They seem so faithful and then they bite you in the face."

"Irina," Lara said, holding me at arm's length with her mummy hands and shaking me slightly. "Think before you speak. I'm glad Osip didn't hear you. What are we fighting for if not the workers? How can you compare them to dogs?"

I took her wounded hand and squeezed it. Nobody likes to be reprimanded especially when they're wrong.

It was my name day. It's what you celebrated instead of a birthday, and since my father had been a gentile, there was always a party in our house in honor of Saint Irine. She was a beautiful clairvoyant nun from the Middle Ages who ate apples from paradise and lived until she was 103. I was sixteen. Saint days weren't something revolutionaries celebrated—we were atheists and the church was as bad as the tsar. Still, Lara could tell that I longed for something festive and she went to great lengths to make me a cake, a French napoleon with cream. Even Osip's depressive sister came out of her room to tie ribbons in my hair. She'd grown more withdrawn in the weeks since the February Revolution. I think she saw the writing on the wall before the rest of us did, and the more Osip seemed to lean in, the more she seemed to lose her nerve.

Osip was still at his Petrograd Soviet meeting at the Tauride Palace, where all the factions were trying to hash out a plan of taking over the government. I decided to bring him his dinner and a slice of cake.

It was raining and I had to make my way through a hostile crowd of sailors. Several men grabbed at me as I passed and one stole my umbrella.

The guard at the front door let me into the big meeting hall. I found Osip at his usual place by the front and handed him the wet paper sack. Even though I knew that he'd expected me to leave, I instead kneeled at his feet.

He took off his sweater and used it to towel off my hair. I leaned into it like a pet. It was my special day and I wanted him to pay attention to me, even though his eyes were on the front of the room, where a member was presenting numbers related to the rural uprisings. I could tell that my clinginess was getting on his nerves. History was happening and I was a distraction.

The crowd outside the palace was growing, turning into a demonstration. In the pauses of the man's speech we could hear shouting in the spaces between his words.

The members of the different revolutionary factions were in a difficult position. The Provisional Government was in a precarious balance. This was something Osip argued about with Boris: Armed demonstrations were premature! We were not yet ready, or equipped, to seize power! It was not yet the time to act! If we seized the land of the gentry and handed it over to the peasants, it would only result in chaos and starvation! It would bait the counterrevolutionary forces! And they would crush us before we even had a chance to set up our own government!

The man at the front of the room had gone quiet and we could all hear the chant coming from outside—"*All power to the Soviets.*"

Osip and a few others got up and went to the front of the room to confer. They decided to send out an older man with round glasses. He'd be a friendly canary in the coal mine to gauge the crowd.

"He'll lull them right to sleep," I heard someone snicker behind me. "His voice is very soothing."

I watched through the hall window as the poor canary climbed awkwardly onto a barrel in the rain and began to speak. I knew that the crowd hated him. I hated him too in that moment, for no reason other than he projected weakness. Osip watched tensely. The crowd moved in closer and closer around the barrel. They shouted over him, not listening to his words.

Most of the crowd wasn't even looking at him but at us, dry and behind the palace windows, looking down at them. There was no sense really of where this evening was going to go. The fact that the crowd was aligned with us, was chanting for the same things we wanted, only made its energy more confusing. They wanted the Revolution to happen faster! So did we! Where was the new world order we were promising? We were bungling it, they were sure, with our excess of caution. Why were we kowtowing to the moderates? Why were we asking always for permission?

I thought the demonstrators were right, but I had a tendency to agree with whoever spoke last.

A sailor raised his fist and shook it inches from the canary's face. "Take power, you son of a bitch, when it's given to you."

It made me think of the several times when I was younger when I'd seen men, drunk friends of my father, declare their love this angrily to my mother. They loved her so much they wanted to grind her down with their bootheels.

The crowd moved as one organism, and the canary in the coal mine was knocked off the barrel.

Osip couldn't take this anymore; he and a small group ran to the man's aid. Someone else had managed to find the old royal trumpet and blow it. The crowd froze and turned to Osip, who swiftly climbed up onto the hood of a black car, into which the canary was being shoved.

The baby was trying to move inside of Zhenia. He was too big already to rearrange himself easily, but the doctor at her last appointment had said he would need to turn upside down.

She felt tangled in Irina's story. "They had cars back then?" she asked absentmindedly.

"Yes, they had cars. I just told you he climbed on top of one."

"Whose car was it?"

Irina paused. "I don't know whose car."

"What would the crowd do with him in the car? Where would they drive him?"

"Most likely they would not have driven him anywhere. They would have simply set the car on fire."

The man's glasses had gotten knocked off and were hanging crookedly over his nose, which was bleeding. He sat in the car, fogging up the window, shouting something.

Osip stood on that car hood like it was a mountaintop—yellow scarf billowing dramatically behind him in the wet wind. He looked like a futurist poster.

"Comrades!" he announced grandly. "Dear comrades! You've come here bravely to declare your will and show the Petrograd Soviet that the working class no longer wants to see the bourgeoisie in power. We agree completely. Why hurt your own cause by petty acts of violence against casual individuals? Individuals are not worthy of your attention."

Osip was so modest. He saw himself only as a servant to the people, to history. His lofty ideas were entirely genuine and the crowd could somehow feel this. That Osip could shift the crowd, reorganize its mood, this was very attractive. I felt aroused at the idea of being his wife.

Osip opened the car door and let the canary out. How embarrassing it must have been for the canary. We don't know who it was exactly who turned on us later, but I always thought it could have been him. Being saved is a humiliation.

"Not being saved—being abandoned—is not any less humiliating," Zhenia said. But what difference did humiliation make? She would've gladly traded her pride for anything more tangible. Childcare. A person who'd hold her hand during labor. A box of diapers that she'd soon need to buy.

Irina waved away this self-pity and kept going.

After Osip saved the day—well, really *a* day, since if you know anything about the Soviet Union, the day was never saved—I had my own moment as history's instrument.

Olga, whom I had not seen much of, but who always seemed to have just left whenever I arrived, showed up at Osip's apartment looking for me. I was surprised to see her dressed as a nurse. She brought me a matching uniform because she needed me to accompany her to the Peter and Paul Fortress—this was the only reason she came.

The Fortress, where we'd once delivered letters, had been taken over by revolutionaries but it was about to fall back into the hands of the Provisional Government. Tensions in the streets were coming to a head. There was a delicate balance with the dual power, between the more moderate Provisional Government and the radical Soviets.

I agreed to go only because otherwise Lara would have made me accompany her to the lessons she was giving women in a cigarette factory about workers' rights, and the repetition of these lessons had begun to feel as tedious as the factory work itself.

I was thinking on the walk over to the Peter and Paul Fortress that Olga seemed to follow Lenin's directives pretty closely, and to her people were either expendable enemies or useful. For now she thought I was useful, but she didn't see me as a person worth buttering up. She seemed perfectly comfortable walking with me in total silence. I tried several times to start a conversation on the subject of Boris, whom she dismissed as politically myopic, or Fräulein Agata, whom she just dismissed without even labeling, with a flick of her wrist. And Osip? About him she was more careful. He had good ideas, she said, she just wasn't sure if she agreed with him on his methodology. He wasn't ready yet to seize power, and she was.

On this point, I agreed with Olga. It felt disloyal to Osip, but power was being handed to us and we were waving our pale arms like an old woman who was being pursued by a dog.

There is a perversity in this, no? Chasing and retreating as soon as you are being granted what you want?

"You said yourself. Maybe the timing wasn't right. They weren't ready."

Irina paused and Zhenia felt herself being inspected too closely.

"There are people who know how to exist only as the underdog. And they deflect any offers that would change this."

"What's wrong with being an underdog?" Zhenia asked, and scratched her ankle with the end of her pen. "Overdogs are all monsters."

If Ben were there, he would have pointed to this kind of thinking as a "limiting belief." The baby tried to shift again but then seemed to give up.

"The underdogs were monsters too. To be human is to be monstrous. No matter how much you sweeten it with your false humility and avoidance."

"And yet, your entire later life was a repudiation of this life."

"My life after, as I've told you before, was somebody else's life. It has very little to do with *me*. But I suspect if you were to track down the other Irina, she would tell you something similar. Stop cowering. Stop wasting your life with your games, your waffling. All you know is how to want!"

Zhenia looked down at the floor.

And what is it she wanted exactly? Ben? The idea of Ben? To be loved and admired? To have her grandmother back and alive?

Of course, there was also something else. A different life that glittered deep in the water, that she couldn't yet dive for, that she didn't even dare look at in front of Irina, for what if then Irina would steal it from her?

Or, worse, what if Irina would force her to act, to take what she wanted herself. No, it was safer for Zhenia to look away and pretend she wasn't even hungry. Let this *want* roil and roil inside of her, but wall it in somewhere. And maybe eventually she could learn to want things so quietly that she might not even know when she was suffering.

Finally Zhenia asked, "So, what happened inside the Fortress? Did you slit that Olga's throat?"

"Ha. I'm sure Olga outlived everybody. I'm surprised she ever died."

Inside the Fortress, we went deep past the cell where we'd once smuggled the letters. The room we went into, a damp cellar with boxes of papers and stacks of rubles against the stone walls, had iron shackles and no windows.

Olga took a candle out of her basket and lit it. She held it carefully and sorted through the boxes, making sure not to drip wax on the papers. It was oddly silent in the room, though we knew that there was mounting chaos outside. Flags whipping wildly, bayonets, mouths shouting into the wind.

The Provisional Government was on the brink of seizing back the Fortress, which was why it was so important that we got certain things out of there. Olga passed me rolls of bandages, and I began to wrap a stack of money like it was a wounded limb.

It was hard not to imagine Hanna in here with us again, swinging from the shackles, laughing like everything was an adventure, like it once had been.

Olga looked at me, and it must've been obvious what I was thinking because she said stiffly, "Your cousin was very brave," and then she began to line the bottoms of the baskets with the important documents somebody had directed her to salvage.

"It should have been you," I whispered, sounding like my aunt, and Olga acted as though she hadn't heard me, just piled the bricks of bandaged money onto the documents and covered this with more bandages.

"You know where they're moving the Soviet," Olga said when she was done arranging the documents. You'd think with my proximity to Osip I'd be more in the know, but I wasn't. I didn't know anything, ever. I nodded noncommittally, and Olga knew me enough to know what this meant.

"Kerensky is kicking them out of the Tauride Palace, and they're being moved to our school," she said. "They sent the headmaster packing."

"But why?" I hadn't thought of our school in some time. It seemed absurd to have the Petrograd Soviet do its important work in the classrooms of a finishing school. I wondered why Osip hadn't mentioned it.

"What happened to the students? The daughters of that general?" I wondered out loud. "The one that had the affair with our teacher? What happened to those girls?"

Olga found these lines of questioning sentimental. "Who cares?" she said, and put out the candle with her fingers.

When we got out into the hallways we could hear that outside there was shouting, banging, gunshots.

It was our last chance to get out and still pass through the barricades. Before we stepped through the door, Olga grimly adjusted my nurse's cap. Her eyes looked small without her pince-nez. She took out a tube of lipstick and painted it on me, then I did the same to her.

Nurses wear lipstick, revolutionaries don't.

We walked out the side entrance. Our heels clacking on the cobblestones, as both of us tried to look like real nurses carrying baskets that were not filled with documents and money. I had to carry mine with both hands. Anybody who cared to look would notice that merely bandages would not weigh so much.

We walked quickly, looking straight ahead, avoiding eye contact with any of the guards.

"What've you got there?" one of them called after us.

"Halt!" yelled another.

Olga kept walking, pretending not to hear, but I turned around and looked him square in the face.

"Dynamite and revolvers," I answered.

"That's in terrible taste," another soldier said, and spat on the ground. They didn't look at us anymore, just waved us along.

Olga and I kept walking, not daring to run or slow down or even make eye contact with each other. We stopped only blocks later when a stampede of riderless horses, neighing and whinnying, galloped down the street in front of us. Their saddles were empty, their manes sprayed with the blood and viscera of their former riders.

"Okay," Zhenia said, and put the cap on the pen. She could picture the gore tangled in the horse hair and it made her queasy. The baby was pressing on something, a liver or a lever.

"You've stopped listening," Irina said with irritation.

This felt like the last straw for Zhenia, who had been listening all night and was very tired. It was clear that Irina did not care what she took from anyone in the process of telling her story. Selfishness in its purest form.

"I'm already full with another person," Zhenia said. "Do I look like I can take on any more, anyone else's stories? I'm about to burst. Whatever you need from me, clearly I cannot give it to you. You should go."

Irina swayed and shimmered, and seemed to slide off the stool. "Yes, okay. But I have nowhere to go but in."

She took Zhenia by the shoulders and stepped inside of Zhenia's body. It felt like the tearing of a membrane. Zhenia's mouth filled with the taste of ash. Bitter and powdery like burnt lilacs.

"What the fuck?" Zhenia screamed.

What would this do to her baby? She belched nervously several times, but the acrid taste only intensified. She retched, but this made it worse; it only settled the sensation of Irina lower into her body.

"*There*," Irina said from the depths.

The clock inside the crocodile.

CHAPTER 36

And then, the sensation of words coming up Zhenia's throat like owl pellets. Fur and splintered bones.

> *We won and yet we seemed to win nothing.*
> *War, more war, civil war, hunger.*
> *Osip and I made love in the dark for hours,*
> *Lara lying beside us, facing the wall.*
> *I would suck on his scarf in my sleep.*

"This is awful," Zhenia whispered. "Please stop."

But Irina wouldn't stop. Couldn't stop. The words kept coming up sharp and scary.

> *To keep warm, Lara and I pried up*
> *parquet floors and banisters*
> *in abandoned houses*
> *and burned them as firewood.*
> *Everybody fled.*
> *The city was quiet and very dirty.*

Talking to Irina before had given Zhenia a dizzy feeling she couldn't pin down. There'd been a disconnect between the flatness of Irina's words and the things these words described. Pain and then denial of pain.

But now that Irina was in her, the pain was undeniable. Shame and terror reciting themselves from inside of her.

The beautiful canals and fountains
full of trash, frozen into the water.
Bones frozen into the water.
Things that couldn't be burned for heat.

Zhenia tried to make herself breakfast. Maybe swallowing food would force the words down. She brewed a tea that was supposed to be good for pregnancies. And spread mixed-berry jam on a piece of stale toast.

But as her jaw mashed the bread, Irina's running monologue continued.

Not enough horses to pull the trash carts.
We saw a dog eating a dead horse,
making ravenous slurping sounds.
"Someone will eat that dog too," I said.

Zhenia stood up and put her plate in the sink.

Lara didn't like it when I talked this way.
Even though everybody knew what was in
the oily Civil War sausage and
when we could get it,
we ate it.

Ben had bought sage when they first moved into the apartment. Zhenia found a bundle of it in the back of a kitchen drawer.

The animals at the zoo had already been eaten.
The giraffes, the bears, the ostriches.
This was nothing.
In some of the more distant provinces
people were eating people.

"Oh, Jesus Christ," Zhenia said, "like you're eating me now," and she lit the sage off the stove.

Zhenia was still coughing when she answered the phone. It was Anton. His voice—something real and outside of herself, jarring her back into the world.

REEKING OF SAGE, Zhenia dragged herself to the prenatal yoga class in Silver Lake. Inhaling sage smoke had done nothing. The thrum of Irina was in her, the bass in her breath. And of course, in her DNA and in her baby's DNA.

There was Chloe, her blond hair back in a dirty ponytail, squatting against the wall. She seemed tall and strong, but also kind of billowy.

The baby was so high up under Zhenia's ribs that all the poses felt difficult and everything was uncomfortable. The heartburn added to the permanent ache in her chest. During Shavasana, when the other pregnant women made contented little moans, Zhenia felt like the baby's foot was creeping up her throat.

When people interacted with Zhenia, the droning of Irina's words would recede almost completely, but in the quieter moments the monologue of pain would break through.

> *The hunger was like a swarm of bees.*
> *I wanted to be fucked into oblivion.*
> *I wanted to be ground up under a boot,*
> *I wanted to be fucked with a boot.*
> *A gentle touch, a feathery stroke enraged me.*
> *I needed all of my nerve endings blunted.*

The yoga teacher came up to Zhenia and said, "Relax your face. Relax all the little muscles around your eyes. Relax your jaw."

> *War, more war, civil war, hunger.*

Zhenia opened her eyes and stared at the teacher. "I can't," Zhenia whispered.

Chloe had not seemed to see or recognize Zhenia in the crowded room, even as Zhenia watched her in the long wall mirrors.

After class, Zhenia followed Chloe. One very pregnant lady with a yoga mat, following another very pregnant lady with a yoga mat. Block after block. Nothing to see here! When Chloe stopped at the intersection and looked back, Zhenia stupidly hid behind a telephone pole, which did not cover her stomach or her mat.

Chloe crossed the street and went into a plant store and Zhenia crossed the street and peered through the window at Chloe lifting up a succulent and looking for the price tag on the bottom of the pot.

The hunger was like a swarm of bees.

Zhenia had to blink away Irina's words that kept making their way up to the surface. What could Zhenia understand about war or hunger? Why would she want to?

She waved at Chloe, who waved back uncertainly, then squinted, recognizing Zhenia, and waved back genuinely. She set the pot down and came outside.

"I think we were at the same yoga class," Zhenia said. "We met at the hospital."

"Right," Chloe said. "My husband sent you."

This embarrassed Zhenia. Was she kidding or did she know? And how much did she know? Did she know about the hookups in the closet and their texts?

"Did you like the class?" Chloe asked.

a hive in my chest

"No," Zhenia said. "I didn't. I don't like to relax."

Chloe nodded. "It's not for everyone."

They both laughed awkwardly.

"Do you want to get ice cream or something?" Zhenia said.

Chloe shrugged. "I'll walk with you."

They walked down the block to Scoops, and Chloe sampled a few flavors and Zhenia got a monster cone.

I would suck on his scarf in my sleep.

"Are you nervous about giving birth?" Chloe asked.

Zhenia licked her cone. "To be honest, I haven't thought about it very much. I haven't really felt like myself. I forget that this is a temporary state and the baby is going to come out soon. When he does, I guess I'm really fucked. I'm not ready for that at all."

Her ice cream had begun to melt and was dripping down her wrist. Chloe handed her a napkin.

The giraffes, the bears.

"Thanks," Zhenia said. She tried to take a deep breath to settle Irina farther down. "Are you? Nervous?"

Chloe nodded. "Yeah. I'm really scared." She bent her sample spoon in half. "It's something I wanted for so long. Wanting to get pregnant became its own engine. It's all I could think about. How I'd look. The bump. It took many years. I'm forty. Now that it's actually happening, and I'm about to have a baby, I feel like I'm not allowed to have cold feet."

Now it was Zhenia's turn to hand Chloe a napkin. Chloe blew her nose noisily, then wiped under each eye and smiled. "What if we're ruining our lives?"

The sudden intimacy of the "we" made Zhenia blush. It was probably objectively true in Zhenia's case, but it hadn't been much of a life. "Most people don't regret it, I don't think," she said.

Chloe snorted. "Well, they can't really say that, can they?"

Someone will eat that dog too

Zhenia nodded. Anton was paying her two hundred dollars for today's session. She wondered whether she had to agree with everything his wife said, like in the internship she'd had in college working as an assistant to one of her professors. Nod, nod, nod. But she found Chloe's fixation on the idea of regret inaccurate. For all the unhappiness she knew she'd caused her mother, she didn't think that her mother regretted having her. Regret was sort of a pointless emotion. To dwell on loss was not practical. Better let that loss seed itself in your organs.

"Well, maybe they only feel it some of the time," Zhenia said, compromising after a long pause.

Chloe laughed. For forty she looked pretty good. She had some small wrinkles around her eyes, but not the jowls that Zhenia assumed awaited her in fifteen years when she'd turn forty. She pictured Anton standing behind Chloe, gripping his wife's swollen breasts and breathing into her ear, then looking up and locking eyes with Zhenia.

The city grew emptier and emptier.

Zhenia stood up suddenly and then sat back down. She hadn't realized it, but she'd peed her pants. This was something she'd done a lot as a child. She put the yoga mat in her lap to hide the growing stain.

"Are you on maternity leave, too?" Zhenia asked Chloe to distract from her weird behavior.

We burned fences. We burned banisters and parquet floors.

Chloe raised an eyebrow, not sure whether she should ask Zhenia if she was okay, but Zhenia was nodding vigorously, so Chloe answered her question. "I don't know what I am. I was adjuncting in St. Louis, teaching creative writing and working endlessly on a book, but I kind of gave up on an academic career because of Anton's job out here. And, I don't know, writing hasn't been going that great either."

> *Trash frozen in the canals.*
> *Dead horses getting eaten by dogs.*
> *I was hungry.*

"Are you . . . are you okay?" Chloe finally asked.

There was quite a bit more pee than Zhenia had expected. Warm and down her legs, dripping in plain sight over her ankles and onto her Teva-ed feet.

> *A swarm of bees in my chest.*

"I've been working on a book too," Zhenia said. This came out just to make conversation and keep Chloe from looking down. It definitely felt like a lie, even though technically, it wasn't. She had a notebook full of words. And now a headful of this looping awfulness to transcribe in the hopes of getting it out of herself by getting it onto a page.

Chloe stood up and pulled Zhenia to her feet, which made a squishing sound in her sandals. "I think your water just broke," Chloe said. She seemed suddenly very competent and not at all like the self-pitying, weepy woman she'd been a few minutes ago. "Let me drive you to the hospital. Huntington? Or are you doing it at home? Do you have a doula or someone I should call? Your . . . husband?"

Zhenia, bug-eyed, let herself be led to Chloe's Prius. The only person she had to call was her mother, who, it turned out, had been waiting for this call with her bags packed.

CHAPTER 37

The contractions started in Chloe's car. Chloe held Zhenia's hand at all the red lights and mimicked deep breathing.

> *Bones frozen into the water*
> *the oily Civil War sausage*

The pain was hard to separate out from the fear of future pain. Zhenia felt like her body was becoming a portal and something deep inside was being pried open. "Not just my cervix, but like, something in another dimension," she tried to explain between contractions. Was Irina doing this to her? Was Irina pulling apart her cervix? No, no, of course not. This was just what was supposed to happen.

> *when we could get it, we—*

The sensation of Irina's presence and her words were finally lost in the noise of the other, louder sensations inside Zhenia's body.

Zhenia nervously drummed her fingers on the dashboard and hiccupped. Then the pain would come back again and knock her sideways.

If she severed the pain's connection to time, it became tolerable. She disappeared into it: A leather curtain. Flesh. A stage, empty, with a bright spotlight, a stool with nobody on it.

In and out, through the pain. Threading the eye of the needle. And then there was Irina's voice again, but now it was singing her a song over all this noise, the same one her grandmother had sung her, the same one she had sung to her belly, to herself. The one about the little gray wolf. The little gray wolf that would steal you off the edge of your bed and drag you into the woods and tear you apart under a willow bush.

The Wolf, Little Red Riding Hood, the Grandmother with a sharp ax.

Crawling down the sidewalk in front of the hospital, the ground tearing up her knees, through the sliding doors, slapping away hands that tried to lift her. This was the only position she could tolerate being in, she'd screamed. Getting to a familiar foot, grabbing the ankle, and trying to look up between contractions. *Are you my daddy?* When had the answer not been "no"?

The foot belonged to Anton. He and Chloe stayed with her as they waited for a room. Her pain intensified but her connection with it grew more distant. A body does not allow you to feel this sort of pain fully.

—Why is she being dragged up here?

—Put some dirt on her, she'll get cold.

—Why does she have to be on my side? There is no space. If you want her so much, put her on your side.

—I heard her baby had an umbilical cord tied around his neck like a noose. Krrrrak.

—No, that wasn't her. That was someone else.

—Remember when we all went to the hospital because we got the Spanish flu? I couldn't stop sneezing for months! Years!

—We had such parties in our hospital rooms! Remember that? Very festive!

—Flutes of champagne. And we'd throw the glasses into the fireplace. Step on them? Yes, very satisfying.

—Remember how much we loved sweeping, swish-swish with the broom?

—Sweeping indeed. Ladies blathering. If she doesn't belong here, we shouldn't keep her. Let's roll her down the hill.

The rabbits and zygotes on the hill multiply, then disappear, multiply then disappear. The zygotes pop quietly like soap bubbles, but the rabbits are noisier,

grinding their teeth, purring like kittens. A clatter of back feet thumping as
they scratch behind their ears. Zhenia is rolled through them, they leap up, over,
under. The one she catches by the ears begins to scream loud, loud, terrified
and human.

Zhenia's eyes flutter open, then closed. A rubber mask over her mouth,
she tries to pull it off, but heaviness is spread through her limbs. She can't
move. She's outside time.

A surgical curtain severs her from her belly. A magician's assistant being
sawed in half. The clinking of metal instruments, figures moving behind
the curtain, the tops of their little blue caps.

What happened to all the rabbits? Returned to an empty top hat. And who
would reattach her to her body? She's like the shadow that needs to be sewn back
onto the boy. From that children's book her grandmother used to read to her. The
boy who wouldn't grow up. Her grandmother was the only one who could sew.
The only one who knew Zhenia's soul. *Zaika*—this was her pet name. Bunny.
Ben had said the reason Russians were so obsessed with their souls was because
they were always on the verge of vacating. There must have been a vacancy in
her. Space enough for a ghost to move in. Where had her own soul been all these
years? Where had it been hiding? Now it was meek and anemic, but there at
least! Gasping for breath. Matted fur over sinew and bone, shiny eyes searching,
searching. A tentative hop. *Zaika, Zhenichka, prosnis, wake up, Zhenichka,* her
grandmother's voice. She couldn't see her, but she could feel her cool hands lift
her up and change the wet sheets under her, change her into a dry nightgown.
She'd peed their bed again. *Ia zdes, I'm here. Davai. Davai. Horosho. Okay.*

A baby's head, raised in someone's hands, black hair, oily and wet, a bloody
face, smushed still, peeking over the curtain. Give it time, that nose will unfurl.

The nurse held the baby on Zhenia because Zhenia's arms were not
steady yet. Zhenia cooed at the baby through the mask as the doctors behind
the curtain sewed her up.

Vova, she said, *my little volchiok. You're not a bunny at all. You have hair*
on your back, you have hair on your belly. You must be part wolf. The little
wolf from the willow bush had torn her open from the inside.

And Irina, maybe there was no room for her anymore, because she didn't seem to be there. Had she been birthed too?

LATER, AFTER SHE was wheeled into the recovery room, Zhenia found out from a round-eyed Chloe that she had almost died. There'd been a lot of bleeding.

"Not a good thing for a pregnant woman to have to see!" Zhenia's mother clucked sympathetically.

Chloe was slightly taken aback by this strangely aimed empathy. "I'm just glad she's okay."

Zhenia's mother still had her neck pillow from the airplane resting on her shoulders. She had arrived while Zhenia was being stabilized. She'd sat on her rolling suitcase next to Chloe as they both anxiously awaited updates that they got through Anton.

It must have been her mother who contacted Ben because he showed up too with his girlfriend, who was pacing in the hallway.

Ben petted Zhenia's sweaty head, waiting for his turn to hold the baby, even unbuttoning his shirt so he could do "skin to skin" as the nurse was explaining.

Zhenia's belly felt numb and she still looked pregnant. The baby's home was mostly intact even if disfigured by stitches, she thought, so he could go back and live there if we're ever in a pinch. She started laughing at this idea. Her laughter—weird and sudden—caused Chloe to pause what she was saying to Zhenia's mother.

"It's whatever they put in the IV," Zhenia explained. "I still feel a little loopy."

She let Ben hold the baby. His feelings—about Zhenia, the baby, the divorce, all of it—were reconfiguring inside of him right now. His face was always too expressive. She'd been waiting, anticipating this moment, but it didn't give her much pleasure.

"I like the name Myles," Ben said. "Also, I had an uncle Simon who I liked a lot."

"I'm naming him Vladimir," she said, watching her red-faced baby curl and writhe in Ben's chest hair. "Vova, Vovachka, Volodya." After one of her grandmother's favorite writers.

"Vladimir? Why?" her mother said in a tone of voice that annoyed Zhenia, but then her mother took the baby back from Ben and put him on Zhenia's chest, so for that she was grateful.

"Are you going to do the circumcision?" Zhenia's mom asked.

"No, people don't do that anymore," Zhenia said.

"What do you mean, people don't do that? Most people still do that," Ben said.

Zhenia could feel the catheter bag on her leg fill with warm pee. She closed her eyes and breathed with the baby, which Chloe took as a cue to round everybody up and leave. Where was Irina now? Zhenia wondered. She didn't feel gone, exactly. And yet the voice wasn't there.

Anton stopped by after she had dozed for a little bit, and her mother was sitting in the chair, also dozing, and the baby was asleep in the hospital bassinet. Zhenia woke up and opened her eyes. She and Anton stared at each other significantly, with feeling, and then Zhenia asked groggily whether he was still planning to pay her the two hundred dollars, and laughed in that weird drugged way, which woke her mother up.

CHAPTER 38

Marina took six weeks off work at her lab and helped take care of both Zhenia and the baby. She made soup and cleaned the filthy apartment of the ants, which wanted to feast on the many liquids coming out of Zhenia and carry her and the baby off to their underground lair. The first few days, Zhenia needed help getting in and out of bed, Velcroing herself into that hospital corset, and walking to the bathroom. Anytime Zhenia coughed or sneezed, the pain in her belly was excruciating, and the blood would come squirting out of her into the lumpy diaper pad. Her breasts were hard and oozy, and Vlad would open his little gummy mouth and wail, turning his head from side to side like a cartoon baby bird. When Zhenia tried putting him on her breast, he'd snap his jaws shut on the tip of her nipple (also excruciating). It was Marina who patiently showed her how to do it, by sticking her finger in Vlad's mouth when he began to do his bird call and prying his jaw open a little farther and then quickly shoving his face onto Zhenia's breast.

There was a precision in the way Marina did it, and the shove wasn't violent but it was forceful. It made Zhenia laugh, little Vlad's expression as he zoomed into her tit. And then her laughter turned to tears because she felt embarrassed needing her mom so much. Maybe for the first time in her life.

She expected her mother to act put-upon or resent this, but this was not the case at all. Marina genuinely seemed happy—making soup, scrubbing the kitchen, fetching water and horse pills of Advil. "Did you poop?" her mother would ask Zhenia, her mother would ask Vlad. She was in the weeds with them. The doctors had said that it was very important that they both poop, and Zhenia's mother's happiness and relief over Zhenia's pooping had seemed insane, until Zhenia then felt that same happiness over Vlad's.

"I wish Babushka was here," Zhenia said one afternoon as she was sitting up in bed, breastfeeding Vlad. Zhenia's mother was assembling the breast pump they'd been given at the hospital.

"Why?" Marina said without looking up. "She hated babies."

"She did not."

"You don't remember the way she was with Greg? You were better with Greg than she was."

Zhenia remembered her grandmother's squeamishness. "Maybe she just didn't want me to feel betrayed."

"You think she was any better with you?" Marina raised her eyebrows and connected the tube to the motor and turned it on and off. "You're lucky I never let her get too close when you were a baby. She was prone to violent outbursts. She was always shoving me, slapping me, hitting me when I was a little girl. She was jealous that Papa loved me." Marina had tears in her eyes retreading these old slights. She dropped the tubes she was holding and wiped her face. "Oh, if I could have gotten away from her, imagine my life!"

"Okay, Mom," Zhenia said, annoyed but not wanting to argue. She stared at the sunlight coming in so yellow onto the foot of her bed. She could feel something in her stirring, but whether it was Irina or just an aspect of herself, she couldn't say, and maybe there was no distinction to be made anyway. Vlad stopped sucking and began to cry.

"Hold him more upright, so the burp will come out. Listen to your baby. He's telling you he doesn't like what you're doing."

"I'm telling you I don't like what you're doing," Zhenia grumbled, and patted his back.

"Well, don't take it out on him," Marina said, and switched on the breast pump, now fully assembled. It filled the room with the rhythmic suctioning sound, like the ocean if it were trying to extract something from you.

After these kinds of fights Zhenia and Marina would avoid eye contact for a while, read things on their phones, or talk and sing to Vlad. If Zhenia didn't protect her grandmother, who would? And yet, she understood too, spending these long nights and days with her mom, shuffling to the park together with Vlad in the stroller, stopping in the fancy little grocery store for olives, waking up together many times in the middle of the night to feed and change him, that maybe since childhood she'd been functioning under a misunderstanding that she'd had to choose between the love of her mother and the love of her grandmother.

"Why did you let her take me from you?" Zhenia asked once as they watched a little girl run in circles on the playground with a dog on a leash. Even this question had felt like a betrayal. Her mother patted her head.

"I'm sorry," she said. "I thought you were both happier that way. I always felt like I was intruding. With Greg it was so much easier. A child that was mine and not hers. I wish I hadn't thought of it that way, but I did."

They got home that day to a large white bouquet from Naomi. It seemed kind of funerary and it activated Marina's allergies, so they left it by some older bouquets on the corner where, a few months earlier, a pedestrian had been hit by a car. Naomi also sent over a cashmere teddy bear, which Zhenia wanted to get rid of on principle, but it was very cute, so she couldn't bring herself to, and anyway, what was the principle? It was a nice gesture from a person who had once been her friend.

CHAPTER 39

Sergio had gotten better at driving Paul's scooter. They would go for rides now, up and down Manhattan, sometimes over the bridge into Brooklyn and Queens, even Long Island. They'd go after Paul's physical therapy and speech and language pathology appointments, a reward for the more grueling ones. In some ways Paul had made a lot of progress. He could walk again with only a barely perceptible limp. Language, though, was more difficult. Paul had always been a talker, and this new silence initially felt like a great absence for Sergio, but then it changed into something more companionable. Paul seemed so present now. Even though he said little, he was there. He held on to Sergio's waist as they zoomed alongside the rivers and the ocean, through the mist and the fog. Sergio loved the feeling of Paul's chin resting on his shoulder. When the wind was in their faces it was too loud to talk anyway.

They liked to stop sometimes in a swamp sanctuary and take turns pointing out all the birds. They did this so often that Sergio even bought an Audubon guide. He would look up each bird they saw in the guide and name it, and Paul would stare so intently at his lips that it made Sergio feel like Adam.

It wasn't that Paul couldn't talk at all. Language was slowly coming back to him. He could say "I do," for example. An old friend and former student of Paul's drove them out to the Berkshires in Massachusetts, where they got married. It was the only state where you could come from outside to do it, since it still wasn't legal in New York. Now Paul would be on

Sergio's insurance, and if there were any other hospital visits, Sergio would be considered family, not treated like a random man off the street.

Their witness had gotten more dressed up than they had. She wore a dress with layers of taffeta. Paul wore an old blue suit that hung loosely on him now, and Sergio wore a collared shirt and jeans. They went out for a celebratory lunch afterward at an outdoor café. Sergio and the friend were catching up, and Paul was staring out at some seagulls that must have been blown inland from the ocean. They circled low over the tables, their weird pink legs tucked straight back.

One seagull separated from the others and landed on the ground in front of Paul. Its body was surprisingly large when it was so close. Paul stared at the gull and the gull stared for a while at Paul. It gave Sergio a chill, seeing this communion.

The waitress hadn't come out yet to take their order or bring them bread rolls so they had nothing to offer the seagull, who, sensing this, eventually waddled over to a table that hadn't been bussed yet, where the other seagulls were already feasting on what remained of the moules-frites.

BEN CAME TO visit Zhenia and the baby before he went back to Atlanta. Marina helped him carry in a lot of boxes from the car, objects for the baby that made their small apartment feel cramped. He came alone this time, without his nervously pacing girlfriend.

The baby had fallen asleep with Zhenia's nipple in his mouth and Marina threw a burp cloth at her to cover up her breast from Ben.

"It's nothing I haven't seen before," Ben said jokingly.

Marina just grunted.

Her mother's choked anger made Zhenia flinch. She must have, Zhenia guessed, seen something of Zhenia's father in this whole situation and this was a subject they never talked about. Zhenia had only ever seen a photo of her father once—balding with a blond goatee, thick glasses, a shirt that was buttoned too tight over his broad chest, his pants and sleeves rolled up. In his hands: a cigarette and a fish. She'd found the photograph in her mother's things when she was little and studied it, knowing instinctively that it was the most taboo object in the house. She'd described it later to her grandmother to confirm who it was, but when she went back to look for it, it was gone. As a teenager she'd turned the house over more than once trying to find it, but her mother must have burned it or thrown it out or flushed it down the toilet.

Ben, Zhenia, and the baby stepped out onto the balcony to have privacy while Zhenia's mother glared at them and unpacked the bulky gifts and broke down the cardboard boxes they came in.

Zhenia herself did not feel angry with Ben. She let Ben hold the baby, and sniff the baby, and kiss the baby's juicy cheeks and flaky fontanel. Ben traced the narrowing path of black hair down the baby's neck. The baby stared back at Ben, at his forehead, at the streetlight over his shoulder.

Ben began apologizing: It was fear. It was behind him now. Zhenia wiped the tears on Ben's face with her hand. She thought about the manifestation, how she had imagined essentially this very scene, and now she knew clearly that she did not want it.

She always assumed that she'd been trying to sabotage their relationship because there was something wrong with her. Because she didn't think she deserved happiness, or because she was punishing herself. Why hadn't it occurred to her that she simply wanted the relationship to be over? For no good reason. But why did you need a good reason? The affection she felt for Ben, the comfort she took in all their patterns and routines, this wasn't love. From the beginning she'd acted as if she were in an arranged marriage and she was making the best of it, but nobody had arranged this marriage.

Marina stood on the other side of the glass door and knocked.

"Let me take the baby. It's cold. Why isn't he wearing a hat?"

Ben muttered, "Wow. She hates me now," and Zhenia shrugged and took the baby and handed him to her mother.

They kept standing outside, but without the drama of the baby between them something deflated. They talked in circles for a while. Both of them taking turns imagining that things could be different from how they were, while the other person would carefully counterbalance this and be reasonable.

Ben tried to hold Zhenia and squeeze her without hurting her. She had been so starved for touch weeks earlier, but now she and the baby felt like a closed-circuit system. Her breasts were beginning to fill up again, hot and hard, and when a cat on the adjoining balcony meowed, she squirted milk into her shirt. Vlad was getting hungry too; she could hear his little yowling. He could smell her through the glass, the little animal, the little pet. Now *there* was a person who lived in the essence of things, who didn't lie to himself about his needs and desires.

PART 4

CHAPTER 40

"When Anton was eight, and they'd just arrived in America, they went to a dinner at a distant great-aunt's house who had sponsored them," Chloe said to Zhenia. Their babies had fallen asleep on them and now they were pinned underneath, sitting on the couch in Chloe's living room. "This aunt had survived the Holocaust and came to the US as a young woman and lived on the Upper East Side. She was wealthy and the dinner was festive, a big spread, and all the relatives Anton and his parents were meeting for the first time were there. Everyone was getting hungry, ready to eat, and finally his great-aunt gets up to serve herself first and she makes a big production of taking *tiny* scoops of everything. And then she announces to the table: 'Look at How Little I Take!' She makes a point of showing her plate to everyone else so that nobody would take more than she did."

"Wait, and you think this explains who Anton is?"

"No! I mean, yes, in that it's his origin story and I think it explains his," she gestured with her hand, tensing it into a claw for emphasis, "oppositeness."

They were both slightly delirious from lack of sleep and incredibly thirsty from breastfeeding.

Chloe reached carefully without waking her baby, Maya, for a glass of water, chugged half, and passed the rest to Zhenia. They had grown close very quickly. Zhenia didn't know whether Chloe knew that Anton paid her weekly. It seemed like the kind of thing that should tick under the floorboards of their friendship, threatening always to destroy it, but Zhenia did not experience it this way. She took the money from Anton like she would an allowance from a benefactor, because she needed money and he had money and it did not diminish in her eyes at all the way she felt toward Chloe. It was perhaps even possible, she thought, that paying her had been Chloe's idea.

"Okay, now you tell me something," Chloe said. She closed her eyes for a moment. She'd stopped sleeping at night. Maya was waking up a lot, and even when she wasn't, Chloe lay on the floor by the crib, watching Maya breathe.

"What's your origin story?" Chloe asked, and twitched her nose because it itched and Maya had slid down in such a way that Chloe couldn't reach her own face without disturbing the baby.

Zhenia scratched her friend's nose. "Maybe this is my origin story," she wanted to say. "This right now. I thought I was a rock, but I'm an egg and I'm starting to hatch."

Instead, she returned to the demise of her marriage. "Ben and I were fighting a lot. He didn't want a baby and felt like it was unfair that I had unilaterally made the decision to keep it."

Chloe nodded and shut her eyes. "I'm still listening," she said, slightly dreamy.

"I didn't think I wanted to have children either. He was more philosophical about it—it was important to him to not contribute to overpopulation and waste. He would talk about it as a moral decision."

"It seems like when people talk about it along the moral dimension, it's usually hiding something else," Chloe said without opening her eyes.

"Maybe," Zhenia said, running her finger against the grain of the velvet couch. "I don't know about people in general. Some people probably *do* think that way."

"Or they *think* they think that way."

"You know his girlfriend right now is pregnant?"

Chloe snorted. "That is not a good vasectomy." She opened one eye and looked at Zhenia.

"I assume he had it reversed." Zhenia shrugged and then shook her head to get rid of the sticky sick feeling she would get sometimes when she thought of her marriage. "The years I was with him are honestly like . . . a blank swamp." She gestured a little too dramatically with her hand, and Vlady stirred, lifting his sweaty little head like a fish and then thumping it back down in a cooler spot. It was easier, maybe, not to have too much nuance about it.

"Look at How Little I Take!" Chloe said in the old lady's accent.

"Yeah. Exactly. Anyway, I'm just giving you the context: my marriage was crumbling, my grandmother, who I've told you about, was dying, and I was pregnant. So, one morning, I got a call. There's a man on the line, and he says my name, and that he has been trying to track me down."

"Did Ben owe someone money?"

"No."

"Not a debt collector?"

"No." Zhenia noticed that Chloe kept trying to guess her stories, but she was rarely right. "You won't guess. It was a man I'd never met. He'd been talking to my great-grandmother."

"Wow," Chloe said. "How old is she?"

"She's dead."

Chloe blinked her eyes open and stared at Zhenia. "So, what does that mean?"

"He's a medium. And he was channeling her to me over the phone."

"Like . . . as an art project?" Chloe said, rotating her wrist slowly.

Zhenia tilted her head and looked at Chloe without answering. "I mean . . ." she finally said when the silence began to feel awkward. "That's not how I was thinking about it? But sort of. I was writing it down."

Chloe nodded, closed her eyes again, and yawned.

"What kind of stuff did he tell you?"

Zhenia started to tell her about Irina, about how she was a revolutionary, about how her cousin was killed when they threw a bomb together, and about the trip Irina took with Olga to the Fortress dressed as a nurse. A bedtime story. She didn't tell her about the part that mattered—that Irina needed something from Zhenia that Zhenia had refused to give her. Or the scarier part that happened later. When Irina came to her.

Chloe's breathing was a smooth whistle. She had fallen asleep.

Zhenia thought, *I'm in a room with three sleeping people*. She closed her eyes too, but quickly opened them. She'd begun to sense Irina's presence again recently, but only in the moments when she was on the verge of sleep, like the sensation of falling. It scared her, and this fear made her hands tingle.

She thought she'd expelled Irina with the birth, but slowly she'd been becoming aware of the jagged sensation of Irina still inside her. Somewhere deep. The monologue continuing, but so distant Zhenia probably couldn't make it out even if she'd wanted to.

And she did not want to. At home she kept the radio on all night to drown out even the possibility of hearing more. Zhenia had been given this fresh start, and listening to all that seemed like a way of sabotaging it, of looking backward right as she'd finally seemed to manage to get free of herself.

Zhenia picked up the book on the back of the couch that Chloe had been reading before she got there. It was a book of essays in translation by the Russian poet Marina Tsvetaeva. Zhenia had read a few of her poems at some point, but didn't really know much about her because she wasn't part of her grandmother's canon. Zhenia leafed through it, scanning for parts that Chloe had underlined.

"*. . . Men are never the first to desire. If a man desires, then a woman already desires . . . and what will we do with tragic love? When a woman—really— doesn't desire? That means it wasn't she who desired, but another woman nearby. He mistook the door.*"

What did it mean, Zhenia wondered, that Chloe underlined this? That Anton desired her because Chloe already had? Reading someone's marginalia, was that like reading their diary?

He mistook the door.

And then through the door came Anton. He took off his shoes, saw that Chloe was sleeping, and carefully peeled Maya off her. Chloe stirred but didn't wake up. Zhenia got up quietly with Vlad and followed Anton out into the yard.

It was starting to cool down outside, but the ground still held the heat.

"Thank you for helping her finally get some sleep!" Anton said, and kissed Zhenia on the cheek.

Anton was so happy when he came home these days. Zhenia, at first, would do this thing, gathering up her sacks and her baby like a little mouse ready to be taken home. And Anton would say, "Where are you going? Stay! I brought takeout." He would pick it up on the way back from the hospital and he would whistle or hum or sing, but always make noise as he would go into the kitchen and put the takeout onto plates. And Chloe and Zhenia would be lying around on the couch or the floor with the babies, and he would kiss Chloe, and then Maya on her throbbing little soft spot. And eventually he started kissing Zhenia and Vlad, too.

How did it happen, really, Anton's love of strays? He loved most seeing these two women together. How solid they were. The way motherhood turned them heavy, their breasts, their thighs, their stomachs. He thought of the Picasso paintings of the women in togas with potato noses and potato fingers. And he loved the little squealing and squawking babies with their startle reflexes flapping their arms. It had been so hard for him and Chloe to have one. It had taken years, and injections and treatments, and a procedure where they'd had to scrape out the sperm from the insides of his testicles, and then Chloe, despairing, had gone on a road trip with another man and came back pregnant. She'd gotten pregnant and that is what matters. Not how.

Maya woke up and Anton set her on the ground. He rolled up his pants legs and his shirtsleeves. She couldn't crawl yet, but she could put dirt in her mouth.

"It's good for her gut biome. Kids should eat more dirt," Anton said when Zhenia tried to stop her.

Zhenia laughed. "No," she said. "Look at her!"

Maya's chin was covered in dirt, and when she saw that Zhenia was giving Vlad milk, she began to wail at the injustice of it. "Let me give her some milk," Zhenia said.

"Yeah, okay," Anton said, and got a shovel out of the shed.

As Anton dug Chloe a garden, Zhenia lay on the ground and nursed both babies at the same time, milk brother and sister, a head for each breast. The earth under Zhenia's back was warm like a body. The sky was turning pink. The feeling of the babies pulling the milk out of her with their mouths was like an electric current passing through her and into them.

Finally, Chloe stumbled out, creases on her sweaty, sleep-lined face.

"I have an idea about an essay on motherhood," she said excitedly, and sat down in the dirt next to Zhenia. She ran her fingers through Zhenia's hair and watched the babies eat. "Or like an idea of an idea. It seemed close a moment ago."

"What was the idea?" Zhenia asked. Dirt was flying off the shovel in an arc behind Anton's back.

Chloe tapped her bottom teeth with her finger as she was thinking.

"It's all jumbled now. It was a feeling more than a thesis, I guess. I felt like I had wandered out and there was the essay waiting for me fully formed." She reached into the air, blinked a few times, more fully awake now.

"Is that what writing is like for you usually?" Zhenia asked.

The babies were full of milk now, unlatched and on the ground, practicing grabbing things and rolling over, and looking around in the pink light at their mothers' faces and at the birds circling the fig tree.

"Sometimes, yeah," Chloe said, and helped Zhenia up. "I used to hear it. A flow of words."

Zhenia tucked her breasts back into her bra and pulled down her shirt. "Is it scary?" She was thinking of Irina.

Chloe shrugged and shook her head at the same time. It was all so distant now.

"Let's plant those seeds," Anton shouted to them. "Get that zucchini out of the freezer."

Chloe got out an enormous zucchini the size of a cudgel and the reptilian green of the Soviet suitcase Zhenia's grandmother used to take down from the closet anytime she and Marina would fight. An empty gesture—Vera never would have left Zhenia, and anyway, where did she have to go?

The zucchini was heavy, frozen like an icicle. There was something about its unnatural size, its color, that made Zhenia hand it back to Chloe almost right away.

"I found it hiding in the garden the day I had to leave St. Louis," Chloe said, carrying it over to Anton along with a plastic bag full of seeds from her other plants.

"Do you think it will still work?" Chloe asked Anton, and kissed him wetly. "Even though I froze it first and it's so fucking hot here?"

"We'll see." Anton shrugged. "Looks like everything grows here."

Zhenia held the babies on both hips and watched Chloe and Anton tuck seeds into the dirt one by one, then turned away when they buried the zucchini whole on the other end of the plot.

Anton drove Zhenia and Vlad home after that.

"Your nails are so dirty," she said, lifting up his hand from the steering wheel and looking at the thick black crescents under his nails. He put his pointer finger in her mouth as he drove and she sucked on it, the taste of the earth, her improved gut biome. He parked out front of her building and followed her inside, carrying sleeping Vlad in his car seat up the steps to her apartment.

Since she spent most of her time at his house except at night, her own apartment felt empty, like a theater set. It was stuffy from the hot day, and she slid open the balcony door to let the night air in. Then she laid Vlad down in his crib by the bed and offered Anton tea.

Anton never liked to stay too long, in case Chloe was waiting.

"Sure," he said, switching over to Russian. He got undressed and lay down in her bed and she watched him and waited for the water to boil.

"You're different in Russian," she said.

"*Da*?" he said, and beckoned her toward him, pulled her into her own bed. "Do you want me to speak in English to you?"

"No, I think in Russian you're your real self."

"There is no 'real self,'" he said, and kissed her neck.

"I forgot to make you tea," she said, looking at the kettle. She wanted to stall, drag this out longer until she couldn't take it, but Anton was ready.

"I don't want tea," he said, lifting up her skirt over her hips and pulling down her underwear. She moaned before he even entered her. The anticipation of it was enough to make her start to come. She'd been waiting for this all day. The hours with Chloe, the hours watching them, all of it foreplay. By the time he was here playing house, she was already panting, on the brink. Her breasts began to dribble milk. He gripped her hips and thrust into her from behind, over and over, as she arched her back and craned her neck, babbling against his stubbled cheek. They both came quickly. He rolled off her and cupped her face, kissed her nose, got dressed. On his way out, he turned off the boiling kettle.

CHAPTER 41

After Anton left, Zhenia couldn't sleep. There was a buzzing in her that wouldn't quiet. A sensation like Irina was struggling to come up to the surface. It frightened her.

Zhenia sat up and called Paul. This time he, not Sergio, answered. It was late in New York. She knew it was rude of her to call like this, but she didn't care. She needed advice.

"Finally," she said.

"Hello?" Paul slurred this word slightly.

"This is Zhenia," Zhenia said. She wasn't clear on how much Paul remembered or understood. "You were channeling my great-grandmother for me. I need your advice. I need to get rid of her. She is here with me. In me."

She waited for Paul to say something. She could hear him breathing. She didn't know whether he could hear her or understand her.

"How are you?" she finally asked him, ashamed suddenly of her self-absorption.

"I . . . am . . . good," Paul answered slowly.

"You . . . sound . . . good," she lied. "I'm glad. Do you still hear spirits?"

"No," he finally said.

"Oh." Zhenia was disappointed. It was hitting her only now what had happened to him, what must have been taken.

"Do you miss it?" she asked. "It must be hard."

"No," he said after a while.

Maybe if it were face-to-face she'd understand this conversation better, she thought. She didn't know how to decipher it, how to read him, how much of him was there and what parts. Was he happier now? she wondered. Was he free?

"Do you know who I am?" she asked.

"The . . . girl," he said, and hung up.

ZHENIA LAY IN bed with the radio on and pressed to her ear. BBC World Service. There was a flood somewhere. The radio announcer's voice provided a steady drone. Zhenia thought about Paul cowering in the closet. She thought about the clothes hanging over him like a curtain. She thought about her grandmother's dead body, the rouged cheeks. She thought of the letters in the leather doctor's case and her grandmother's unmet needs and desires. She thought of the photo of Zhenia's mother as a lonely girl who would get slapped. She thought about how having Vlad made her aware of herself in a chain and connected her to death. She thought about the feeling of absence that would always be in her. The bed missing from her grandmother's room. The smell of lotion. A cool hand on her forehead. A ripped envelope as a bookmark. A plastic bag full of stale bread for everybody but the pigeons. Piece by piece the furniture inside of her would be dismantled, broken apart and used for kindling.

Zhenia woke up with Vlad in the morning, brought him into bed with her, and fell back asleep.

> An unheated concert hall. Strings. Everybody wearing coats and hats including the musicians. A cloud of cold breath hovers over the woodwinds. You're standing on the balcony. The floor below is littered with shells from sunflower seeds. Lara, it must be her, she has the hump on her back and is very thin. She stands beside you, swaying to the music with her eyes closed, transported away from here. It's a pleasure you can't access. To you the music sounds like noise. You keep looking down at the orchestra seats, scanning for faces of anybody you might know, anybody who can help you.

Someone is tugging at your sleeve. A girl of about four. Vera.
She wants you to lift her up so she can see the people playing.
She's heavier than you expected. She doesn't want to look at
the musicians after all. No. She buries her face in your neck.
Her nose is wet like a puppy's. She wants to burrow inside of
you and you feel an impulse to drop her and run away but
instead you squeeze her and squeeze her until she cries out:
"Mama, you're hurting me!"

Zhenia woke up again to the sound of knocking.

Chloe usually called when she was on her way, then waited in the car, but this time she came up and looked around before setting the car seat down on the bed and unbuckling Maya.

The radio was still on, a steady stream, and when Zhenia switched it off, the silence felt strange on her face. The dream from Irina still hung in the room for her. *Mama, you're hurting me!*

"Hi, Maya," Zhenia said to Maya, and kissed the baby on the cheek. Then she quickly did the same to Chloe, but she felt nervous having Chloe in her space. Zhenia busied herself changing Vlad's diaper, wiping his poop and not looking at her friend.

The truth was that Zhenia wasn't sure how much Chloe knew. She didn't know whether she and Chloe lived in a shared reality or not, and she was too scared to talk to her about it in case they didn't. What if Chloe didn't know about Zhenia and Anton at all, and what if it was something that would cause her pain? The arrangement was fragile and precious to Zhenia, and she didn't want to lose it by defining things and realizing that maybe all of it had been a misunderstanding. Zhenia vaguely knew that she left a trail of destruction in her own wake, but to admit this was somehow lending herself a level of agency and power over other people she didn't really believe she had.

"You ready to go to the lake?" Chloe asked, and slid the balcony door shut. Chloe was taking Zhenia for a rendezvous with Ben's parents at Echo Park Lake. They were in town and wanted to meet their grandson.

They'd been warm enough to Zhenia over all the holidays she saw them, but puzzled by her and the marriage. She imagined the divorce left them feeling relieved.

"Do you want to take a shower? I can keep an eye on them," Chloe suggested gently, watching Zhenia disappear into herself.

Zhenia took a very hot shower until the hot water ran out. She forced herself to keep standing under the water as it got colder and colder. Finally the water was very cold and she stood under it as long as she could tolerate, shrieking the whole time. It was something that her grandmother had taught her to do, *zakaliatsa*, the idea that it would make your immune system stronger going from hot to cold. The shock was its own pleasure. She felt returned to her body as she got out, her teeth chattering as she squeezed the cold water out of her hair.

When she came out of the bathroom, wrapped in a towel, she found the babies on the ground, Maya sucking on Vlad's foot, Vlad not quite understanding what was happening to him. Chloe was sitting at the counter, reading Zhenia's notebook, engrossed. She turned the notebook sideways, following a line up the margin of Zhenia's messy scrawl.

She looked up at Zhenia and did not appear the least bit apologetic.

"Zhenia, this is really good," Chloe said wondrously, as if the words had come from Zhenia herself. "Why didn't you tell me? I mean, you told me, but why didn't you tell me?!"

Zhenia blinked. She wanted to take the notebook out of Chloe's hand and throw it off the balcony.

"We should feed the babies before we go," Zhenia said, and picked Vlad up off the floor, removing his wet foot from Maya's mouth.

Chloe kept staring at Zhenia. "I think I feel jealous of you right now," she said.

This upset Zhenia even further. "You're acting as if it's something I created. I was just transcribing this lunatic's voice."

"Whatever your process is, you should keep going with it. Don't squander it."

Zhenia didn't say anything, just looked down at Vlad and cooed at him.

"Let's not fight," Zhenia finally said.

THEY DROVE TO Echo Park and walked around the lake with their babies in strollers. The fountains were on, shooting high up into the cloudless sky. They stopped to watch people rent paddleboats.

"I feel like I'm brilliant," Chloe said after a long silence, "but my brilliance has not found a physical manifestation for itself yet."

Zhenia took Chloe's hand and held it. Why did it need a manifestation? Zhenia didn't understand. She could feel it there and that seemed like enough. Who was the proof for?

Chloe started to cry. "I hope Maya isn't *it*. My mother was like that too. All her creativity went to me. When I was a teenager I was horrible to her. What a waste, I thought about all her effort—the time she spent on Halloween costumes or baking cakes in the shapes of organs. And now, I still think that: what a waste." She blew her nose.

Zhenia thought all of that sounded very nice. "She probably had fun doing those things."

Chloe waved this away. "I need to make something."

Maya had started to fuss, so Chloe lifted her up out of the stroller. "If I don't do something you will just end up pitying me," Chloe said to Maya, and sniffed her butt, then lifted her higher and put Maya's toes in her mouth.

"I could just eat you up, though," she said, something in her going slack. She hugged the baby tight. "I could."

Zhenia thought all the time about eating Vlad up. She'd asked her mother about this, slightly worried, and was relieved when her mother told her that there was a scientific term for this—"cuteness aggression." People are just so overwhelmed, capsized with love, and this is how they climb back in the boat.

Chloe stayed and showed Maya the geese while Zhenia went to the coffee stand and presented Vlad to Ben's parents. They took turns holding Vlad and sniffing his head and Ben's mom showed Zhenia baby pictures of Ben where, from certain angles and with certain expressions, he looked similar. They made vague promises to help Zhenia and to stay forever in her life, but when Vlad started to cry they seemed to take it personally.

"It's time for his nap," Zhenia said, finally able to pry him away and leave.

"He smells like her perfume now," she muttered to Chloe as she buckled him, wailing, into the car seat.

His crying set off Maya and the car began to fill with tears.

"*Shush, shush, shush, kiss, kiss, kiss,*" Zhenia cooed from the front seat. *I can't take this for one more moment,* she thought. *I'm going to open up the car door and roll out.* And just like that, the babies were asleep.

Chloe was cheerful now. A second wind. Sleeping babies. A car. Remnants of melted ice coffee in the cup holder. A gulp each.

"Let's go somewhere," Chloe said. "Let's go to Sequoia and see the oldest tree in the world. It used to be a logging commune, you know, and the biggest tree was named Karl Marx, but then the government seized the land and made it into a national park and then they changed the tree's name to General Sherman."

"Now?" Zhenia asked, confused.

"No, I guess not," Chloe said. "Someday."

They found themselves instead at the beach. A strange one, right by the airport. The sun was so hot, and Chloe fell asleep facedown in the sand, while Zhenia squatted in the shade structure she made from the strollers and blankets. Both babies ate a lot of sand and were very pleased with themselves.

"You know what my mother's first word was?" Zhenia said to Chloe when her friend woke up.

"What?" Chloe asked, picking sand out of her eyebrows.

"*Dira,* 'hole.' My grandmother loved that story. 'Your first word was *babushka,* and your mother's first word was about absence. She was always dissatisfied.'"

Chloe blinked in the bright sun and tried to swallow. "I'm so thirsty," she said hoarsely.

There was a strange commissary shop on the beach that had one of each item and felt like a front for something else. A Diet Coke was seven dollars, which was all the cash they had. They sat in the shade of the squat cement commissary and breastfed, passing the bottle of Diet Coke back and forth, taking sips and belching as planes erupted over their heads. For some reason this whole scene sent them into a fit of giggles. Neither of them felt very sure about how they got here or how they were responsible for little beings. The parts of Chloe's back that Zhenia had missed when applying sunscreen had clearly burnt. Red negative space.

"You know," Chloe said, "a hole is also the first thing a child can do, can dig. Maybe when your mom said it, it wasn't about absence but about mastery over her surrounding world."

"Wow," Zhenia said, looking at Chloe. That story had been presented to her in this pat way for so long, she'd never really thought to question it.

"But," Chloe said, letting out a loud belch. "I do think it's really weird that her first word had an *r* in it. That, to me, is what's suspect about that story."

Zhenia nodded, thinking it was totally possible that all of it had been entirely fabricated and that maybe her grandmother was not the most reliable narrator.

Vlad kept unlatching from her breast and looking over Zhenia's shoulder. Each time she would turn around to see if there was someone looming behind her.

"Do you notice the way he keeps looking at something?" she asked Chloe.

Chloe followed Vlad's gaze to the empty space behind Zhenia.

"Well, you know what they say about babies and dogs . . ." Chloe laughed.

"What do they say?"

"They can see ghosts!"

Zhenia didn't laugh. This was probably true. Vlad could probably see a lot of things clearly that would disappear once he had the language to describe them.

THAT NIGHT, ZHENIA didn't turn on the radio. She lay in the quiet of her studio apartment. Outside: cars drove by and parked, a couple was arguing. Inside: Irina was waiting. She could feel it.

"What?" Zhenia finally whispered in Russian. "What do you want from me?"

Irina floated out and Zhenia immediately felt a lightness. This was surprising—that so much heaviness had been there without Zhenia's even knowing. She didn't miss the heaviness, but lightness like this felt dangerous. Maybe now there was less of her.

She and Irina were nose to nose. She could see Irina's outline in front of her in the dark.

"Please listen." Irina sounded so piteous that Zhenia stopped being scared. She'd never outrun this poor woman and her sorrows. What was the point of resisting?

"I'm listening," Zhenia said. "I'm listening." And she was.

CHAPTER 42

Things came apart gradually and then all at once. Osip's sister was the first to leave. Her whole life had been structured around building the Revolution, and now that she got it, it brought nothing but death, destruction, degradation, and this was only the beginning. She begged for us to come with her.

"Petrograd is a cemetery," she said. She took the silk scarf that had once been yellow from Osip's neck and tied it around the handle of her suitcase. His neck looked so bare and naked without it there, it was hard to look at him.

Boris placed himself in front of the door. "How can you turn your back on everything now? We're so close," he said.

But what were we close to?

The world the Bolsheviks were creating was different from life under the tsar, yes, but not better. The same bureaucratic machine; forms filled out in triplicate. The power no less cruel, the cruelty less predictable. A permanent state of war. The ax could fall on any of us, and it would.

After she left, a man began to follow Osip. The man would wait openly in the stairwell of our apartment building, relieving himself against the wall. We had to step over his puddle, one by one, to go down the stairs, and then he would trail behind us, saying nothing.

A few weeks later, Boris was arrested for planning a general strike and shot without a trial. The tsar, tsarina, and their children had been shot too.

We were already talking about leaving when Osip was arrested. There was a crackdown on all revolutionaries who weren't Bolsheviks—the Mensheviks, SRs, and others were forced to either flee or go underground.

Lara and I went to the bureaucratic offices and begged but nobody could help us. Nobody even had a record of his arrest. Then, a few days later, the man who followed Osip was back in the stairwell. We ran inside to find Osip sitting on the couch. He'd been badly beaten. His face was swollen to a monstrous size.

Why they didn't kill him, I don't know. But they wanted him out of the country. We were to leave the next day on a train to Zurich. Him and me. Lara refused to come. She said her place was in Petrograd. The workers at the factory needed her, her city needed her. She'd left once before many years ago to follow Osip to Siberia and must have regretted it.

"What was it like without her?" Zhenia wanted to know. She remembered the figure in the dream smoking out the window. If Chloe wasn't there, would Zhenia be happier with Anton? She didn't think so—she loved Chloe too.

"I thought that without Lara I'd get closer to Osip, but this didn't happen. He lived for her letters. We both wanted to go home. We were desperately homesick, but for a Petrograd that didn't exist."

"You didn't like Switzerland?"

Irina had floated over to Vlad's crib, where he was sleeping with his arms up over his head, a faint wheeze in his breath. Irina's proximity to him made Zhenia nervous.

Maybe Irina sensed this, because she floated back to Zhenia. "I don't know. Switzerland was an absence."

Our four years there felt baggy and bland. How do you explain civil war to someone who has only known peace? I don't know. It was exhausting. Death and death and death. And yet the absence of all this wasn't peace. It had stretched us out, and we could not return to polite society. I behaved erratically and rudely, and Osip often had to make excuses for the way I talked to people. I couldn't control myself, or maybe I just didn't care to.

Osip got a job as a groundskeeper at a sanatorium and they gave us a little thatched cottage on the side of a mountain. We ate cheese and milk and bread. Probably because we were so well-fed now, I got pregnant. Having a family would allow us to create firsthand the future that we wanted—this was how Lara responded to the news.

Osip wrote that he hoped this would calm me. This stone growing inside of me. It sedated me, but it didn't calm me. I suppose the modern term for it was that I got depressed. I was in a foreign country. I felt like I'd been torn out at the roots and transplanted to a place that was peaceful and beautiful, but had nothing to do with me.

Time was measured now in dirty diapers. The world of ideas and adventures was gone, and I was forced to care for a creature that had little to offer me in return.

"Don't you feel this way now that you have this one?" Irina gestured toward Vlad.

Zhenia shook her head. "No. The opposite. I feel like I'm only now becoming a real person."

Irina shrugged.

Osip was also happy with the way things were at first. Domestic life agreed with him. He carried Vera around under his arm and sang her songs. He started a little kitchen garden, which felt like a signal that we would be staying long enough to see the seeds grow. We had enough food, for once. White bread, milk.

It was strange drinking milk and making milk. Things felt hopeless, but I wasn't fighting it. And then, when Vera was almost a year old, I came back to myself. Osip was visited by a man with a gray goatee and glasses. A face I had not forgotten since Hanna, Olga, and I had delivered bullets and letters to him in prison. He and Osip spoke in the house while I paced outside with the pram, trying to get Vera to take her afternoon nap.

When they were done talking, the man came outside and I followed him.

"Do you recognize me?" I asked, following him down the path with the pram. "We've met once before."

He said he did, but I didn't believe him.

"It was an eternity ago," I said. "You were in jail. I visited you. Was that not you?"

He stopped and looked at me through his round golden glasses. "Yes, yes," he said, and then I seemed to come into focus both for him and for myself.

"It's nice to hear a Russian voice," I said.

He pulled out a pocket watch on a chain and looked at it.

"Would you like to visit?" he said.

"Very much."

He was staying at the sanatorium. Supposedly recovering from tuberculosis, but I don't think his reasons for being there were medical. He was hiding out.

He held the door to his room open for me. We left Vera in the pram outside, sleeping in the fresh air.

We stood in his neat room, looking at each other, then he put his hand around my throat and pressed me up against the wall. He began to choke me very carefully, watching my face. Things started to go dark around the edges when he kissed me. He pushed me to my knees and unzipped his pants. This, it turns out, is exactly what I had wanted: to be debased with a firm and neutral hand by a person who did not pity me. Vera woke up outside and started to scream. I begged him to keep going, but he wouldn't. He pulled up his pants, went out and got Vera, brought her into the room. He bounced her on his knee and cooed at her, and she giggled with tears still wet on her cheeks and reached for his glasses. He handled her expertly, with charm, but not a deep interest.

He came the next day to talk again to Osip. And this time, Osip invited him into our house with less enthusiasm.

Their meeting was brief, and when this man came out, I followed him.

"Are you following me?" he asked without turning to look at me.

"I'm just walking the baby to help her sleep and you happen to be on the path." It's true that Vera only slept when she was in motion.

I could feel him smiling through the back of his head.

He made love to me against a tree on the path. He pressed my face into the mossy bark, and rubbed my cheek and chin raw as I gasped and Vera slept. I understood that the man was completely indifferent to me, and in this lay the appeal.

For the month that this continued, I was giddy and enthusiastic about life. I washed Vera's dirty face, made her little flower crowns to match my own. I don't know how much Osip knew. He was wary, I think. In a letter to Lara that he had not intended for me to read, he mentioned various misgivings. He worried about me. He did not think that I was well, but he was not the least bit jealous. It was clear he saw me as his burden and responsibility.

The man, it turned out, had been asking Osip to work for the Cheka, the Bolshevik secret police. Osip said he was not interested in doing this. The man persisted, trying to entice him in various ways.

And then one day, the man stopped coming. I went to the man's room at the sanatorium and it was empty. I made a scene. The nurses made Osip come and get me. Oh, I completely fell apart after that. I don't know why I thought that man was my salvation, but when he was gone, the promise of something interesting in my life went with him, and I descended again into despair.

I refused to feed Vera, and my breasts became swollen and hot and leaked milk into the mattress. Osip had to hire a nurse for the baby and he fed me with a spoon.

"Do you think all of your horror and grief just caught up with you then?" Zhenia asked.

Irina was floating by the balcony door, looking out at the lights of the city.

"I suppose so," she said. "In the absence of the horror, the horror only seemed to grow louder. Before, I knew at least how to escape from it with noise. And here, in that boring town, knee-deep in milks, there was nowhere to hide from it."

Osip didn't know what to do with me. It disgusted me that he wasn't disgusted. He was so good to me. I would lie in a darkened room and he would stroke my arm. He felt responsible for my collapse.

He regretted leaving Russia by then, though what choice had he really had?

Months went by and I got better. Vera and I were wary of each other. I got a job working at the little shop on the grounds of the sanatorium. I sold people robes and slippers if they didn't bring theirs from home. I took visitors on tours of the woods, to see birds and mountain goats. I would go out of my way to touch the tree where that man had fucked me, but aside from this small tic, I would say that I was fully recovered.

It was only after the letters from Lara stopped abruptly that something in Osip shifted. He wrote to everyone he could to find out what had happened to her, and finally he got an answer from a downstairs neighbor who said that Lara had been arrested and taken away. He had heard it all take place a few weeks earlier. The fact that this letter had not been censored or redacted, as most letters with this sort of content would have been, was odd. Maybe the neighbor was working as an informant and this was bait, though it's possible that the letter had somehow just escaped censorship on a fluke and gotten passed through.

Without hearing from Lara, Osip was not himself. He went for walks at night alone. He said it was to clear his mind and he never let me come with him. Who was he meeting? I'm not sure. Perhaps nobody.

I begged him not to go anywhere without me. Not to leave me in this godforsaken place with the goats and everybody's coughs echoing off the mountains. I got on my knees and pleaded.

"Irina," he said, pulling me up. "Cut it out."

But I slid back down to the floor and hugged his legs, so he sat down next to me. He kissed me on the forehead, on the nose.

"What is for us here?" he said. "Everybody we love is back there."

And so it was decided. He did not tell me the details of his arrangement, but he must have agreed to whatever terms they asked.

THE DAYS WE spent in Switzerland, after we decided to go back, were very happy ones. That sense that this easy, boring life was temporary made it tolerable. Now when Osip would give Vera her bath I'd hear him whistling. I was less stern with her too. She was speaking more, and I began to see in her something closer to a companion.

She would often say things that were unintentionally apt and poetic, and I would feel a momentary delight, like I had said those things myself.

I remember us going on a picnic. It was early summer. We had borrowed a straw basket from our landlady and filled it with cheese and bread and milk, and even apricots. We were laughing and strolling through a meadow. We set up our blanket under a spruce tree, and Vera wandered away to pick wildflowers for a bouquet and Osip and I drank our milk, happy and safe, looking up at the clouds, living already in a Russia of our imaginations. It was probably our happiest moment together as a family, one full of hope.

CHAPTER 43

"Do you think it was a mistake to leave Switzerland?" Zhenia asked.

"No, of course not," Irina said. "What kind of life would that have been?"

"But what was the point of coming back? You ended up leaving again anyway. You went to New York!"

"No," Irina said stubbornly. "You haven't been listening. I did not go to New York. Someone else went to New York. I, I came back to Petrograd. And that, let me tell you, was a shock. In the four years that we were gone, the city was renamed Leningrad, and Lenin's face was suddenly everywhere—on buildings and factories, in flower beds, hanging in the corners of people's apartments where icons used to be. That bald head and ugly goateed face. As soon as he died, he was everywhere."

"Did you see him in the afterlife?" Zhenia was curious. Her own earliest memory from before they emigrated was of dragging around Lenin's picture everywhere she went and kissing it. The warmth she felt toward that face was something her mother and grandmother discouraged, but they were careful not to do so very directly since that could get them, in their already precarious position, into trouble. Because Zhenia didn't know her father, she must have projected all her feelings toward him onto Lenin's picture. In fact, as she thought about it, she realized that the image she had of her father, bald and goateed, from the photograph she'd seen only once—maybe it had been some sort of confabulation, her father's indistinct face overwritten with the more familiar features of Lenin.

"Lenin wasn't anywhere near me in the afterlife," Irina said.

"Why?" Zhenia pressed. "Because he was in a deeper circle of Hell or something like that?"

"How should I know?" An exasperated edge in Irina's voice. "He must not have felt any regret. I'm telling you my story, not his."

Zhenia put down the knot of hair she was picking at and closed her eyes. Maybe Zhenia was asking Irina these questions to stall what she could already sense was about to happen. Realizing this caused something in her to flutter. "Sorry. Continue."

Vera had never seen a real city. "Imagine crowds of people, everyone you know multiplied, out in the bustling streets," I told her.

The things I missed most were the smells—the bakery by my aunt's house, Lara's lilac perfume that she'd let me wear, the horses and wet wool coats and scalding-hot tea and the air before it started to snow. My childhood, I suppose.

The canals and the streetcars and the long summer nights were still there and yet the city we'd left was gone.

Lara had been released from jail and was waiting for us back in the apartment. Osip wept and held her for a long time. The apartment had been deemed too large for her, and a man and his mother now lived in the room that once housed Osip's sister. The old woman watched our reunion with suspicion.

Lara was cheered by Vera's presence. I thought Vera might be scared of her because of the hump, but Vera loved Lara immediately. She petted Lara's ravaged face.

"What happened to Lara while you were gone?" Zhenia asked.

Irina did not answer right away. Her space in the room seemed to darken and pulse.

"I never asked her," Irina finally said. "I didn't want to know."

Not long after we came back, I was walking near Trinity Square with Vera. We were arguing over something. She had wanted to dawdle more, to look in the shop window at a display of matryoshkas, the nesting dolls set up in a neat row, but I needed to get in line at the cafeteria if we were to have any dinner. A fat man with a stained collar got in front of me, blocking my path. Another man took Vera by the hand and led her away.

I didn't understand what was happening at first. I tried to push around the fat man and grab her. Anyway, there's no use fighting in situations like that, but it's instinct.

"Of course you were fighting. You were her mother and you wanted to protect her," Zhenia said, not understanding why Irina was denying something this obvious.

"It's not moral or loving. It's just instinct," Irina continued as though she hadn't heard.

They brought me in for questioning to a repurposed room in an old palace. There was a beautiful stained-glass window mostly blocked by a large shelf. Every opportunity had been taken to rebuke whatever small beauty was available.

The man questioning me had yellow teeth and long yellow fingernails and was smoking one cigarette after another. I was afraid the way an animal would be. Dread made my body feel heavy. I kept yawning, which did not escape my questioner's attention.

"Are you bored?" he asked sardonically. Even though I'm sure he'd seen the whole gamut of fear responses.

Though what did I know about him? As little as he knew about me. I thought about the matryoshkas Vera had been admiring in the display window. Of course this was our national toy—your real self needed that much armor, that much posturing, that many identities before you got finally to the smallest one, featureless and dense.

The questioner lit one cigarette with another and asked me about Osip. He kept circling around the same question, asking it from all the different angles. He asked if Osip associated with some man I'd never heard of. I said I didn't know.

They had constructed a lie for their records, and they needed me to corroborate some aspect of it. Why the perversity of a paper trail when they did whatever they wanted anyway? I don't know.

He began to talk menacingly about Vera, but even if he hadn't, I would have probably signed my name to anything he wanted.

WHEN I HAD thrown the bomb I had thought myself very brave. But what bravery had been involved? None. Here was an opportunity to be brave, to refuse to turn on a person who'd taken care of me, who'd fathered my child, who in my own way I loved.

But I was not brave. I agreed and said what they wanted, because they were going to have me say what they wanted anyway.

The man who questioned me, he told me a long story about a horse he had as a boy, a beautiful horse he'd loved that needed to be killed. Tears came to his eyes, he was so moved by his parable. I couldn't stop staring at his hands. Why had his nails been so long? It was something that haunted me afterward. Long nails on a man. Who had he been in his previous life before rising up the ranks? He would not have been in the military, not with nails like that. A bookie? A butcher? I don't know. My mind hung on to details like this to avoid the larger question of what I'd done.

When I finally got home late that night I found Vera sitting on Lara's lap. People had come by to search the apartment. Papers were in disarray. Pillows torn open, loose goose feathers scattered in piles. The small geranium plant in its shattered pot swept to a corner. The old woman who now also lived there stood in the doorway to the kitchen, watching us.

Osip hadn't come home. This time he was gone for good, though we didn't know this yet. There was always hope to torture us with.

Zhenia was sitting on the edge of her bed beside Irina. She scrunched up her face.

"Why would they lure you back to Russia just to do this? It doesn't make sense."

"Sense? No, none of it made sense," Irina said. "They were not interested in making sense." They were interested in something else. Poor Irina.

There was not enough food in the city. We had to take the train out to the countryside and this was no easy task because the trains were packed. If you wanted food you had to go out to the farms yourself and trade for it.

We went with everything Lara had at her disposal—a silver hairbrush, a gold locket, two winter coats, which we wore on top of our own, and lighters. For some reason, lighters were what everybody wanted. We were able to get them from the factories where Lara taught literacy. The factories were a mess—they'd stopped manufacturing whatever it was they'd been set up to make because there weren't enough materials, nor interest on the part of the workers. The machinery was being dismantled piece by piece and sold off or repurposed for making lighters, which were in high demand in the countryside. It was Lara's students who told us where to go, which train to take, who to bribe. They had all by then grown very fond of Lara because, I suppose, it was impossible not to be.

We had to take Vera with us because I did not have anywhere to leave her. I didn't trust the old woman alone with her in the apartment. I caught her once in the kitchen bending back Verochka's fingers. Vera was staring at her with round eyes, not making any sound at all.

The train was so packed that an old lady wearing three fur coats had fainted, but other people's bodies were propping her up. On a train this crowded you wanted to be close to the openings so there was air and you wouldn't be crushed to death, but you also didn't want to be too close or you could fall out.

Vera was upset to be in such a crowd. She'd grown up with goats in the mountains. A crowd like this was a shock to her system. She wailed into Lara's coat, then finally fell asleep standing up.

When we got to the countryside, it was not easy to find anybody to sell us grain. They didn't have any to spare. There was already a lot of robbing and requisitioning happening—the government coming in and demanding all the grain from the peasants. They had nothing they could part with, they told us.

For a winter coat, one lady offered us a laughably small bag of potatoes. I thought that if people saw Vera they might take pity on us and give us more, but instead, when they saw a child, they saw weakness and desperation. At home they had their own children they needed to feed, and they knew we would settle for less than items were worth because we had no other choice.

I left Vera and Lara back at the train station and struck out on my own. I found a man who took all the lighters and the coats for a pood of potatoes. I could smell that the ones on the bottom had already gone soft and rotten. But in any case, the quantity was good, and I dragged it back to the train station through the snowy street.

Lara and Vera were playing some sort of memory game called "I Am Packing for a Vacation," where they went back and forth repeating long lists of items and adding on. We waited for the train home huddled together for warmth next to the potatoes.

We watched crows circle and land in a field, circle and land.

"Look," Vera said stupidly, "sausages!"—as one crow flew up, entrails hanging from his beak.

Vera was still in the clothes she'd gotten in Switzerland, which were too small and too fancy and got her looks from passersby, but we didn't have anything else to put her in.

On the ride home she sat on the sack of potatoes and talked with Lara about Osip. Lara said that soon there'd be a letter from him, she was sure of it. Considering the shortage of paper, and the general unlikelihood of this, I thought it was wrong of Lara to raise Vera's hopes, and I suppose mine as well.

Dragging the sack of potatoes back from the train station, I saw a face I recognized but couldn't quite place. A girl of about fifteen. A prostitute, but clearly, from the awkward way she hunched, she was new to it. She stood there, not knowing what to do with her hands, swaying in place. When a man came up to her, she didn't look up fully but hooked her arm in his, and they walked off.

Later at home, as Lara and I fried some potatoes with dried mushrooms, which we had picked in the park, it hit me where I'd seen this "former person"—she was one of the general's daughters who, a lifetime ago, my teacher had sent me to spy on.

"What, Mama?" Vera had asked. "What's so funny?"

I was laughing even though of course it wasn't funny.

Who knows how long we all would have hobbled along if Lara hadn't been taken away again. After that, I had increasingly fewer options. There was only one person who I thought might still be able to help me, and though I didn't want to ask her, what choice did I have?

"Who?" Zhenia asked.

"Olga, of course." Irina sniffed. "She lived in Moscow now with her lover, a bigwig Party official, but she was in town for a meeting and staying at the Hotel Astoria, where I met them for dinner."

"Where did you leave Babushka?" Zhenia rubbed her hands, thinking of that horrible old hag bending back her grandmother's little pudgy fingers.

"I brought her and put her to sleep on the couch in the lobby."

It was surreal to be in the hotel only a few years after I'd thrown a bomb there and everything in my life had changed. The restaurant looked mostly the same. They'd renovated it after what I did, and now instead of aristo-crats and the bourgeoisie, it was full of Soviet officials. Olga and her lover were staying a floor below where I had killed somebody. From the dining room's window, I could see the bakery, and the apartment building where I'd dragged Hanna's dying body.

Zhenia had an impulse to stroke Irina's invisible arm. She thought about how she'd felt on her most recent trip to New York, seeing the city move on without her. The buildings were the same but the stores and people inside them were all different. Or like at her mother's house, where the rooms were repurposed, and lives had continued without her, and then ended without her.

"Have some more bread," Olga's lover said to me. "White bread. You'll probably like it. I don't think it's any worse than what you were eating in Switzerland." He smiled—I suppose that's how a person might describe this grimace.

"Thank you," I said. I wanted to tell him that I'd been to this hotel under different circumstances, but that I'd never eaten there because I'd never been able to afford it, not before and not now. That maybe being able to afford it was, in itself, suspect. But of course I said none of this. This man had the power to crush me, and I tried only to recede from his attention.

It was strange that Olga was with him. She had always seemed so principled, so staunch. Maybe she grew out of it? I could tell from her coat and from her watch that she was no longer principled in the ways I would have expected.

Her companion stood, seeing another official who stopped by our table with a woman wearing a strange clash of sparkling necklaces.

"Did you see the jewelry shop window around her neck?" Olga's lover said piously after they passed. "The bribery is out of control."

"Loot the looters." Olga shrugged noncommittally and pushed her glasses up the bridge of her nose. This was the party line and what every single person in that room was doing.

He left to go talk to men at other tables.

Olga stared at me blankly.

"I have a favor to ask," I finally whispered.

Olga already seemed to know what I wanted. "I can't get him out." She licked between the tines of her fork.

I nodded. I had figured as much. I didn't think anyone could, if someone had wanted him enough to lure us back. The rule was: kill first, ask questions later.

"I can get you out, though," Olga continued. "But only you. Nobody else."

I blinked, not quite understanding. I glanced toward the lobby. Surely she didn't mean that I would have to leave Vera behind? Without Osip or Lara we had grown closer and closer out of necessity. She felt now like an extra limb. We went everywhere together. She was my only companion.

"Children have to stay. They're important to the agenda. But I can put your daughter in a special place."

The comrade waiter brought dessert.

Should I have had no appetite for dessert? Should I have shook my head and said, "Who can think of sweets in times like this?"

Olga passed me a napkin. "Why don't you bring it home to Vera?" she suggested, but only after I'd already shoved most of it into my mouth.

"I have no need to put her into a place like that," I said with my mouth full.

"You will." Olga nodded. "You will. Do you really think they will let Lara out for long with what she was doing? And who do you think would take on another mouth to feed right now?"

"Maybe my aunt."

Olga blinked and straightened. She was watching her man talk to someone I recognized as a former friend of Osip's. I put my hand up to cover my face from him.

"Stop that," Olga said. "Listen, I can help you, but the offer will not stand forever. I think we both know that your aunt can't and won't take care of your daughter. This is not a regular orphanage, which is where she will end up if you leave her with your aunt, or if you stupidly decide to stay." She knocked back her drink and dabbed at her lipsticked mouth. "Who comes back?" Olga suddenly whispered under her napkin, and for a moment I saw again a person whom I'd once known.

So could this be hell for her too? Was she admitting this?

"I saw the general's daughter," I said, wiping away a tear and changing the subject.

"Well, it looks like you solved that mystery for yourself, then."

"Don't you want to know what became of the older one?"

Olga smiled at my stupidity. I always thought I was holding a trump card and it was always a handful of trash.

"I'd be more concerned about what will become of you," she said.

A few days later, I took two trams with Vera to the address Olga had given me. It was a large brick building on the outskirts of town. We stood outside the gates and waited.

Eventually some kids came outside and I watched them through the bars, appraising how well-fed and well-dressed they looked. Then the groundskeeper came and unlocked the gate.

The wave crests finally and crashes inside Zhenia. The undertow pulls her under, deeper, deeper, and then darkness.

There's Baba Vera, hair combed with water and put up in a bow. Her lips are shiny and red from the lollipop she's licking. It's shaped like a rooster. How happy she looks to be getting such a treat.

She takes it out of her mouth and makes it crow: *koo-ka-re-koo.*

The sticky smell of burnt sugar and faintly rancid sunflower oil.

She's still looking down at the rooster and smiling as she's being led through the gate, realizing a moment too late that she's been handed off.

She twists around and tries to grab on to Irina's hand—it's stretching out to her between the iron bars—but the groundskeeper picks Vera up and carries her toward the brick building.

Vera claws the air over his shoulder, but he doesn't slow his pace. "Mama! No!" she shrieks. "Mama! Don't leave me!"

In Irina's chest everything violently contracts, tightening into itself, until it's only a pinpoint of light—and then the clicking, clicking of heels, faster and faster, as Irina starts to run.

CHAPTER 44

So that's where this Irina's story ended. From then on it felt like another Irina continued to live in her body.

"Do you want to move on?" Zhenia finally asked, wiping her eyes on her sleeve. "Are you ready?"

"It seems wrong," Irina said, "disgusting, to keep going in the face of tragedy. In the United States this sort of resilience is celebrated. You are an American. I was expecting you to say, 'You are so brave.'"

"Maybe you were brave."

"Of course I wasn't brave! I was never able to stay pure in the face of endless violence, deceit, and lies. I couldn't be unbendable. Someone like Boris, he could, only because he didn't live long enough. But tell me, all of these gestures of bravery, these sacrifices that end in death, who do they benefit?"

"I don't know," Zhenia said. "I guess society. Seeing someone else's bravery makes you braver."

"Does it?"

Zhenia didn't know. The darkness outside was beginning to thin. The sunrise was coming.

"And, now that I have heard your story, you need me to help you." Inside of one painful story, another one nestled, and inside of that one too, forever.

Zhenia put the pen down and closed her eyes.

She saw a meadow in Switzerland with her grandmother, lying on a picnic blanket, a grown-up as Zhenia knew her, looking at a book of poetry, her lips moving soundlessly as she read. And beside her were a scattering of Zhenias.

A little Zhenia doing somersaults, an older Zhenia holding her grandmother's hand, Zhenia the teenager with hair dyed with Kool-Aid, looking up at the sky. Zhenia beckoned all her old selves and they floated toward her. What would she need to whisper into each one's ear to tell them not to hold on? She took a deep breath and instead sucked them all up inside herself, the pine needles, and the basket, and her grandmother, and all of her past selves.

She opened her eyes and looked at Irina, poor Irina, Irina who had never been able to forgive herself. Zhenia crawled toward her and gathered her in her arms. With one hand she loosened her breast and stuck her nipple into Irina's mouth. "Shh," she said. "Shush, shush."

And as Irina drank, she shrank and shrank to nothing.

—*Gone!*

—*Well, good riddance.*

—*And what about us? It doesn't exactly seem fair.*

—*So many feet under the table. None of these ankles are familiar.*

—*Adieu, adieu!*

—*Now imagine me throwing you my monogrammed handkerchief. Picture it floating down from the deck of the ship.*

—*Yes! Or flower petals. Flower petals, when thrown, are nice too.*

The next morning Zhenia spent with Chloe, dozing with the babies on the couch. They lay head to foot, babies on their chests.

When Zhenia woke up, Chloe read her something in a paperback from a neighbor's giveaway pile that they'd found on their walk.

"'The Mayoruna Indians in South America,'" Chloe read, "'sleep in hammocks woven from vines that are tied to the central pole of the hut. In order to sleep and keep the structure counterbalanced, they need to all sleep at the same time.'" She folded the corner of the page and sat up. "They can't sleep alone."

"Like you." Zhenia smiled and closed her eyes again.

When Anton came home, Zhenia and Chloe sat on both sides of him on the couch with the babies on their laps. He read the babies a book in

English—about a sweet bunny which Maya kept trying to put in her mouth, and a book in Russian—about a cat whose house burned down because her neighbors were too incompetent to help her.

"Jesus," Chloe said, laughing. "The poor cat."

Then she reached across Anton and tucked a strand of hair behind Zhenia's ear. The moment felt electric and slowed down, and Anton reached forward and kissed the inside of Chloe's elbow.

That night after Anton dropped her off, Zhenia lay awake for a long time, feeling Irina's absence. It was very quiet until Vlad woke up crying. Zhenia ran her finger along his gums. Did they feel swollen? He was drooling more than usual, she'd noticed. He was probably teething. She paced with him back and forth across the apartment, singing snatches of the lullaby about the baby and the wolf until finally she got him to fall asleep.

WHEN IT WAS so late that in Boston it was already morning, Zhenia called her mother. It was too early still and Zhenia woke her up.

"What's wrong?" Marina said. "Was there an earthquake?"

"No. Everything's fine. I just felt lonely."

Her mother sighed. "I don't know what's keeping you there anymore."

"Mom, I'm in love." She really was.

Marina was quiet for a while. "You're getting yourself into another mess," she said sadly. "You don't see that?"

"Maybe," Zhenia said, closing her eyes. "But I want to." She was so close finally to dozing off.

"What are you going to do with Vlad when you go back to work? Who is going to watch him? That friend?"

"I'm fine, Mom. Mama, can you sing me the lullaby? I keep forgetting the end of it when I'm singing it to Vlad. The one Babushka and you always sang."

"Yes, okay," Marina sighed.

Zhenia heard her mother swallow and then begin to sing.

ACKNOWLEDGMENTS

Thank you to my grandparents, paternal and maternal—trying to understand their stories is what inspired this book. And thank you to my parents for reading versions of this book for historical and emotional accuracy. And my brother, Matthew Shifrin, for our long talks about our family history, which is a source of artistic inspiration for him as well. None of the characters in this book are based on actual people or relatives of mine, but the emotional process of listening and taking in my family's stories ended up in these pages.

Thank you to David and Fais for being so patient and loving with me as I wrote this sometimes difficult book. Fais, watching you grow up has connected me backward somehow to my childhood and ancestors in really unexpected ways, and I definitely would never have been able to write it without you. I love you!

Thank you so much to my wonderful editors, Tina Pohlman and Zack Knoll, as well as Taryn Roeder, Regan Mies, and the rest of the team at Abrams/Overlook, a place I interned at when I was a college student. That Katya wouldn't have believed this Katya's luck!

Thank you to Bill Clegg and everyone at the Clegg Agency. Bill—your sharp eye and brain made this book so much better. My books always feel deeply understood by you. Thank you, Marion Duvert, MC Connors, Simon Toop, and everyone else!

Thank you to Emily Robbins, Shannon Robinson, and Lia Silver for reading so many versions of this book in our workshop. I'm so grateful for all your wise notes on all the many, many, many drafts you read.

Thank you, Elif Batuman, Lauren Groff, and Michelle Huneven for being such generous readers.

Thank you to Lisa Locascio, Betsy Medvedovsky, Alexander Nemser, Kim Samek, and Sara Finnerty Turgeon for your notes.

Thank you to Rabbi Rosner and Rabbi Chorny for some historical advice.

Thank you to Anna Medvedovsky and her family for giving me a Cambridge writing residency over the summer.

Thank you to the residencies at VCCA, Art Omi, and the Jan Michalski Foundation.

Thank you to the Bruce Geller Memorial Prize for the Word Grant. Word is a program of American Jewish University's Institute for Jewish Creativity.

Word: Bruce Geller Memorial Prize is made possible by the late Jeanette Geller in memory of her husband, Bruce.

A lot of research went into the historical storyline of this book. In the section where Osip is standing on the car, I drew heavily on an incident that happened to Trotsky, and in fact, I put part of Trotsky's speech into Osip's mouth. The original speech read:

"You've come to declare your will and show the Soviet that the working class no longer wants to see the bourgeoisie in power. But why hurt your own cause by petty acts of violence against casual individuals? . . . Every one of you has demonstrated his devotion to the Revolution. Every one of you is ready to lay down his life for it. I know that. Give me your hand, Comrade! Your hand, brother!"

I also was inspired by the many journals and memoirs from the time period—particularly the ones of Teffi, Korney Chukovsky, and Marina Tsvetaeva.

The book referenced by Chloe that discusses the sleep habits of the Mayoruna Indians was adapted from *The Secret History of Dreaming* by Robert Moss. The quote from the Tsvetaeva book that Chloe is reading is from *Earthly Signs: Moscow Diaries, 1917–1922* (NYRB).